Also by Samantha Chase

One More
Promise

SAMANTHA
CHASE

sourcebooks
casablanca

Published by Sourcebooks Casablanca, an imprint of Sourcebooks, Inc.
P.O. Box 4410, Naperville, Illinois 60567-4410
(630) 961-3900
Fax: (630) 961-2168
sourcebooks.com

Printed and bound in Canada.
MBP 10 9 8 7 6 5 4 3 2 1

For my own wonderful musician, who reminds me every day that I can do anything I put my mind to. Your encouragement is what keeps me going when I don't think I can. Thank you for always being there for me unconditionally.

And to Jon Bon Jovi, for creating the music that inspired so much of this series. Whenever I couldn't find the words, Bon Jovi was there for me.

Prologue

IT WAS ONE OF THE MOST LUXURIOUS ROOMS HE HAD EVER stayed in, and yet it was beyond unappealing. It wasn't a comfort—it was a prison.

Even if it did come with Egyptian cotton sheets.

Dylan Anders paced the living space, counting each step. He'd gotten in the habit of pacing over the last eighty-nine days. It was a way of making him focus on something other than the hell he was living in. Okay, maybe *hell* was a bit strong, but…this wasn't the life he wanted to be living.

But it was the life he had screwed himself into.

By being stupid.

By being selfish.

By…simply being.

A soft knock on the door had him stopping and waiting. He knew who was coming and although it offered some comfort, it also brought on a fresh wave of anxiety.

What if I mess up?

What if I fail again?

The door opened and in walked his parents—both with huge smiles on their faces. His mother walked toward him carrying a covered plate, which Dylan was certain contained his favorite dessert—chocolate chip pound cake. His father was a few steps behind her carrying a piece of luggage.

Wait…luggage? What?

Carol Anders stood all of five feet tall, and as she reached up and cupped Dylan's face in her hands—while standing on her tiptoes—her smile was one of pure love. There was nothing Dylan wanted more than to keep that smile on her face.

"One more day," she said in a fierce whisper. "One more day and you'll be free to come home."

Free? Somehow Dylan doubted that. He might not be stuck in the rehab facility, but that didn't mean he was well and truly free. The actions that led him to being admitted here were never going to leave him. And he didn't want them to. No. It was important for him to remember how far he had spiraled out of control and how much those actions had cost him. The only saving grace—if he had to find one—was that he hadn't killed anyone.

But it had been close.

Tomorrow, he'd finish his required ninety days in rehab and be let loose upon society again. And yet, he didn't want to be a part of it anymore. He didn't know what he wanted.

After a few silent moments, he nodded toward the suitcase at his father's side. "What's with the suitcase?"

Steven Anders smiled. "When you arrived here, your clothes were shoved into a ripped-up duffel bag. We thought it might be nice to leave here and celebrate your fresh start with fresh luggage."

Dylan couldn't help but chuckle. Leave it to his parents to think all he needed to get started on this new life was a new suitcase. Not that it was wrong—it was incredibly sweet of them—but it wasn't how he tended to view things. His view was a tad bit darker. Sometimes there wasn't a silver lining. Sometimes people made bad choices and bad things happened because of them.

When he looked up, he saw both of his parents were watching him with the same patient smiles they always had. Sometimes he wished they'd yell at him, curse him, tell him what a disappointment he was.

But they never did.

And how twisted was he that he hated it?

Just once, he wished they'd call him out on his bad behavior and demand that he change his ways. Not that it mattered at the moment. He was changing his ways. And not only because his legal team and manager told him he had to.

It was because he was ready.

Sort of.

For most of his life, Dylan had accepted that this was the way his family was—he screwed up; his parents forgave him. They never talked about what went wrong or why he did the things he did. As he studied the two people he loved more than anything in the world, he came to a very serious life decision—if he was going to change, then his parents needed to change with him. Maybe it wasn't going to be comfortable. And maybe it would all blow up in his face. But if there was one thing he had learned through all his therapy sessions, it was that he had to stop hiding from his feelings. That meant no hiding out in a bottle of vodka to avoid his fears, disillusions, or just about anything.

During the last two weeks, his parents had come to his counseling sessions. It was considered helpful for them to do family counseling—mainly because he had initially started drinking because he was trying to get attention.

This was the first time, however, that he was initiating the conversation on his own—without a counselor present. Part of what he had learned after three months of being in rehab was that he needed to take responsibility for his actions.

So if ever there was a time to take that step…it was now.

Taking a steadying breath, Dylan let it out slowly and felt some of the tension leave his body. "Mom? Dad?" he began hesitantly. "It's going to take a whole lot more than a new suitcase to get me on the right path."

The next day, as Dylan walked away from the rehab facility that had been his home for the past three months, he felt a lightness he hadn't felt since he was fifteen years old.

And he walked away carrying his ratty, old duffel bag.

Chapter 1

DYLAN PROWLED AROUND THE HOUSE FEELING RESTLESS. His skin felt tight and he was a little jittery.

And that was how he felt nearly every night.

After touring with his band, Shaughnessy, for years and then taking time off to join other bands on their gigs, it seemed odd to have nothing to do. Not that he missed it. Much. Now he could look back at the last ten years of his life and realize that while he loved playing the bass—loved the music—the lifestyle had damn-near killed him. He'd spent too many years drinking too much and partying too hard and had paid the price. Dealing with a normal, everyday life was something completely foreign to him.

He was at loose ends and didn't know what he was supposed to do with himself. He'd played chess with his manager earlier, and Mick had hung out for most of the afternoon, but he couldn't be expected to stay all day and into the night. He was entitled to a life of his own. Except…Dylan kind of resented it. Not Mick. Not exactly. But anyone right now. Right now, everyone he knew was doing something with their lives—having lives—and he wasn't.

"Maudlin much?" he murmured, walking through the kitchen on his way to the deck.

Outside, the night air was cool and the sky was clear. He sat in one of his lounge chairs and stared up at the stars. It was peaceful and relaxing and…beyond boring! No matter how hard he tried, Dylan knew he wasn't meant to sit around and lead a quiet and tranquil life. Of course, that didn't mean he had to resort to drinking or getting high, but he certainly needed more than this.

He was holding himself back. He knew that. Right now, he still felt a little fragile, like any small step back into the life he knew with the people he used to hang out with would lead to a relapse.

And he refused to relapse.

Again.

There had been a night not long after he'd come home—he'd gone out with his ex for dinner. Heather had called him up out of the blue and offered him a night out, no strings attached. After months of no sex, he had eagerly jumped at the chance. Unfortunately, the night had been a complete disaster. Without alcohol fueling their time together, Dylan had felt awkward and uncomfortable. Heather, oblivious to his struggles, had ordered herself drink after drink, and by the time they'd finished dinner, he was more than a little turned off by her behavior.

They'd gone to her place and, even though his brain was saying yes, his body had no desire to take things any further. Funny—he'd always imagined it would be the other way around. Regardless, Heather had not taken the rejection kindly and had screamed all kinds of profanities at him while taking direct aim at his masculinity.

When he'd gotten home, he'd managed to find one well-hidden bottle of vodka.

The morning after hadn't been pretty.

Actually, the end of the bottle hadn't been pretty.

And now—because of that—he was afraid to get near the temptation. Maybe eventually he'd feel strong enough, but for right now, Dylan knew he wasn't. So where did that leave him? He couldn't keep living in isolation and he couldn't exactly go back to his old haunts.

With a muttered curse, he got up again and walked into the house. Closing the French doors behind him, he stalked into the living room and spotted the folder on the coffee table beside the chessboard—the literacy campaign information Mick had brought over earlier.

With a long and drawn-out sigh, he walked over and picked it up.

It would probably hurt him more than help him, but damn if he wasn't desperate for something to fill his time. From the look of the schedule Mick had included, the entire thing would take about three months between the organization and planning phase—which he fully intended to be a part of—and the actual campaign itself. There would be speaking engagements, commercial shoots, print ads... It would certainly fill his time and get him into the public eye in a positive light.

Maybe.

Dylan wasn't comfortable talking about the struggles he had endured in learning to read when he was young. He knew there was no shame in it, but that didn't mean he wanted to share it with the world. A man was entitled to keep some parts of his life private, wasn't he? But by sharing it, it could potentially help the cause—help him be more believable in his role for the cause.

Great. Now he was looking for a way to work the thing to his own advantage. How selfish was that? Unfortunately, it was the nature of the beast. In his world—or at least the world where his public persona lived—you never did anything that didn't ultimately serve your own interests. Sad but true.

Another sigh escaped as he sat on the sofa and began to read the documents. All of them. All twelve pages. His eyes hurt, his brain hurt, and he wasn't quite sure he understood half of what he had read.

At the bottom of the last page was the name of the contact person—Paige Walters. She was probably some spinster librarian who was trying her best to drum up interest in reading to keep her local branch of the public library open. He chuckled at the image. Tomorrow, he'd take the first steps and reach out to her. He'd explain who he was and how he wanted to help and, hopefully, do it all without having to bring up the community-service angle. And if it did come up, he'd simply pour on the charm.

And how hard could it be to charm a sweet, old librarian?

"Okay. You got this. It's all good. Be firm. Be strong." Paige studied her reflection in the ladies' room mirror. These mini–pep talks were coming with more and more frequency and yet she wasn't feeling any more confident.

In ten minutes, she was due to make a presentation on the status of the literacy campaign. It had been her brainchild, and to say that she was the only one excited about it would be an understatement. Reading was Paige's passion, and when she had gone to her monthly book club meeting and the topic of doing some fund-raising for the local libraries had come up, the ideas for something bigger began to spring forward in her mind. And, of course, once she started talking about it with her group of friends, it became obvious that she should be the one to head the campaign.

Public relations, marketing, and promoting were in Paige's blood. Her father owned a very successful PR firm in LA—PRW—and she had been wandering the office halls since she was a toddler. Now, as one of the senior account managers, she was free to pick causes and pitch them to the board and know she would be heard.

Or at least somewhat heard.

Okay, they only partially listened and then someone else would step in and take over, but still…if it meant she could finally be working on a campaign she was passionate about, then she'd deal with the petty behind-the-scenes nonsense.

But this one was her baby. No one else was going to want to swoop in and steal her thunder because it wasn't glamorous or trendy. It was reading. And if there was one thing Paige knew about her family, it was that none of them read for pleasure the way that she did. Other than her book club, she didn't know anyone else who read as voraciously as she did. And for all the hours—years!—of pleasure reading had given her, she was ready to give something back.

Yes, she had ideas—so many that it made her brain hurt—but that didn't mean she was going to shy away from the challenge. Reading programs. Tutoring sessions. Story time for all ages. Her heart began to beat faster as she thought about all the possibilities. If everything went smoothly, she was going to have a roster of distinguished authors in all genres and present them to the world as ambassadors of reading—well-spoken individuals who would show all the ways in which reading could enrich a person's life! They'd start at the preschool and elementary-school levels to help build a foundation, and then move on to find those who still struggled or who had gotten lost in the school system.

This campaign was her way of saying thank you to the thousands of authors who put their work out there and found ways to put their books in readers' hands—and encouraging the world to pick up a book even if they struggled with reading.

"Whew!" she chuckled as she fanned herself. It all was so exciting that she knew, in a matter of minutes, everyone on the board was going to feel it too.

"That's not what you're wearing, is it?"

Paige turned as her sister, Ariel, walked into the ladies' room. Ever the glamor gal, her sister looked impeccable—porcelain complexion; long, silky, pale-blond hair; blue eyes; and, at five foot ten, her willowy frame towered over Paige's mere five feet four inches.

"What's wrong with my outfit?"

Ariel gave a delicate snort as she faced her sister. "Do you see my suit?"

Hard not to, Paige thought and then nodded.

"This is an Ann Taylor suit." She struck a pose and smiled serenely. "And the shoes?"

Another nod.

"Manolo Blahnik." She pointed her foot for emphasis. "This is how an executive dresses, Paige. You need to throw out your wardrobe and let a stylist help you. It's time to stop dressing like your office is at a coffeehouse. It's not the image Daddy or any of us want for PRW."

Paige sighed. "The only one who seems to have an issue with my wardrobe choices is you. No one has said a word about it."

"Actually, they have. To me. This is me telling you—from everyone—that you need to start dressing the part."

For a moment, all she could do was stare. "Um… excuse me? What?"

Carefully, Ariel leaned against the countertop and then made a pinched face at her suit touching the surface. "Look, you're an executive now, Paige. College is over. I mean…honestly. If you weren't my sister and I saw you walking around here, I'd swear you were an intern."

Looking down at herself and then at her reflection, Paige still didn't understand what all the fuss was about. "I'm wearing a skirt!"

With an eye roll, Ariel studied her. "It's a knit skirt. And clingy. And…are those tights you're wearing?"

"Um…yeah. Why?"

"Oh God," Ariel murmured and smoothed a hand over her hair. "Okay, let me try another approach. Turn and face the mirror." They both did. "Look at us side by side. What do you see?"

"That genetics clearly favored only one of us?" Paige joked.

Ariel didn't smile. She rarely did. She thought it caused wrinkles.

"Okay, fine. I'm looking."

"And?"

"And I see that you are wearing a suit and I'm wearing a skirt and sweater." She shrugged.

"You're overaccessorized," Ariel pointed out. "The scarf, the bracelets, the giant watch, and don't even get me started on those clunky boots."

Okay, now she was getting pissed. "Look, I happen to *like* all these accessories, and there's nothing wrong with any of it. I'm not you. I'm not going to wear a suit or stilettos. That's not who I am! And even if I went out and copied your entire wardrobe, I can guarantee you it won't look the same on me as it does on you."

"Obviously."

"Why are you always like this?" Paige asked wearily. "It's like you purposely choose the worst times to pull these stunts."

"Stunt? What stunt? I'm trying to help you, Paige! You're about to go in front of the board with your whole… book thing. I want you to put forward the right impression. Gosh, excuse me for trying to be a good sister."

And there it was—the start of the martyr act. If she had a dollar for every time Ariel…

"I mean, every time I try to do something nice for you, you get mad and make me feel bad. I don't know what else I can do to prove to you that I have your best interests at heart."

Okay, she is still going…

"Remember when we used to play together and you would tell me how much you wanted to be like me when you grew up?"

Um…no.

"What happened? What did I ever do to you to make you so ungrateful?"

"That's enough," Paige said finally. "I'm not ungrateful. I'm not. I'm sorry you feel that way. It's just that

I'm stressed enough right now, and if you were really concerned about my choice of wardrobe today, you could have told me sooner than three minutes before the presentation." She did a quick double take at her watch and gasped. "Three minutes! Oh crap!"

"Language, Paige," Ariel said with disdain. "Daddy would have a fit if he heard you cursing like a sailor."

Seriously? That was cursing like a sailor? Then it was a good thing her father wasn't in her head right now because he'd probably have a stroke.

With one last glance at herself in the mirror, she couldn't help but be self-conscious. Her hair was a mess compared to her sister's. Where Ariel's was pale blond and silky, Paige's was more of a honeyed blond and wavy. Even tied back like it was now, it didn't look neat. And she wasn't kidding on the genetics comment. Besides the height difference, Paige was...curvier. And not in a way that made her feel like a model. Her curves were... Well, they were everywhere and tended to make her look chubby rather than shapely.

Dammit.

This is exactly what always happened. She'd be feeling good about herself and then her sister would walk by with some stupid comment and undo the girl-power pep talk she had just given herself.

Straightening her glasses—oh yes, she wore glasses too—she resigned herself to going in front of the board looking less than executive worthy and hoped everyone would be more focused on the facts and figures of the campaign than her choice in fashion.

One could hope, right?

As they exited the ladies' room, Paige immediately

switched gears and went into work mode. "Okay, did you send out those invitations I asked you to for participants?" Paige had given her that simple job in exchange for helping Ariel negotiate the fine points of the Hernandez contract. Invitations were one of Ariel's strongest points. No one liked to refuse her. That's why Paige hadn't assigned the task to one of their assistants.

Ariel nodded as she glided elegantly down the hall. Paige had to take two steps to her sister's one. "I did. And I even reached out to several more. This way if anyone backs out, we have substitutes at the ready."

"Perfect. Good job. Thanks," Paige replied. "Have you gotten any responses yet? I mean to the new ones?"

Ariel nodded again. "It's all in the folder."

"What folder?"

"The one I gave you."

Paige huffed loudly as they turned and made their way toward the corner conference room. "You didn't give me a folder, Ariel."

"Well, I put it on your desk," she said flippantly, and then her entire face broke out in a smile as their father stood to greet them. "Hi, Daddy! You're looking handsome today!"

Ugh. Seriously?

"Hey, Dad," she said with a smile after Ariel stepped aside.

"There's my girl," Robert Walters said proudly. "All set for your big presentation?"

"I am. I was just…"

"Didn't you forget that folder on your desk?" Ariel asked sweetly, and Paige wanted to kick her.

Their father looked at Paige expectantly.

"Um…thanks for reminding me. Give me five minutes." She took two steps back, then turned and did her best not to run from the room.

Of course, once she was out of the conference room's line of vision, she bolted. Down the hall, around the bend, and she almost tripped and fell as her assistant, Daisy, jumped out from behind her desk.

"Hey! Where's the fire?" she asked and then gasped. "Oh my God! Is there? A fire? Are you coming here to warn everyone? Should I make an announcement? Everyone—"

"No! No!" Paige quickly interrupted. "There's no fire. I forgot a folder I need for the meeting. Ariel said she put it on my desk." Walking past her assistant, she went into her office and began a frantic search of her desk. There were papers and files and calendars and Post-its but…no folder. The one she had given Ariel was a pretty pastel blue with the logo she was thinking of using for the campaign on it. "Where the heck…?"

"You know, if you cleaned that surface off once in a while, you'd be able to find things much easier."

"Uh-huh… Where could she have put it?"

"In the conference room."

Paige instantly stood. "Excuse me?"

"The folder? The pretty blue one with the logo you think looks good but needs to be tweaked because it's too generic for something like this? Personally, I think you should go with something—"

"Daisy! Focus! Where is the folder?"

Daisy sighed and said, "In the conference room. You had already left when Ariel floated in here on her cloud of superiority, and I told her you weren't coming here before the meeting. But did she listen? No. So after she left, I took the folder to the conference room for you. It's on the little podium stand and everything. Oh, and I left you a bottle of water and a little thing of hand sanitizer."

This time she didn't bother hiding that she was running and simply sprinted down the hall and back to the conference room. Her footsteps echoed as she entered the room and all eyes were on her.

Dammit.

With a quiet clearing of her throat, she apologized and took her seat at the table and then waited for her father to do as he always did — go over their agenda and open the floor to any new projects — and then he'd let her get up and do her thing.

Relief swamped her as she got comfortable and realized that no one was particularly paying attention to her and she could take a few minutes to catch her breath and collect her thoughts. She wished she could have grabbed the folder to glance through it before she had to stand up and present. Her curiosity was piqued about who else Ariel had reached out to. For starters, she didn't think her sister knew of any other authors who would achieve Paige's goals.

Paige followed along on the agenda and made notes where she knew she'd need to step in and finalize details and finally — *finally!* — her father called her up.

At the podium, she smiled and immediately started sharing one of her favorite stories about when reading had become so important to her. She had been eight, and it had been storming and she couldn't go outside and play. Her mother had suggested sitting quietly with a book. That book had been *Harry Potter and the Sorcerer's Stone*. For several minutes, Paige described how it felt to be transported to another world, where she could forget about the storm and about her disappointment about not being able to go outside and instead enjoy the wonders of the written word.

When she looked up, she saw some interest, some boredom, and her sister filing her nails.

Clearing her throat, she straightened and went in for the hard facts and figures. "The statistics haven't changed much in the past decade. Thirty-two million adults in the United States are functionally illiterate. Over twenty percent of adults read below a fifth-grade level. And it's not getting better, as schools are graduating teens who can't read. Libraries and schools want to change this. With the introduction of projects such as International Literacy Day, we have brought this problem more into the spotlight, but it's not enough. We may not be able to help everyone, but I believe with the right campaign, we can put a dent in this alarming statistic."

Opening the folder, she only gave it a cursory glance before continuing. "I've been actively working with Literacy Now for some time on a personal level, and when they came to me and asked for help with a new campaign, I knew we could do something amazing for them. My plan is to bring on a host of A-list authors for promotional spots on TV and in newspapers and magazines to talk about the issue. On top of that, they will go to schools and talk to teachers and students, to encourage them not only about the importance of learning to read, but also to share the joy and wonders of how reading can enrich their lives."

"Who have you recruited so far?" her father asked, and Paige was thrilled to see the genuine interest on his face.

Pulling out the list, she was about to read it and then stopped. *What the…?* She glanced over at Ariel, who was now texting on her phone. "Ariel?"

Her sister looked up. "Hmm?"

"What is this list?"

"The one you asked me to work on."

"Uh…no, it's not. This is not a list of authors. I have no idea who these people are. My list had *New York Times* bestselling authors from multiple genres—Marta Hayes, Mitchell Blake, Stephen Cane… Who are these people you've contacted?"

Robert Walters looked over at his older daughter and waited. Paige knew immediately that the waterworks were going to start and the excuses were going to fly.

"That is *not* what we talked about, Paige! You said you wanted big names. You didn't specifically say authors."

"It's a *literacy* campaign! Who else would we need? And, need I remind you, I gave you the list. All you had to do was reach out to their agents. I didn't ask you to contact anyone new."

"Oh, that's just great! I do you a favor by finding you better people—more famous people—and this is the thanks I get?" Ariel cried and then looked at their father. "Honestly, Dad, I was trying to make this campaign a success. No one will pay attention to people they don't know talking to them about things they don't care about. There was no one famous on her list!"

"Now, Ariel, Paige had a specific plan for this campaign—"

"But it wasn't going to work," Ariel countered. "And besides, I was trying to do a good thing. I've been feeling so weird lately, and then it came to me that this was what we needed to do. So while I was at the doctor's office—"

"Why were you at the doctor?" Robert asked, concern instantly lacing his voice.

Paige was certain she was seeing her own brain from rolling her eyes so hard. How was it that nobody else saw through this ridiculous act?

"Well," Ariel began with a coy grin, "I was going to wait until lunch to tell you, but…" She looked around the table to build anticipation. "I'm pregnant! Dennis and I are having a baby!" Then she squealed with joy and waited as everyone jumped up to congratulate her.

With a sigh of resignation, Paige stuffed the papers into the folder and simply joined the line to wait her turn.

--~~--

The next day, Paige begrudgingly sat and looked over Ariel's list. The rest of the previous day had been a bust. After the big pregnancy announcement, the meeting had ended. Her father promised they'd get together later in the week to talk about the campaign again, but he had been too far gone with joy at the news of becoming a grandfather to concentrate on anything else.

There was a part of Paige that was excited at the thought of becoming an aunt, but really, it was the image of her sister getting fat and throwing up that put the slight grin on her face.

"Uh-oh. Someone looks like they're plotting something!"

Looking up, Paige chuckled as Daisy walked in. She was a little bit younger than Paige—fresh out of college—but there was something about her that made you feel like she had been living under a rock or something. She was a hard worker but a bit…quirky. Clueless. Not in a bad way, Paige thought, but there were times when it took far too much energy to reel the girl in.

"What could I possibly be plotting?" Paige asked sweetly. "There's too much work to be done to focus on anything else."

Placing some messages on her desk, Daisy took a seat facing her. "So how did the meeting go yesterday? I had to head out early. Did everyone love the list of authors we're going to get?" She sighed happily. "I mentioned to my mom—who loves to read—that we were trying for Marta Hayes, and she about fell out of her chair! I mean she screeched, and I thought she was going to hyperventilate! So I had to calm her down and get her something to drink and before you knew it—"

"Daisy?"

"Hmm?"

Paige took a moment and studied her assistant. "Remember when we talked about asking questions and waiting for the answer before you start talking again?"

Confusion came first. Then remembrance. Then a smile. "Right. Sorry," Daisy said with a sheepish smile. "You were going to tell me about the meeting."

"I had just started going into my pitch about the list of authors, except when I looked it over, it was all different. Ariel changed it," Paige said.

"What? No!" Daisy cried with disbelief. "Why would she do that?"

"Because she thinks we need bigger celebrity names—not authors. I mean…she doesn't even understand what it is we're trying to do here. It's a literacy campaign! We need to have authors! I know there have been other campaigns with sports stars and celebrities, but that wasn't the angle I was going for." With a huff, Paige pulled up the list of names Ariel had made and handed it to Daisy. "Honestly, I can't even look at the stupid thing. I get aggravated just thinking about it. I don't even recognize some of those names!"

Taking the paper from her boss's hand, Daisy scanned it and then gasped excitedly. "Oh, come on! You have to know who Mick Jagger is!" Then she looked up at Paige and shook her head. "Not that I expect him to do the campaign. I mean, let's be realistic."

"I know there are some big names on there—none of whom are probably going to do it—but that's not the point. The point is, I had an outline for this campaign and she disregarded it. Now I'm going to have to redo my approach and still reach out to authors and their agents and publicists and publishers when I'm already swamped!"

"I can help with that, Paige. That's part of my job."

Paige smiled. "I know. And thank you. But…I had this whole thing worked out in my head and now it's going to be completely different."

"What did your father say? Didn't he question why she changed everything without telling you?"

"He never got the chance," Paige said.

"How come?"

"Because in the middle of it all, she dropped a bombshell. She's pregnant."

"No!"

Paige nodded. "Oh yes."

"And she decided to share that? In the middle of your presentation?"

Another nod. "I don't think she would have if it weren't for the fact that I was calling her out on making these changes without my permission and she was trying to take the focus off that."

"Kind of an elaborate tale to tell just to get out of getting reprimanded."

Tale? "Wait…are you saying you don't think she's pregnant?"

Daisy's eyes went wide. "What? Oh, no. That's not what I meant. Although…nothing would surprise me where Ariel's concerned." Then her hand flew over her mouth as if she couldn't believe she had said that out loud.

Unable to help herself, Paige burst out laughing.

"Oh God, oh God, oh God, oh God!" Daisy cried, jumping to her feet. "I'm sorry! I'm really, really sorry. I can't believe I said that!"

Wiping tears of mirth from her eyes, Paige waved her off. "It's okay. Seriously, Daisy, you're fine. It's fine. Sit down. Please."

Daisy murmured "Oh God" a few more times, then sat, her face beet red with embarrassment. After a moment, she calmed and let out a slow breath. "That was completely unprofessional of me. Ariel is your sister and an executive, and she deserves my respect."

Color me impressed. "It's all right," Paige said. "No one heard except me and…well…you know my frustration with my sister, so we're good."

"Honestly, Paige, you need to say something to your father. Or to your mother, and have her talk to your father. What Ariel does it's…it's just wrong."

Don't I know it. "The thing with her is she's good at her job. Really good. I'm not trying to take that away from her. But she's not good at finding a cause and getting a campaign started. She's good at taking over once all the groundwork is done."

"So why not let it be known that it's not fair that she's coasting on other people's ideas?" Daisy asked.

"Because I'd end up looking paranoid. I'm not good at responding on the fly when she pulls one of these swoops. I'm normally stunned and then I turn mute."

"Or you come in here and talk to yourself."

Paige's eyes narrowed at the comment.

"Sorry."

"Don't be. You're right. I just don't know how to be heard. I've tried to show that I can handle a campaign on my own, I really have, but…" She paused. "Do people think I dress weird?"

"Um…what?"

"My clothes. You hear the things people comment on around here. Has anyone commented on what I wear?"

"Why would you ask that? You are, like, the coolest person fashion-wise in this office! We all love your clothes! Very hipster-ish."

Sighing, Paige pinched her nose and thought of how to respond. "I don't think the executives are looking at how much of a hipster I am. That's who I'm worried about."

"Did your sister put this idea in your head?"

Paige nodded.

"Look, I talk to all the assistants here, and believe me when I tell you we talk about everything. No one has ever mentioned your wardrobe to me, so I think if anyone has an issue with it, it's Ariel and Ariel alone."

They sat in companionable silence for a moment before Daisy spoke again.

"So, a baby in the family. That should be nice."

"I guess. Although, I have to admit, I have a hard time imagining Ariel dealing with pregnancy. I don't think she realizes that she won't be rocking her designer suits and heels quite like she's used to."

Daisy chuckled. "Well…maybe she will. You see all those glamorous actresses walking the red carpet when they're nine months pregnant, and they do it with such ease! Remember Beyoncé at that awards show? I can barely walk around in high heels now. I couldn't imagine doing it while I had a baby belly."

"I guess we're going to find out soon enough how she'll do." Honestly, no matter how snarky her thoughts, Paige knew her sister would come off looking like it was all a breeze. If it were Paige, however, there wasn't a doubt in her mind that pregnancy would make her look like a bloated, beached whale.

Great. Something to look forward to.

Not!

Clearing her throat, Daisy picked up the list that had fallen to the floor and glanced at it again. "Honestly, Paige, it's not that this is a bad list. It's random—almost as if she were simply picking names of people who have been in the headlines lately. I can't see a correlation between any of them and this particular campaign."

"That's what I thought too. I just wish she had—"

Daisy's loud gasp cut her off.

"What? What's the matter?"

Daisy glanced at the list and then at Paige before her gaze returned to the piece of paper. "Did you see who's on here?"

"Um…yeah. Sort of. Maybe. Why?"

"Dylan Anders is on here! Oh my God! I can't believe it! I love him!" She jumped to her feet again. "Do you think he's going to do it? Did Ariel mention if she'd talked to him already? If he comes here, I think I'll die. No…no…I *know* I'll die! Oh my God…Dylan Anders!" she cried and began to fan herself with the paper. "That man is sex on a stick!"

Paige sighed. Great. Just what she needed—sex on a stick when she hadn't had sex since…well… Heck. When *was* the last time she'd had sex?

"He's got great arms! Oh my gosh, have you seen them? I bet he has great hands too! He must, from playing bass! And he looks incredible in jeans and when he's all scruffy—he's one of those guys who can totally pull that off and make it look incredibly hot, you know? But oh…that would be amazing if Ariel got him! Don't you think it would be amazing?"

"Not five minutes ago we were talking about how her list was ridiculous!" Paige snapped. "And now one look at a name of some random guitar player—"

"Bass player."

"Whatever! One look at a name on a page and all of a sudden Ariel's right and I'm wrong?"

Daisy gave her a patient smile. "No one said you were wrong, Paige. I just think this could be, you know, exciting! Rock stars and authors. It could make for a very cool campaign. You'd be appealing to a wider demographic this way, wouldn't you?"

Dammit, she didn't want Ariel to be right. She didn't want this to be a good idea at all. This was her baby. Her brainchild. She'd worked for weeks perfecting everything down to the tiniest detail, and her sister, being her typical self, just happened to stumble upon a great idea? How unfair was that?

"Look, I'm not saying what she did was right," Daisy went on. "I just think that maybe, this one time, she might have happened upon a good idea." She shrugged. "It's up to you what you want to do with it. You're the one who's going to make it great."

Paige gently face-planted on the desk. "I don't know what to do with it," she mumbled. "If I agree with her, she's going to be so smug. And if I don't go along with it and the campaign fails, then it will all come back on me how I screwed up because of my ego."

"I certainly wouldn't want to be in your shoes."

Slowly, Paige lifted her head and gave her assistant a stern glare. "Thanks."

"Why don't I get you a bottle of water and some ibuprofen and close the doors so you can concentrate? I won't let anyone in unless it's an emergency and I'll hold all your calls. How does that sound?"

"Make the water a soda and throw in a bag of chips and you've got a deal."

Daisy left and, for a minute, Paige let the silence wash over her. It was after three in the afternoon and a Friday. Would it be a bad thing for her to pack it in and call it a day? She had a feeling that maybe she'd get more accomplished and perhaps think a little clearer about this list of potential celebrities if she was some-place a little more soothing. Peaceful.

And not her office.

That was the key.

If she was going to relax and look at the situation objectively, she knew she needed to put a little effort into unwinding. Maybe she'd leave and stop at the grocery store on the way home and find something fun to make for dinner—and grab some cake or brownies for dessert. And wine! Yes, a nice bottle of wine to get her through the weekend would help with the situation.

Looking around her office, she spotted her satchel and immediately snapped it up and began organizing papers, folders, and reports and stuffing them inside. With a quick glance at her emails, she noted that there wasn't anything urgent waiting for her, and without an ounce of guilt, she shut down her computer. Walking around the room, Paige scooped up her phone, her charger, and the small stack of books she had on a corner table that she'd been meaning to bring home.

Once everything was packed, she scanned the room one more time and was pleased to see that she had everything she needed. At the thought of leaving early, the tension began to ease from her shoulders, which she rolled to confirm that fact. All she needed to do was let Daisy know. No need to tell anyone else—it wasn't as if she punched a clock. Everyone worked crazy hours as needed and no one ever questioned her whereabouts. Not that she ever took advantage of it, but it was a nice perk.

"Okay, boss! Here's your soda and… What are you doing? Are you going somewhere?" Daisy asked as soon as she stepped into the office.

"I have decided to head home and look over this stuff and try to make sense of it all. You know I see things more objectively when I'm not stressed."

Daisy smiled and then sighed. "I wish you weren't tense all the time. You're so good at your job, and you know everyone here thinks the world of you. It wouldn't be such a bad thing for you to just...relax!"

"That's why I'm leaving early. I'm going to go home and unwind and..."

"Do some yoga? I love doing yoga. It really helps me—"

"No yoga," Paige interrupted before the story went any further. "I'm going to pick up something good to make for dinner, something yummy for dessert, and some wine."

"Yoga's better for you."

"You relieve stress your way, and I'll relieve it my way. Okay?" she asked, forcing a smile on her face.

"Fine. Go and grill a cow or eat a vat of ice cream. See if I care. I'm going to do hot yoga tonight and maybe a Zumba class in the morning."

"Good for you," Paige said, taking the bottle of soda from Daisy's hand. "And I hope you have a great weekend. I'll see you Monday." She began to walk away, but Daisy got in step beside her.

"Can I ask you something?"

"Sure."

"Do you ever do anything...you know...fun?"

Paige looked at her as if she was crazy. "Seriously? That's your question?"

Daisy nodded. "Uh-huh. It's just that I've noticed how you take work home every weekend, and you never talk about doing anything fun, like going on a date or out with friends. You should do that."

They were at the elevator, and Paige hit the Down button and then turned toward Daisy. "Things have been busy but…sure, I go out with friends."

"When was the last time you did that?"

Oh God. When was that? Probably around the last time she'd had sex. Not that she was having sex with friends but… Oh. Wait. Mitch. Mitch Stevens. Sex and a friend. Sort of like a two-for-one based on this conversation.

"Okay, I'll admit it's been a while. But it's all good. Once this campaign stuff falls into place, I'll be able to step back a bit and take time for myself. I promise."

Daisy's gaze narrowed. "I'm not sure I believe you."

Behind them, the elevator dinged its arrival. Thankfully.

"Don't worry about me," Paige said reassuringly. "I'm fine. You enjoy your weekend and hopefully on Monday all of this will have sorted itself out. And maybe…" She stopped as the look on Daisy's face changed.

Paled.

Her mouth opened and closed but no sound came out. Her eyes widened.

"Daisy? Are you okay? What's going on?"

"I…I… It's…it's…"

Panic swamped Paige. She stepped forward and grabbed her assistant by the shoulders and gave her a gentle shake. "Daisy? What's wrong?"

"*Sex!*" Daisy hissed.

"What?"

Daisy began to tremble as she leaned forward and whispered to Paige, "Sex on a stick. Oh God. He really is!"

Paige took a step back and immediately bumped into someone. "Oh…excuse me. I'm sorry. I…" She turned her head and froze.

Good Lord.

Tall, dark, and a bit scruffy. He wore faded blue jeans, a gray T-shirt, and a leather jacket, and smelled like a sexy combination of heaven and sin. Paige's eyes wandered up to his strong jaw and dark-chocolate-brown eyes as she swallowed hard.

Holy. Crap.

"Hey," he said casually, smiling. "I'm looking for Paige Walters. I was told her office was up here."

"You're…you're…" Daisy stammered.

He laughed softly and held out his hand to her. "Dylan Anders."

Of course he was.

Chapter 2

DYLAN SHOOK HANDS WITH THE WOMAN WHO WAS STILL wide eyed and slack jawed, but it was the one directly in front of him who held his attention. She was petite and curvy and maybe it was the glasses but…her eyes looked huge. They were such a deep shade of brown they were almost black and maybe it was his imagination but she hadn't blinked. At all. Taking his hand from the first woman, he asked, "And you are?"

She giggled. "Daisy. I'm Daisy Garner and I'm a huge fan." She studied her hand and then sighed. "Wow. I can't believe you're here. I was just saying how I was hoping you'd come in and here you are! Can I get a picture of you? Will you wait while I get my camera? I swear I'll only be a minute and—"

"Daisy!" the woman in front of him snapped, but she didn't look away from him.

"Oh…right. Sorry. Give me a minute."

When she was gone, Dylan relaxed. Smiling, he said, "She's a bit chatty, huh?"

"You have no idea."

He waited a minute to see if she'd introduce herself, and when she didn't, he prompted, "I don't believe I caught your name."

She blushed. "Oh…um. Paige. I'm Paige Walters."

Uh-oh. This threw his plans for a loop. He was all set

to charm an elderly librarian type. And Paige Walters was as far from an elderly librarian as they came. She had a studious look to her, but those killer curves and the fact that she was probably younger than him blew that plan to hell. Now what? Maybe she was a fan like Daisy was. That could work in his favor.

"So," he began, "you're exactly who I was hoping to see." Then he noticed her satchel and it dawned on him that she had been waiting for the elevator. "I'm sorry. Is this a bad time?"

"Did we have an appointment?" she asked, her voice sounding a little gruff and shaky.

"Uh…no. We didn't. I was hoping to talk to you about this campaign that you're working on."

Her eyes got wider and then narrowed at him. "Really?" she asked with both sarcasm and disbelief.

Dylan nodded. "Yes. So…do you have some time right now to talk? If you're heading somewhere, I can walk with you, or we can grab some coffee or—"

"Oh, take her to get some coffee!" Daisy said excitedly, as she walked toward them, smiling from ear to ear. She snapped a couple of pictures of him and then asked Paige to take one of the two of them together before she got back on topic. "Paige was heading out, but she loves that great coffee shop on the corner. They have amazing cake pops."

"I'm standing right here, Daisy," Paige said wearily.

"I know you are, but I also know if I didn't say anything, you'd probably pass on taking the time to talk with Dylan. I'm being helpful."

"You're being rude," Paige murmured and then offered Dylan a tight smile. "Anyway, um…I am heading out for the day, but I can spare a few minutes for coffee if that works for you."

"And cake pops?" he teased and almost sagged with relief when she smiled. And damn, did she have a great smile.

"And cake pops," she said as she ducked her head and blushed again. Turning to Daisy, she said, "Go and man the phones and I'll see you Monday. If anyone comes looking for me—"

"I'll take care of it," Daisy replied, clearly suppressing a grin. "Have a great weekend." Then she looked at Dylan and giggled. "It was nice to meet you!" Then she spun and practically skipped away.

Beside him, Paige shook her head.

"Is she your assistant?"

She nodded and then reached around him to hit the button for the elevator. A few minutes ago, she couldn't take her eyes off him, and now she would barely look at him. They waited in silence, and once the elevator arrived, he motioned for her to precede him into it and then stepped in behind her.

"If you'd rather not get coffee, you know, I'm sure I can schedule a time to meet with you here next week," Paige said as soon as the doors closed.

Wait, was she trying to get rid of him?

While looking straight ahead at the doors, she went on. "I'm sure you're a very busy man and I don't know if you can have coffee without people swarming you or something, and to be honest, if we're going to talk about the campaign—and your possible involvement in it—I prefer to do so without fans hovering for pictures."

Her voice was almost void of emotion, and Dylan realized Paige clearly wasn't a fan of his.

"I don't normally get bothered," he supplied. "I mean occasionally a fan or two, like your assistant, will come over to say hello, but it's not like my presence in a Starbucks is going to incite a riot or anything."

"Still… I think it would be better if maybe we scheduled something for…"

Dylan stepped in front of her—directly in her line of vision so she couldn't ignore him. "How about a compromise?"

She looked at him quizzically but silently. Great. He hadn't thought about where he was going with this. All he knew was that he didn't want to wait until next week to talk to her. True, he hadn't known that until this minute, but there was something about her that… intrigued him. And more than anything, he wanted to know if she had an aversion to working with him because of his history or because of something else.

Maybe he was paranoid, but he was getting a strong vibe that Paige was trying to get rid of him.

"A compromise?"

Think fast! "Um…yeah. A compromise." *Brilliant. Keep repeating the same words. That oughta make her want to work on a literacy campaign with you. Moron.*

The elevator came to a stop on the first floor, and when the doors opened, Dylan again motioned for her to go first as he frantically tried to think of a reasonable compromise.

"Like what?" she asked as she came to a stop in the middle of the massive lobby. There were a few people walking around, but no one was paying any attention to them. Maybe that would work in his favor, if she noticed he wasn't one of those mob-inducing celebrities.

"Well, you seemed like you were on your way out to…someplace. Maybe I can tag along and we can talk. Like in the car. We'll grab our coffees—if you want one—and drive for a bit. No one's going to chase after the car or anything," he said with a small laugh and instantly stopped when he saw she wasn't laughing.

Or smiling.

"I'm going to the grocery store," she stated. "And then home. I don't think that's going to work. We can do this next week. I'll have Daisy call you. I think we have your number on file so—"

"No!" he quickly interrupted. Okay, this time he was definitely being paranoid, but he knew if he didn't talk to her today, didn't convince her to let him in on this project, that he wasn't going to get another chance.

"Excuse me?"

He sighed and figured he had nothing left to lose. "Look, I get it. You know who I am and I can tell you've got no real interest in working with me. Actually, I don't get it. If you feel like this, why reach out to me at all?"

"Actually…I didn't," she said hesitantly and then instantly looked down at the ground.

"I don't understand."

Now it was her turn to sigh, but then she looked up at him. "I had… And then my sister…" She stopped and sighed again. "Maybe we should go get that coffee."

Two minutes ago, Dylan would have considered that a victory, but now he had a feeling she was using it as a way to let him down easily. "Yeah. Okay. Sure." She gave him a brief nod and then led the way out of the building. He got in step beside her, and neither spoke as they walked along the sidewalk to the corner coffee shop.

Once inside, they still didn't speak except to give their orders. He breathed a sigh of relief that no one seemed to recognize him, and when Paige offered to get a table, he agreed to wait for their drinks. Dylan motioned to the barista and asked for a couple of cake pops to be added to their bill. He noticed Paige hadn't ordered any, but at this point, he wasn't above using whatever he could to get on her good side.

As he waited, his mind raced. Why was this so important? When Mick had first mentioned this project to him, it wasn't something he'd wanted to do. Then he'd made his peace with it, but it wasn't as if it were mandatory that he do this project in particular to meet his community service commitment. There were plenty to choose from. Maybe it was ridiculous for him to be getting in a snit over it and trying to win over a chick who didn't seem like she wanted to be won.

Dylan looked over to the table in the far corner that Paige had snagged for them and smiled. She looked flustered, and she fidgeted with her hair and then her glasses as she looked around the room as if waiting for some sort of flash mob to jump out at any moment and demand he perform with them.

"Oh my God! Are you Dylan Anders?" a voice whispered from behind the counter.

Dylan turned and smiled at the young girl holding his tray of cake pops and coffees. He leaned in a little and whispered. "I am."

She blushed and slowly handed him his tray. "I

thought it was you and I didn't want to say it out loud and embarrass you—or me, in case I was wrong. Wow! I...I'm such a big fan. Really. You're awesome."

"Thanks," he replied and looked at her name badge, "Tammy. I appreciate that."

She looked over her shoulder as if gauging the line. "Would you mind signing something for me?"

"Not at all." He waited as she reached for a cup and then grabbed a Sharpie and handed it to him.

"Sorry. It's all I can find, and I don't want to draw attention to you or get in trouble with my boss."

"No worries," he said, still smiling, as he signed the cup and handed it to her. "And thanks. I appreciate you keeping it quiet."

"Oh," she sighed happily. "Sure. No problem. Enjoy your coffee!"

With a wave, Dylan made his way to the corner where Paige was waiting, frowning.

Great.

Deciding to ignore that look, he put the tray on the table and smiled. He handed her the white chocolate mocha Frappuccino and then the plate of cake pops. He saw her eyes light up briefly and decided right then and there that if he managed to get her to agree to let him work on this project, he would have to remember that she clearly had a sweet tooth.

Placing the empty tray aside on a vacant chair, he stripped off his jacket and was about to sit down when he saw the horrified look on Paige's face.

She was staring at his arms—at his tattoos—with more than a hint of disgust. Okay, not everyone was a fan of tattoos, but his weren't anything to freak out over.

It wasn't as if he were covered in demons and skulls, for crying out loud! His sleeves were deeply personal to him. Every drop of ink on his skin held a special meaning—his latest tat finished the sleeve on his right arm and said, "Inhale the future, exhale the past." It was a good motto to be living by right now. The rest on that arm had to do with music and was filled in with roses, which were symbolic of deep love, passion, and balance. Or so he'd been told. They were also sometimes seen as a message for healing, rejuvenation, and courage.

That described his journey of the past several months.

Not deterred by her reaction, Dylan sat and took a sip of his dark roast. Not that he didn't enjoy a good latte or espresso, but right now, he really needed some straight coffee.

"So," he began after his first sip, "I read the packet you sent along, and I have to admit, it sounds great."

Paige took another sip of her drink and then put it down before speaking. He watched her eye the plate of cake pops, and he had a feeling she was fighting the urge to at least taste one before talking to him. But she looked up at him and gave him a small smile.

At least she wasn't sneering or looking at his arms anymore. She cleared her throat and straightened in her chair.

Here we go.

"Mr. Anders—"

"Dylan," he corrected with a smile.

That seemed to relax her a little. "Okay…Dylan. There seems to be a bit of a…misunderstanding." She paused. "You see, my original plans for this campaign involved using well-known authors and *only* authors.

After all, who understands the love of reading and the importance of it more than an author?"

"That makes sense."

She nodded and took another small sip of her beverage. "Well, that was the plan I laid out to my firm, and the person I asked to reach out to those authors took it upon herself to…expand upon my list and reach out to…"

"Me?"

She nodded again. "And others."

"And that's a bad thing?"

That had her hesitating, and he watched with a mixture of annoyance and amusement as she eyed the cake pops again. Knowing he'd never have her full attention at this rate, Dylan reached over and picked one up and held it out to her. "Here. Eat it. Please!" he said with a forced chuckle. "Just…get it out of the way so we can talk."

Her cheeks turned a deep shade of red, and Dylan realized it probably wasn't overly proper or polite of him to point out that she was agonizing over a piece of cake, but they had bigger issues to discuss, and dammit, he deserved her full attention.

"Sorry," he murmured as she reluctantly took the pop from his hand. "I hate sitting here watching you argue with yourself over this. Take it and enjoy it. I got it for you."

"Thanks," she said quietly. "It's not very professional, or ladylike, for me to be paying more attention to cake than a client so…I'm sorry." Then she took a delicate bite of the pop and groaned with pleasure.

Dylan's immediate thought was how the cake was bite-sized and wondered why she took such a small bite, but as soon as she groaned, he realized he didn't give a damn how many bites it took for her to get through it. Never had he seen someone take such extreme pleasure in their food—especially such a tiny bite of food!

He shifted in his seat and thought of helping himself to one of the pops but immediately reconsidered. If they had to sit here for the rest of the afternoon, he was willing to torture himself and simply listen to Paige enjoy each and every bite.

"Oh, that's good," she said and smiled at him. "Thank you."

"My pleasure," he replied, and meant it. "So...someone messed with your list..."

She took another bite, moaned, and nodded.

Dylan shifted again to ease what was sure to become a very evident reaction to the sound of Paige's throaty voice.

"My sister," she said. "She doesn't think authors— bestselling authors—are a big enough draw for the campaign. So she decided to reach out to bigger names, but to be honest with you, I don't understand her reasoning." She studied him for a moment. "I mean, overall I do. Many literacy campaigns in the past have used athletes and celebrities to help sell the cause. But...is there something about you that would have her believe you'd be a good fit for a literacy project? Have you ever done anything for this cause before?"

He shook his head. "Honestly, I've never worked on anything like this before." He paused and tried to work out in his head what he wanted to say, but his mouth didn't want to wait. "Look, I'm a musician. Normally my time is spent on tour or in the studio. There was never time or a need to do anything like this. But right now? I've got nothing but time on my hands and this is a project I'd like to get involved with."

With a tilted head, she looked at him, and he noticed the slight frown. "Why? Why do you have so much free time?"

"The band's on hiatus."

Straightening, she nodded. "Oh. Okay. For how long?"

"I don't know. Things are a little…complicated right now. But from what I saw of your timeline, it's not going to cause a conflict."

"How can you be so sure? What if things worked out and someone wanted to perform next week? Then what?"

"Then I'd make it work out so I would honor my commitment to you first," he said quickly, feeling the first twinge of hope since this conversation began. "If I sign on with you, Paige, then I promise I will see it through to the end. Although I can't imagine that you'd need me to be an active participant 24/7 for the entire run. But the campaign would be my first priority. You have my word on that."

That seemed to please her. She took another sip of her Frappuccino and then picked up the next cake pop. Dylan almost leaned in with anticipation.

"I, um…I wasn't sure which flavors you liked," he said as she studied the pop. "That one is red velvet, I believe."

She gave him a shy smile. "Red velvet is my favorite, but they're all good." Then she took a small bite and— God help him—let out another little moan.

He felt a bead of sweat start to trickle down his neck.

Was she aware that she was doing it?

Clearing his throat, he said, "I think what you have

planned is impressive. I can imagine it's going to be successful and I want to be a part of it. So what do you say, Paige?"

Rather than answer, she took her second bite and finished the cake pop. Dylan had to distract himself until he was certain she was done.

Clearly, it had been way too long since he'd had sex if he was getting this hot and bothered over a woman eating dessert. He made a mental note to work on rectifying that.

Tonight.

Paige shifted a bit in her seat and studied him. "Dylan, I'd like to say yes to you, but…I can't."

Dammit.

"I was leaving early today to look over all the information Ariel changed and sort of wrap my head around it all and see if it makes sense or if we should stick to my original list of contributors and authors. It's nothing personal—"

"It feels personal," he muttered.

A small sigh escaped her. "I don't know enough about you to make this personal," she countered. "Honestly, Daisy told me who you were, but before that…I had no idea. I'm sorry."

For a minute, he could only stare. Was she for real? Not that he thought that highly of himself, but he knew that in current pop culture, he was a pretty big name. And she had no idea who he was?

"Do you listen to music? At all?"

She laughed. "Of course I do. And I'm sure if you told me what band you're with—"

"Shaughnessy."

"Oh! Oh yes! I really liked your last album," she said with a genuine smile. Then she shrugged. "But I'm the kind of person who can listen to the music and not give any thought to the people behind it. I know that sounds horrible but…there it is."

Okay, this wasn't a bad thing. It could totally work in his favor. If he could convince her to sign him on without having to get into the whole community service requirement quite yet, he'd be thrilled.

Relaxing, he crossed his arms over his chest and smiled at her. "It's okay, Paige. I don't have *that* big of an ego, where I expect everyone to know my name. Still, I feel like you're cutting me off—and anyone who isn't an author. I don't know what your sister's logic was behind the changes, but maybe she's onto something. I'm not saying you shouldn't have authors in the bunch. You totally should. But there's something to be said for adding another demographic. I'll bet we could organize a concert of some sort to raise money and awareness."

And if she agreed to sign him on, he'd make it happen come hell or high water!

Her eyes went wide. "A…a concert? I didn't think of anything like that. But then again, I haven't had the time to look at this from every angle. I was so set on having authors doing this that a concert wasn't even on my radar."

"Between the band and my connections, I'd like to think I could help you put something together that would get the attention your cause deserves." Then he leaned forward and took one of her hands in his. "And I truly believe in this, Paige. I think what you're doing is very…noble. There are a lot of kids who grow into adults without learning how to read—or who can't read beyond the basics. With any luck, this campaign will not only raise awareness, but it will also provide the funds needed for programs to help people of all ages."

When he stopped talking, he saw how Paige's eyes were bright with unshed tears.

What the…?

"I'm sorry. Did I say something wrong?"

She shook her head. "No. No, not at all. You said something completely right."

He looked at her with confusion.

With a quick swipe of her eyes, Paige looked at him with a small smile. "I feel like I've been fighting an uphill battle with this particular project. It's something that's personal to me, and I can't seem to get that same excitement from anyone else at the firm." She paused. "I mean, don't get me wrong. It's not like anyone's sabotaging it, but—"

"But they're also not going out of their way to support it either," Dylan finished for her.

"Exactly." She sighed. "I was in the middle of my presentation yesterday when I discovered the changes to my list. Then my sister… Well…never mind. It's not important. Let's say that my presentation got cut short and now I need to decide how to move forward."

It hit him then that he wasn't going to get an answer today. Clearly, she was a person who thought everything through, and from what she she'd said, this particular campaign was her baby, and she wasn't going to take to making changes kindly. He knew when to throw in the towel and let things go. And he would.

For now.

Picking up his cup of coffee, he took a long drink and then put it down. "Well, I guess I've taken up enough of your time." Standing up, he smiled and held out a hand to her. "It was nice meeting you, Paige, and I hope to hear from you soon."

His abrupt change of action seemed to fluster her. She went to stand and shake his hand at the same time and ended up almost knocking her chair over and did succeed in dumping her satchel. With a muttered curse, she apologized and dropped to her knees to pick up her things. Dylan crouched beside her, and they both reached for a book that had fallen out. Dylan grabbed it first and smiled.

"I finished this last night," he said, handing it to her. "I love a good whodunit, don't you?"

For some reason, that seemed to fluster her too. She accepted the book and hugged it to her chest as she frantically scooped up the rest of her things. With a muttered thanks, she stood. Dylan straightened and studied her. Paige kept her back to him as she repacked her satchel and he wondered if she was going to turn around or acknowledge him again. He was about to tap her on the shoulder when she faced him.

"So um…yes. I mean…I do love a good whodunit too," she said softly. "Do you have a favorite author?"

Dylan motioned toward her satchel. "I like his entire series. I started it about three months ago, and now I'm bummed because the next book won't be out for another couple of months."

"You… I mean… That's book eight in the series. You read all eight in three months?"

He nodded. "And a few others. Like I said, I'm a

sucker for that kind of story. There were also a few Stephen King books, and I'll admit to a couple of graphic novels that I threw in for variety. It's a great way to pass the time."

For a minute he thought she was going to comment, but all she did was nod.

All righty then.

Deciding there was more to Paige Walters than he was going to figure out today, Dylan knew it was time to go. "I hope you have a great weekend and enjoy your book," he said and then grabbed his empty cup and walked away.

"Dylan?"

Was it wrong how he got a little bit excited at the thought of her calling out because she had changed her mind and was going to sign him on the spot? Taking a steadying breath and hoping he didn't appear too anxious, he turned around.

"Thanks," she said, smiling. "I appreciate the coffee and cake."

"Oh…uh…sure. No problem."

"Have a good weekend," she said and then gave him a little wave.

The urge to ask her for a definite confirmation of at least a callback for next week was fairly strong. But he knew it would only hurt his cause. He had to be patient and give her time to think. With any luck, he'd given her enough information to at least consider him for the project.

Walking out onto the sidewalk, he slipped his sunglasses on and took a moment to enjoy the sun on his face. It felt good. And he enjoyed the smell of the city air. In rehab, he had been up in the mountains of Colorado and it had been beautiful, but he was a city boy at heart. The noise, the people…even the smog—it made everything seem right.

After a minute, he started toward PRW's building, where he'd parked his car. Glancing at his watch, he saw it was a little after four. Traffic was going to be a bitch, but it wasn't as if he was in a rush to get anywhere. Well, there had been that thought of getting laid tonight, but it was something he had to think about—no need to repeat what had happened with Heather. Or what hadn't happened. The thought made him shudder.

Pulling his keys from his pocket, he approached his Mercedes-AMG GT and used the remote to start it. The sporty convertible had been his first purchase after rehab. It was the first time he'd trusted himself to own a nice car. Now he was able to enjoy driving himself around—something he hadn't done in years—and it felt good. It gave him a sense of pride, and then he felt foolish for it. After all, most people were capable of driving themselves around town.

And now he was one of them.

With a grin, he opened the door and slid behind the wheel and sighed with pleasure at the feel of the soft leather and how the seat hugged him. Yeah, life was good.

And if he could get Paige Walters to take a chance on him, he might be able to say that life was great.

—∿∿—

"Brilliant. Just brilliant," Paige murmured as she placed her trash in the pail and carefully wove her way through the crowd of people in the coffee shop. Over and over in her mind, she replayed her clumsy act of knocking her stuff to the ground.

And that was after practically orgasming while eating a cake pop.

Okay, two cake pops.

She groaned as she exited the shop and walked toward the parking garage. *Why* had she agreed to go for coffee with Dylan Anders? Why hadn't she stuck to her guns and had Daisy call him with an appointment? Not only could she have avoided making an idiot out of herself, but she also could have kept her previous clueless opinion of him intact and not have to deal with the fact that he was a nice guy who seemed to get what she was trying to do.

Other than Daisy, he was the *only one* who seemed to get what she was doing.

And now she realized she had a fascination with tattoos. Tattoos! When Dylan had first taken off his jacket, she was shocked and a little repulsed by the sheer amount of ink on his arms. But after a little while, she couldn't help but keep noticing the artwork and found it to be… exquisite. Beautiful. More than once she had to stop herself from reaching out and touching his arms — which, forgetting about the tattoos, were muscular and sexy — and asking him to tell her what had inspired the choices.

Why? Why him? Why couldn't one of her favorite authors have come in and talked with her like this? Why did it have to be a scruffy, tattoo-covered rock star who not only didn't look the part of anything she was trying to do, but who potentially would also be a distraction for… well…her and probably any female in a ten-mile radius?

Although, she had to give him credit — other than the

barista who handed him their order, no one bothered him. No one came looking for autographs or pictures. He blended right into the crowd. How was that possible? When she got home, she would do a thorough Google search and see what else she could find out. Yes. That's exactly what she'd do. As charmed as she was by him—and she truly was—she had a feeling that part of it was an act to get her to agree to have him join the campaign.

But why? Why was this such a big deal to him? He wasn't going to be paid for it. And compared with being in one of the biggest rock bands in the world, this was nothing. It wasn't doing anything for him on a professional level, so why was he so anxious to be a part of it? What could he gain?

If there was one thing Paige prided herself on, it was being a good judge of character. And Dylan didn't strike her as the selfless type. He had a swagger and a confidence that seemed in direct conflict with the image she was hoping to project with this campaign.

So was this personal? Did he know someone who struggled with reading? He was clearly well read based on what he'd shared with her, so she knew he didn't have the issue. Someone who struggled with literacy didn't read *that* many books in a three-month time span. Should she decide to work with him, she'd have to ask.

With a groan, she pulled out her keys as she approached her Toyota Prius Prime. Her sporty little hybrid was shiny and new, and she loved how she was doing something good for the environment at the same time. It had been a fight to get her father to install charging stations in the company garage, but he had relented and now…

She stopped and noted that her car wasn't charging.

"Dammit, how could I have forgotten to plug it in?" Then she remembered how she had hurried in this morning and feared she was late. Honestly, it wasn't the first time she'd forgotten. But as she stepped closer, she saw that was the least of her problems.

She had a flat tire.

"Dang it," she hissed. With a loud sigh, she opened the door and tossed her bags in and then popped the trunk to get at her spare tire.

Then she really started to curse.

It wasn't until that moment she remembered how this model no longer came with a spare but with a patch kit and a pump. Great. Like she had even the slightest clue how to patch a tire! She let out an aggravated growl and slammed the trunk shut.

"Everything okay?"

Great. Just great. Turning around, she forced a smile. "Oh…hey, Dylan. What are you still doing here?"

"I wasn't in a rush to get anywhere and I got a call, so I decided to take it rather than be distracted on the road. So…what's going on? Everything okay with your car?"

And for the life of her, she didn't know why her temper chose *that* moment to snap, but it did. "No. It's not. And you know why?"

Dylan was about to answer, but she cut him off.

"Because life sucks, that's why!" she cried. "Or maybe it's just me. I forgot to put my car on the charging station. Why? Because I'm too worried about how it will look if I'm three minutes late for work! Then— because that's not enough—my front tire is flat. Flat! It was fine this morning! And my super-new, super-cute, super-efficient, great-for-the-planet car doesn't come with a spare tire. Oh no. That would have been too easy. No, this car comes with a patch kit and a pump. So I have more trunk space, but now I have to figure out how to patch a tire!"

"I'm sure it's not—"

"Do you see the lighting in here? My glasses? Do I look like someone who is going to be able to spot a hole in a tire and then patch it? Take the tire off and put it back on? Do I look like I even want to?" she asked, her voice going into the hysteria category.

Slowly, Dylan climbed from his car and walked toward her. "Okay, okay. How about we call AAA or something? Maybe they can send someone to do it for you?"

While it was a completely reasonable suggestion, it pissed her off even more. "But I wanted to leave! I wanted to leave an hour ago! And now I'm never going to get to leave or go to the grocery store to get brownies and wine, so I can go home and Google who the heck you are!"

"Who I…? Um…"

A rather unladylike snort of disgust came out before she could stop it. "I know who you are, Dylan," she snapped. "Sort of. But…what's your deal?"

His dark eyes went wide. "My deal?"

"Yeah. Why would someone like you—a rock star with the whole…I don't know…rebel-look thing going on—why would you want to be involved in something so boring as a reading campaign? It doesn't fit. So the way I see it, there's got to be something in it for you, or you lost a bet."

"A bet?" he croaked. "Paige, look…I know you're

upset about your car and all but…you're talking crazy here. Let's call AAA or a mechanic and get your tire fixed so you can get your brownies and wine. Okay?"

If he wasn't so darn tall, she would've slugged him.

It wasn't his fault—not completely. She didn't know if her tire was flat an hour ago, so she couldn't say with any great certainty that he was the reason she was stuck here right now.

But she was.

"Fine," she sighed, pulling out her cell phone. It didn't take long to get AAA on the phone, but unfortunately, at four thirty on a Friday afternoon in downtown LA, she was going to have to wait.

Goodbye, brownies.

Goodbye, wine.

When she slipped her phone into her satchel, she looked at Dylan and gave him a weary—and apologetic—smile. "They can't get anyone here for two hours. So…I guess I'll hang out up in my office until they get here."

He studied her for a minute. "Where were you going to get your brownies and wine?"

"Why?"

He shrugged. "I've got absolutely nothing to do right now and I feel bad that I interrupted your afternoon. Maybe I can take you to pick up what you need and this way you don't have to sit around and wait. And besides, you seemed like you wanted to get out of the office today. It would majorly suck if you had to go inside."

You got that right, she thought.

"I'm not going to ask you to take me grocery shopping. That's ridiculous."

Dylan chuckled. "Really? Why?"

"Seriously?" she asked without hiding the sarcasm. "When was the last time you went grocery shopping?"

He laughed a bit harder before saying, "Last Tuesday." At her shocked expression, he looked a little smug. "Believe it or not, I'm not so much of a diva I can't do things for myself."

Somehow Paige had a feeling that wasn't necessarily the whole truth. "So no one does your shopping for you on a usual basis?"

He shook his head. "They used to, but not for a while now. Ever since re…" He stopped and cleared his throat. "Ever since the band went on hiatus, I found I was tired of never having anything in the house I wanted to eat. It was easier to shop for myself."

Still, she couldn't hide her disbelief.

"And shame on you for making assumptions," he said, leaning closer, but she could tell he was teasing.

"Sorry," she mumbled.

Tucking his hands into his front jean pockets, he gave her a lopsided grin. "So, come on. You know you don't want to go into the office. You'll get sucked into working, and before you know it, it will be late and everyone will be gone, and you'll still be sitting at your desk doing the work you wanted to put aside for the weekend." He paused. "We'll shop and by the time we return, AAA should be here and your tire will be fixed and you'll be free to go. What do you say?"

She'd say he was crazy, but she had a feeling that of the two of them, right then, she had clearly come off as the crazier one.

"Only if you're sure," she began. "I don't want to put you in a situation where…"

"We've been over this already, Paige," he said patiently. "I'm not going to cause a riot at the Whole Foods. Or anywhere, for that matter."

For now, she'd have to take his word for it. "Okay," she finally said. "Thanks."

They walked over to his car and Paige was surprised when he opened the passenger door and waited for her to climb in.

Quite the gentlemanly move.

When he climbed in beside her, she noticed several things at once: First, the car was incredibly high-tech. Second, the leather seats felt like butter and hugged her like they were made for her. And third, Dylan Anders smelled really good.

Like really, *really* good.

So not the thing to focus on right now.

"There is a Whole Foods not too far from here," she said.

Beside her, Dylan nodded. "I don't live too far, so I'm familiar with it. Is that where you normally shop?"

"Um…yeah. It's close to the office, and I go by it on my way home."

"I love their deli department. They have some great salads," he said conversationally. "I'm not a great cook, so I appreciate their selection of ready-to-go stuff. And their salads are always so fresh. I'll probably grab some dinner for myself while we're there."

Were they seriously having this conversation? He was a rock star with one of the biggest bands in the world and this was the kind of conversation she inspired? Grocery shopping?

Well, that was a depressing thought. She was so plain

and boring that this particular rock star was talking produce with her.

Fabulous.

She made a mental note to add ice cream to her list.

They made it to the store, and while she had been having an inner dialogue over the pity party that was about to be her weekend, Dylan had kept up a running dialogue about shopping and how much he was enjoying doing things for himself. Obviously, there was an extended period of time when he'd had hired help to do everything for him.

Tough to feel sorry for the poor, little, rich rock star.

"I can tell by the look on your face that you're making assumptions again," he said, his voice soft and somewhat close to her ear. They were walking through the produce section, and he was practically pressed up behind her as he spoke. Paige nearly jumped out of her skin.

Maybe it was his nearness. Maybe it was the heat coming off him, but either way, she wasn't copping to it.

"This is just…bizarre to me," she said instead.

"Because…?"

She shrugged and picked out a head of romaine. "I guess when I think of celebrities, I don't envision them shopping for themselves. Or if they do, they're incognito or something."

"So if I had on a hat and sunglasses, and maybe a fake mustache, you'd feel better about this?"

The image that flashed through her mind made her laugh. "I don't know if I'd feel better, but I'd certainly be more amused."

"Duly noted," he said with mock seriousness as he stepped around her and began perusing the fresh vegetables.

For almost an hour, they walked around the store, talking about everything and nothing, and Paige had to admit, it was quite…pleasant. Dylan Anders seemed like a nice guy. Genuine. So maybe she had jumped to conclusions earlier. Maybe he could make a good spokesman for the campaign. And, if she thought about it, he could add a certain edginess to the whole thing that could hit a demographic they wouldn't have had before.

Her mind made up, Paige was willing to give him a try. Not that she was going to tell him today—she didn't want to seem overly anxious—but she would call him on Monday and let him know. Plus, this would give her the weekend to rework some of the promotional spots to include him. And maybe his band. Oh! How cool would it be to have his band do a spot for the campaign and have her be the one to bring them back after their hiatus?

Ideas immediately began to swirl in her mind, and as much as she was enjoying wandering the grocery store with him, now all Paige could focus on was getting home, so she could finesse her ideas.

As much as it pained her to admit, maybe Ariel had been onto something. With the potential of using bigger names in pop culture, it would open up advertising opportunities—they could get onto the music sites and magazines where they could reach out to teens or get national interviews on TV! Her heart started to race with excitement at the possibilities.

Pushing past Dylan, Paige made her way toward the checkout.

"Hey!" he called after her with a small laugh. "Where's the fire?"

Looking over her shoulder at him, she gave him a distracted smile. "Oh…um… I'm just afraid the AAA guy is going to show up sooner rather than later and thought we should wrap things up here. Is there anything else you need?"

His eyes narrowed like he wasn't quite sure he believed her, but it lasted only a second. Then he followed her. "Nope. I'm good. I have enough to get me through the weekend."

Paige looked at their shared cart and frowned. He had purchased an awful lot of food. Single servings. Was it possible he didn't lead some glamorous social life like she always imagined musicians did? Would that be too personal of a question to ask?

"So…all of this is for you? For the weekend?" she asked and then immediately wanted to kick herself.

"Sure is. I had thought about going out but"—he shrugged—"I think I'd rather stay in. And besides, did you see this grilled salmon salad? That is definitely tonight's dinner."

Was he for real? If this was the life of a rock star, she was seriously disappointed. "Wow," she said with a chuckle, "and here I was thinking guys like you were eating steak and lobster and caviar and drinking until dawn and then being driven home because you overindulged."

He paled. There was no other way to describe the way his entire appearance changed. Oh God. Did she offend him? Why couldn't she keep her mouth shut?

"I mean…" she stammered, immediately trying to backpedal, "that's the way I envisioned the life of a rock star. I didn't mean to offend you. I guess I've watched too many documentaries on musicians in the eighties.

It was the decade of decadence, right? I guess I didn't think anything had changed. Sorry." When he still didn't move or blink, she stumbled on. "I need to stop making assumptions about you. I swear that was the last one. Really. I...I'm sorry, Dylan."

Finally, he seemed to snap out of his daze, and he blinked at her and then began walking. "No big deal. Don't give it another thought. There are people who live like that, but right now, that's not me. I'm perfectly content to have a quiet weekend at home."

At the checkout, they divvied up their orders and paid and then made their way to his car. Paige was too afraid to say anything, so instead she sang along to the radio.

Back at the parking garage, he pulled up beside her car and parked. Her tire was still flat, so she hadn't missed the repair guy. With a sigh, she turned to him. "Thanks for killing time with me. You were right. It was much better than going up to the office. No doubt by now I would be deeply entrenched in things I was hoping to get away from."

He gave her a small smile. "No problem." Looking around, he seemed to be considering his next words. "We can grab another coffee or something. You know, since they haven't called to say they're on the way yet."

It was a tempting offer, but she felt bad about monopolizing his time. Although she could argue that she was using the time to get to know him and make sure he'd be a good fit for her project, but...that seemed a bit wrong.

"Thanks, but...I know you've got a trunk full of perishables. And besides, I'm sure they'll be along soon."

As if on cue, her cell phone rang, and two minutes

later, she confirmed that a truck would arrive within thirty minutes. She relayed the info to Dylan.

"Well, I feel bad leaving you in the parking lot," he said, shifting in his seat so he could face her. "I have a feeling if no one's watching, you'll go work."

Was she that transparent?

"Maybe…but by the time we transfer my groceries and I check emails on my phone, they'll probably be here. I can hang in my car for a few minutes and not be tempted to go upstairs."

"I don't know," he said teasingly, but then he shut off the car and opened the door. "I think it wouldn't take much for you to get annoyed with waiting and go inside."

Okay, yes. Yes, she was *that* transparent.

Paige climbed from the car and met him at the trunk and it didn't take long to move her groceries.

Like, less than a minute.

Dylan shut his trunk and then leaned against it, arms crossed over his chest as he studied her. "Look, far be it from me to tell you how to spend your time or whether you should work or not work. All I'm saying is I don't mind hanging out if it will keep you from…you know."

They both chuckled, and for a minute, Paige considered asking him about his career, so she could plan the campaign. Would that be wrong? Inappropriate? Could she—

"Paige? What are you still doing here? Daisy said you left hours ago," Ariel said as she made her way toward them.

Great. Now she could feel small and insignificant with an audience. Awesome.

"Oh, um…I've got a flat and I'm waiting for AAA,"

Paige replied and then noticed her sister staring at Dylan. "Ariel, this is—"

"You're Dylan Anders, right?" Ariel said, ignoring Paige's attempt at an introduction. "The guitar player?"

Nodding, Dylan glanced at Paige before extending a hand to Ariel. "Bass player, but yeah. And you are?"

"Ariel Blake," she said smoothly, shaking his hand briefly. "What are you—?"

"Dylan stopped by about the campaign," Paige said quickly. "Apparently your invitation got to him and he came by the office to talk about participating."

A serene yet knowing smile played at Ariel's lips as she looked at her sister. "You see? Just because it wasn't your idea didn't mean it was a bad idea."

"I never said it was a bad idea, Ariel," Paige murmured, completely mortified that her sister would choose to have this discussion in front of Dylan. "You just sprang it on me. I would have appreciated a heads-up."

"Either way, I think people will be way more interested in hearing people who are relevant to pop culture, instead of a bunch of literary nerds no one recognizes," Ariel said and then turned to Dylan. "You agree, don't you? If you were a kid struggling to read, who would you rather take advice from—a famous guitar player or…or…that Shakespeare guy? I mean, what's he going to say to kids about reading?"

"Um…probably nothing since he's dead," Paige pointed out.

"Exactly," Ariel agreed, totally missing the sarcasm in Paige's tone. "He has no idea what today's teens want to read. But Dylan will be able to relate to them. And he's got more going for him than anyone else on your list."

"He does?"

"I do?" Dylan asked, his voice a bit squeaky.

Ariel looked between the two of them and nodded. "Absolutely! We can talk about how important reading is to a musician—you know, because he has to read the music."

Paige slowly closed her eyes and lowered her head in embarrassment, catching the smirk on Dylan's face as she did so. Didn't her sister realize that what she said made no sense whatsoever? She had to fight the urge to laugh.

"And then there's the angle on how he needs to have more advanced reading and writing skills to write music."

Oh God. She was still talking, wasn't she?

"Ariel," Paige said, interrupting her, "I don't think you need to—"

"But more than anything," Ariel went on, ignoring Paige's words, "Dylan can show teens that reading is cool."

Oh. Okay. "Well, that's true," Paige agreed, seeing the somewhat roundabout way her sister came to this conclusion. As a musician, most kids—and some adults—would look at Dylan's profession as something cool and to be envied, and if he could impress upon them his own love of reading, it might encourage them. She looked over at Dylan and saw him almost sag with relief. Was he as thankful as she was that Ariel was done?

"Anyway, it's something to consider. I need to go. Dennis is taking me to dinner, and I don't want to be late." Ariel turned and extended her hand to Dylan again. "It was nice meeting you and I hope to see you as part of the campaign."

"Thanks," he said, shaking her hand. "I hope to be a part of it."

With a little wave, Ariel started to leave, and Paige's mind raced about how she could end this conversation with Dylan without offering him a part right now. She was seriously considering it, but she needed a bit more research.

Ariel climbed into her sporty little red Porsche and backed out. When she came up alongside them, she lowered her window, her gaze on Dylan. "By the way, I meant to tell you that I hope you're doing okay. I hear rehab can be a struggle. It's good to see you out and about." She paused and smiled. "And I spoke with your manager, and we're totally cool with you doing this as part of your community service. I'm sure Paige will sign off on whatever you need. Take care!" And with another little wave, she was gone.

Paige felt a little…shocked. Dazed.

Betrayed.

She looked over at Dylan and saw he was frozen to the spot, his gaze wary.

As it should be, she thought to herself.

Why had no one mentioned this to her? How had she not known? And dammit, why was her sister so completely oblivious and insensitive that she thought it was okay to drop that bombshell here, like that, and right in front of Dylan?

No! Don't think about Dylan's feelings, she chided herself. *Think about yours!* Not only had Ariel gone and messed with her plans, but she was also doing it by asking addicts to help her out? What kind of message was that going to send to people?

"You…you were in rehab?" she asked cautiously.

Dylan nodded.

"For…?"

"Alcohol. Drunk driving. There was an accident. I went and—"

"Was anyone killed?" she asked, hating both the tremble and disgust in her voice.

He shook his head. "No."

"So all this today—the coming here and schmoozing me—it was to guarantee that you could check community service off your list?"

He seemed to stiffen and Paige could see the anger in his eyes. "It's not like that."

Like she could believe him now. "Right. Whatever," she said with a huff and was saved from saying anything else by the arrival of the AAA truck. There was no point in hiding how she felt. She couldn't. "Excuse me." Rather than say anything else to Dylan, Paige greeted the driver and showed him her car. With any luck, Dylan would take the hint that their conversation was over and leave.

Unfortunately, five minutes later, when she looked over her shoulder, he was still there, leaning arrogantly against his car, arms still crossed. He thought he could wait her out? *Fine*, she thought. *He can stand there all night if he wants to, but once my tire is fixed, I'm out of here.*

And she wouldn't give Dylan Anders a second thought.

Chapter 3

HE KNEW THE INSTANT PAIGE HAD COMPLETELY WRITTEN him off. She had a very expressive face, and she didn't even try to hide the disdain she was feeling toward him. Well, he had a surprise for her—he wasn't feeling too kindly toward her either. It was one thing to judge a person when you had all the facts, but it was another to do it when you knew nothing!

Why he was surprised, he couldn't say. After all, he was used to people judging him, but usually they had good reason to. One flippant comment from her sister, and all of a sudden the camaraderie they had established this afternoon was gone? What did that say for the kind of person she was?

And why should he care? From the beginning, he hadn't been interested in doing this. He'd told Mick so. The best thing for him to do would be to move on.

It probably wouldn't be hard to find a way to get his hours in without being made to feel worse about himself than he already did. Hell, if he looked hard enough, Dylan had no doubt he could find a place or a cause that would love to have him—even be grateful for him—and then he'd be able to tell Miss Paige Walters to kiss his ass and good luck with her boring campaign.

That had him laughing a little—imagining the look on her face if he said that to her. It would be the most satisfying thing to happen to him in months.

"Thank you so much," Paige was saying to the AAA driver. "I appreciate your help. I had no idea how to go about finding the leak."

"You need to take the car in and get the tire replaced. The patch is all fine and good as a temporary fix, but it's not a long-term solution."

"I'll take it in on Monday," she replied. "And again, thank you."

Dylan watched as she signed some paperwork and then took out some cash to tip the man. With a word of thanks, the AAA representative turned and seemed to notice Dylan.

And then he *noticed* Dylan.

Great.

"Oh, man! You're Dylan Anders, right?"

It would be pointless to play dumb, and the man had Paige blocked in, so the longer Dylan stood here and talked to the guy, the longer she'd have to stand there and stew.

"Yes, I am!" he said with a full-blown grin. He held out his hand and gave the guy a hearty handshake and then proceeded to talk to him about everything from his favorite Shaughnessy song to his taste in other music.

Paige cleared her throat. Loudly. But Dylan ignored it.

"Would you mind signing something for me?" the guy asked.

"Not at all! I'll sign as much as you'd like. Take something to the guys at the garage too!"

"Um…excuse me," Paige said with a hint of annoyance, "but I need to get going. Could you move the truck?"

Dylan looked at her and grinned. "We'll be done in a minute. Maybe you should go inside and see about calling the Toyota dealer about that new tire."

Her dark eyes narrowed at him. "I don't want to go inside."

"And we're not ready to move the truck yet," he countered.

"Oh, *we're* not ready?" she mocked. "Seriously?"

"What can I say? I can't disappoint a fan." Turning his back on her, he walked over to the driver's side of the truck and then spent another five minutes signing papers, flyers, hats, whatever the guy could get his hands on. When he was done, he looked at Paige, who was fuming, and felt like poking her some more. "Is that it? I've got time."

"You know, my girlfriend would go crazy if you spoke to her," the man said hopefully. "Would you...I mean...would you mind if I called her and you could get on the phone and say hi? I swear it won't take long and you'll really make her day!"

"I would love to! Go for it!"

Paige looked like her head was about to explode.

Was it wrong that he was having so much fun?

Before he knew it, a phone was thrust into his hands, and he was saying hello to a shrieking female. Dylan did his best not to wince at the high-pitched squeal and forced himself to smile at the AAA guy. As he listened to the squeals turn to excited chatter, he noticed an older gentleman walk toward Paige.

He also noticed her stiffen.

Was this guy someone she worked with? Someone she had a problem with? Her body language told him she wasn't comfortable and yet...she smiled at the man. Curiosity got the better of him and he had a gut feeling that this was a man he needed to meet.

"Well, I need to go, sweetheart," Dylan said cheerfully into the phone. "I hope you have a great night so… take care!" Handing the phone to the driver, he wished him a good night as well and then walked to where Paige and the older guy were talking.

"It wasn't a big deal," he heard her saying. "The tire's repaired, and I'll take it into the dealer Monday and get the tire replaced."

"Are you sure it's safe to drive? Maybe you should have it towed and I'll drive you home."

"That's not necessary, Dad. But I appreciate the offer."

Dad? So this was Robert Walters, the head of the firm. Interesting. Dylan straightened a bit as he strolled over, smiling. Paige glanced at him and frowned, and Dylan noticed how her father caught on to her instant change in demeanor as well.

"Paige?" her father asked. "Is…everything all right? Do you know this man?"

Still smiling, Dylan walked up and extended his hand. "Dylan Anders. I'm hoping to be working on Paige's literacy campaign."

Robert Walters shook his hand and visibly relaxed. "Splendid! Are you an author?"

Paige coughed and turned away to hide what was— no doubt—a snort of disgust.

"No, sir. I'm a musician. Your daughter Ariel reached out to me about the campaign and I came by today to talk to Paige about my participation."

"Nothing's confirmed yet," Paige interrupted, shooting him a warning glare. "I'm still not convinced Ariel's suggestion is how I want to go."

Robert studied Dylan for a moment and then turned to his daughter. "I looked over her proposal—she gave me a copy after the meeting the other day—and I have to admit that it does sound intriguing. Getting members of various arts could extend our reach with the campaign, Paige. It's not an uncommon approach, and it's proven to be successful in the past. I know you wanted this to be your baby, but that shouldn't mean you automatically dis-qualify suggestions just because they're not your own."

For a minute, Dylan felt bad for her—she was getting reprimanded by her father in front of him. That had to be embarrassing.

"Well, to be fair," Dylan began, having a sudden urge to clarify, "I don't think she's against all non-authors, just me."

"Wait…now I remember. I read your bio," Robert replied. "You're with a band, you play the bass, and you're fresh out of rehab for your drinking, correct?"

Okay, right to the point. Dylan nodded. "Yes, sir." Then he braced himself for the condescension and disapproval.

Crossing his arms across his chest, Robert gave him a hard look before turning to his daughter. "And you have a problem with this? With him?"

Her cheeks turned a light shade of crimson as she studied the pavement. "It wasn't exactly what I had in mind."

"Paige," her father began sternly, "it's not like you to be so judgmental. Personal feelings should *not* play into what's going to help your cause. I think you'd be doing the campaign a disservice if you eliminate willing volunteers based on your own bias." He paused. "You should reconsider." Turning to Dylan, Robert extended his hand. "I'm looking forward to seeing you on this project. I'm sure my daughter will do the right thing."

And then he bade them both a good evening, walked over to his car, and swiftly drove away.

Leaving the two of them standing in awkward silence.

Just when Dylan thought he'd go mad, Paige spoke.

"I'm sorry," she said softly, not quite meeting his gaze, and he knew she was uncomfortable.

A few minutes ago, it would have been fun to make her work for his forgiveness, but now it seemed mean.

"It's okay," he said, his voice equally quiet. "I get it, you know. I know you had envisioned someone completely different for this project and then I walk in and ruin it."

This time her eyes did meet his and what he saw there was gratitude, plain and simple.

"It isn't personal…"

He laughed softly. "I think it's a little bit personal."

That had her laughing with him. "For the sake of total honesty, fine. I do have an issue with your…past. I can't help it. I lost a friend to a drunk driver so…"

Dylan held up a hand to stop her. "I'm sorry. Truly." Then he stopped and raked a hand through his hair. What was he supposed to say to her admission? "I'm sorry for your loss. I am. But you have to know that I am trying to get my life straightened out. I hate how I let it spiral so far out of control, and I'm thankful I didn't kill anyone in the accident. I've worked hard to clean up my act and become a better person. Every day is a struggle, Paige, and it continues to be a struggle when people want to pass judgment."

She sighed. "I'm sure, and I hate how I added to that. I'm normally not like that…I don't usually act that way."

Somehow he had a feeling she didn't realize how transparent she was. And while he had her pegged as the kind of woman who would be a total pain in the ass to work with, there was also something about her that he found…appealing.

"I'm not saying you have to like me," he said. "Most of the time I don't particularly like myself. I'm still trying to figure out who I am now that I'm not wasted all the damn time. All I'm asking is for you to give me a chance. In the grand scheme of things, I'm going to be a tiny part of this project. You'll probably only have to spend like fifteen minutes with me."

With another soft laugh, she shook her head. "It would probably be more than that."

"Just…just promise me you'll think about it. Don't write me off because of something I did in the past. I'm trying hard to stay positive and look to the future, but I can't if people keep forcing me to relive the past."

She pointedly looked at his arm—where his new tat was—and he knew the instant she made the connection.

"I need to keep looking forward," he said gruffly.

Paige's expression turned serious. "The past isn't going to change, Dylan. I'll admit I don't know the specifics about what you did or about you in general, but your actions had a definite effect on people. You can't erase that because you're ready to move on."

"I get that, I really do, but I'm not going to let it define me for the rest of my life either. I have to live with what I did every day. Trust me when I tell you it doesn't just go away. But I think I deserve a chance to prove to the world that there's more to me."

His heart hammered in his chest as he waited for her to respond.

"Why this?" she asked, her voice so soft Dylan almost wasn't certain he'd heard her.

And her eyes.

Damn.

They looked up at him with so much emotion and conflict that he almost didn't know what to say.

"Honestly? I don't know. When my manager first presented me with it, I thought, *No way.*" And when he paused, he knew exactly what he needed to say—to share. And not because he was using it as an angle to win her over, but because she deserved the truth.

"When the band first got signed by Mick, our manager, I could barely read. I struggled with it all through school, but I was too embarrassed to tell anyone and I sort of…I don't know…fell through the cracks, so to speak. I dropped out of high school at sixteen." He shrugged. "Mick hired tutors and helped me pass the GED, but it took a couple of years for me to realize what a gift it was."

"Dylan, I…I had no idea."

He shrugged again. "I don't talk about it. Ever. I don't think the guys in the band know about it. I was embarrassed. Ashamed. Up until then, it didn't matter to me, but when we had to sign contracts, and there was so much to read and learn, Mick figured it out. He never made me feel bad about it. He simply stepped in and offered to help. I owe him a lot for that."

"He sounds like a good person."

That had Dylan laughing out loud. "Sorry. It's just…

Mick's…Mick. He can be a complete asshole most of the time and he's a hard-ass about a lot of things, but deep down? Yeah. He's a good person. But he doesn't want anyone to know."

Paige smiled. "Then I won't be the one to tell them."

All the tension started to ease away. "I'm not saying I want to put that information out there—about my learning struggles—but let's say I understand now why reading is so important."

She nodded. "And if I said I wanted to use it for the campaign, what would you do?"

Dylan's first instinct was to get defensive, to get mad, but he squashed it immediately. "I'd probably say I'm not comfortable with it, but if you thought it would help, then I'd agree to it."

"Wow."

"Exactly."

She gave him a sad smile. "I wish you had been honest with me earlier."

Dylan took a moment to let that sink in before responding. "Would it have made any difference? You still would have been disgusted. You took one look at me—the leather jacket, the tattoos, the whole image—and you formed an opinion. Nothing I said was going to change that. The only difference is that we wouldn't have gone and had coffee and cake pops," he said solemnly before adding with a sheepish grin, "or gone food shopping together."

The sound of pure feminine laughter echoed around the parking garage, and Dylan's grin grew.

"You're crazy, you know that, right?" she asked.

He shrugged. "Part of my charm."

She sighed. "Oh, Dylan—"

He knew that tone, knew where it was leading, and he had to stop her. "Don't!" he quickly, but lightly, interrupted. "Don't make any decisions yet. Please. Take the weekend to think about it."

When she didn't immediately respond, he began to feel desperation clawing at him. Reaching for her hand, he clasped it in his. "I promise you, Paige, from now on, I will be one hundred percent honest."

"But you—"

"I know I should have been that way from the moment we met, but…can you blame me? You know how you reacted to the news, and you're not the first one to respond like that, so I'm a little cautious about putting it out there. It was wrong of me, and I'm sorry. Please. Give me a chance to prove to you that I'm not a bad guy."

"You don't understand." She carefully removed her hand from his. "This project…I had it all mapped out. I wanted authors and only authors."

"But from what your father and your sister said earlier, you need to consider some other options. Let me be one of those options!"

"I don't think—"

"What about the clients?" he asked, almost frantic now. "Don't your clients deserve to have a say in this?" Wait, did she have clients for this campaign, or was it well and truly hers to do with as she wanted? Why hadn't he thought of that?

But by the look on her face, he knew he had her.

There was hope.

For him, at least.

"I…I hadn't thought of that," she admitted slowly.

"Look, I'm sure you'd like nothing more than for me to leave and let you get on with your weekend."

"Well—"

"But," he quickly interjected, "promise me, Paige, that you'll think about this. Okay?" He paused and then almost sagged with relief when she nodded. "And would it be all right with you if I came by on Monday? I do have an AA meeting at noon, so maybe I can come by in the afternoon, like I did today?"

"I think Daisy would faint at your feet," she said with a smile.

"I'm sure she'll be fine. I want you to know I'm serious. I'm willing to do whatever it is you need from me—even let you go home and have brownies and wine for dinner when I'd like to keep talking to you and pleading my case."

And he realized that was only partially true. He enjoyed talking to her. He had a feeling if they didn't have this conflict over the campaign between them, they'd be able to talk about any number of things at length.

Paige looked at him as if she was trying to figure out if he was serious or not. It was enough to make him squirm. "Why don't you come in around four on Monday?" she said finally. "I'm not making any promises though, Dylan. I am going to talk to my friends over at Literacy Now, and if they're not okay with the changes Ariel and my dad want, then I have to honor their wishes."

He nodded. "Okay, but you need to promise me you're not going to try to sway them to your way of thinking," he countered. "I mean, I know where you stand on this, and I can respect that. But like you don't know me, I don't know you. For all I know, you're going to get on the phone with them and paint them a picture of a guy out of rehab who's a hot mess."

"I wouldn't do that," she said stiffly.

"I have no choice but to take your word for it, don't I?"

Paige at least had the decency to look contrite. "Point taken."

"Okay then. As long as we understand each other."

She nodded. "I am sorry, Dylan. That was crappy on my part to…to jump to conclusions. It's a sore subject with me…the whole drinking thing."

"I get it. And I am sorry about your friend."

"It was a long time ago. High school. But it still…it still hurts. She barely had a chance to live, to experience anything, before it was all taken away," she said sadly. "It doesn't take much to bring me there, to that place where it breaks my heart to think about all Marni missed."

There wasn't anything he could say. For months, Dylan had been telling himself he was thankful he hadn't seriously hurt or killed anyone with his drunk driving, but he knew he could have. And standing here now and hearing Paige put it so simply—how those actions affected others—it was powerful.

Unable to help himself, he reached out and took one of her hands in his again and gently squeezed. "It's not fair," he said softly. "I can't imagine what that kind of loss is like."

"You're lucky. It was hell. In some ways it still is for me. I keep in touch with Marni's parents. I go to the cemetery with them every year on her birthday and the anniversary of her death. And when I'm with them, I can't help but notice how ten years later, it's still heart-breaking for them."

With her hand still in his, he nodded. "That's very nice of you to go with them. I'm sure they appreciate it."

"They seem to, and honestly, it means a lot to me to spend time with them. Marni was their only child, and I was in the car with her that night. Part of me feels guilty that I'm here and she's not."

"You can't think like that, Paige," he said earnestly. "You know they can't possibly think that."

"No, I don't think they do. It's just how I feel. Marni was… Gosh…she was so amazing. She was student body president, captain of the tennis team, and had been accepted to UCLA and had this incredible future ahead of her! She had so much more going for her than—"

"Don't you dare finish that sentence," he said fiercely. For the life of him, Dylan had no idea why this bothered him so much, but it did. How could she possibly think her life wasn't worth as much as her friend's?

Those big, dark eyes looked up at him, and she gave him a sad smile. "You're right. I know I shouldn't think like that but…I do. Like I said, this is a sensitive subject for me. So while it's personal, it's not about you. Not really."

They stood there in silence for a time, and Dylan realized he was still holding her hand and was reluctant to let it go. But he needed to. He needed to let her go and have her weekend, and he needed to… Well, there was nothing he needed to do. Again.

Earlier, he had envisioned going out later that night and finding someone to hook up with, but now? Now it didn't seem nearly as urgent. So he'd go home, eat one of the meals he'd purchased, and...read. Or watch TV. Or...stare at the walls.

Slowly, he let go of her hand and took a step back. "So...I should go."

"Yeah. Me too."

"Monday though, right? Four?"

Paige nodded. "Monday at four. Yes." She smiled.

He smiled.

Funny thing was how she seemed as reluctant as he was to walk away. Was it possible her night wasn't looking any more promising than his? Should he ask her to dinner? To a movie? Or maybe—?

"Have a good weekend, Dylan. And...thanks. For listening."

"Oh...um...yeah. No problem. Anytime."

With a small smile and wave, Paige turned and walked over to her car. Dylan watched as she climbed in and stood back and waited for her to pull out and drive away.

With nothing left to do, he got into his car and made his way home.

To his personal prison.

—⁓—

It was as if the entire world was against her.

By three o'clock on Monday, Paige was fairly certain she was the only person alive who understood what had made her concept for this campaign so perfect. Now, as she made her way to her office, she felt completely defeated.

And more than a little pissed off.

After lunch, she had been summoned to her father's

office, which was never a good thing. He'd sat her down
and explained, in his gentle yet condescending manner,
how he had gone and talked to the Literacy Now people
and they were thrilled with Ariel's revisions.

Revisions? Ha! More like sabotage!

She had meant to call them earlier, but the morning
had gotten away from her after going and getting her
tire replaced. By the time she'd arrived at the office, it
was time for a meeting with another potential client for
a new restaurant opening in Hollywood. Paige wasn't
going to be in charge of the campaign, but her coworker,
Xander, asked her to sit in with him.

Either way, she hadn't made the call and what it
all meant was that she was no longer heading up the
project. Ariel was. Not that they were cutting her out
completely. Oh no. That would have been too kind. No,
now she had the task of playing a supporting role in
babysitting the talent.

Namely, Dylan Anders.

As she turned the corner and strode past Daisy's
desk, all she could think of was how badly she wanted
to punch something.

Or someone.

"Hey, Paige!" Daisy called out as she walked by.
"You have a couple of messages from—"

"I'll call them tomorrow," Paige said firmly as she
crossed into her office and slammed the door.

It wasn't until she was alone in the silence of her
office that she realized her heart was ready to pound
right out of her chest and she was trembling.

"Dammit, dammit, dammit, dammit," she murmured
as she began to pace. This was supposed to be *her*

chance—*her* turn to head up a project and stop being the gofer! Literacy Now was *her* baby—those contacts were *her* friends—and as usual, she had been tossed aside while being patted on the head.

"I know you're disappointed," her father had said, "but you're an important part of the team."

Yeah right, she thought miserably.

Babysitter. She was relegated to playing babysitter to a rock star who had a reputation for being hard to handle. Paige had argued how Dylan wasn't that guy anymore—and it had come as a bit of a shock to her as the words poured out of her mouth!—but no one was ready to believe it. His past was in the tabloids and no one was ready to take him without a handler.

"Paige seemed to hit it off with him," Ariel had said when their father had called her in to join their meeting. And when Paige had argued her point, her sister had pulled the pregnancy card and claimed she felt queasy and made a run for the bathroom.

And never came back.

That had led to her father gushing over how excited he was about becoming a grandfather and how they needed to not upset Ariel in her delicate condition. Then he added how this sort of project would be perfect for Ariel because she could delegate so many of the tasks because of all the groundwork Paige had already done.

Even now it still made Paige roll her eyes.

She stalked over to her desk, sat, and face-planted on the paperwork.

If this were a job where she wasn't working with her family, she'd quit. She'd seriously be packing up her office right now and storming out the door.

And while quitting seemed like a good plan, Paige knew she'd never go through with it. Some way or another she'd be guilted into coming back—because her father was all about appearances, and having a daughter leave the firm looked bad—and then everyone would think she was a sore loser.

There was no way she was going to let that happen.

No matter who she had to babysit.

So unfortunately, quitting wasn't an option, and she was stuck. Again. Doing a job she hated. Again. And what was worse was how no one seemed to notice or care. She thought about her conversation with Dylan on Friday and realized that *now* it was personal. Her resentment toward him went up several notches.

Then she closed her eyes. All weekend, he had been on her mind. She'd done her research, and even though he had a colorful reputation, he wasn't a bad person. She almost wished he were; it would have made things so much easier right now. But no, Dylan Anders was sexy and charismatic, and she'd been darn mesmerized by watching video clips of him all weekend long.

Not something she would be willing to admit aloud.

He was a talented musician, he was incredibly sexy, and he had the perfect amount of swagger that she discovered she found attractive too.

It was like the tattoos all over again.

"God, what is happening to me?" she murmured. Four days ago, she was completely content listening to John Legend or Ed Sheeran, and now? Now she had all of Shaughnessy's music on her iPod and had it on a continual loop.

There was a light knock on her door, and Paige lifted her head as Daisy peeked in.

"Sorry to bother you, Paige," she said softly. "I heard about Literacy Now. I'm so sorry."

Straightening, she asked, "Who told you?"

"Ariel stopped by with her revisions for the schedule and wanted me to give you a copy." Placing the folder on Paige's desk, Daisy gave her a sympathetic smile. "You could look at this as a good thing, you know."

"Really? How?" Paige asked sarcastically and didn't even feel bad about it.

"For starters, there's less pressure on you. It's all on Ariel now."

"True but…I've already done all the hard work—the research, the recruiting, booking photographers and banquet spaces. I mean, all she's doing is stepping in and taking the spotlight!"

"Okay, there is that," Daisy said, frowning. "But, between you and me, with her pregnancy announcement, I'm sure she's going to need a lot of help. I'll bet you anything you'll be in charge in no time."

"And by then, she will have made a mess of everything, and I'll have to clean it up," Paige said with a sigh. It was a scenario that had played out more times than she cared to count. "It's so typical of her. Why am I the only one who sees it?"

Daisy pulled up a chair and sat. "Trust me. You're not the only one who sees it. There are a lot of us here who do. I don't get why your father doesn't see it."

"He's always been blind to Ariel's doings. And whenever I try to point them out, I get accused of being jealous." She sighed again. "And it's not that. I swear it's not. It's just that somehow, I always end up getting screwed and I'm so tired of it!"

"So what are you going to do?"

"I'm going to do what I always do. My job," Paige said after a moment. "We're a team and I have to remember that just because I'm not the captain, it doesn't make my job any less important."

Daisy rolled her eyes. "Oh, please. We all want to be the captain, the head cheerleader, the star of the show. There's no crime in that, Paige. You need to take a stand, and when Ariel crashes and burns on this, you need to put your foot down and tell them you're not taking over. Let her deal with the mess she makes for once."

"I would love to, but she's pregnant and said she was sick and—"

"Right. Sick," Daisy said with a snort of disgust. "I saw her run from your father's office earlier, and as soon as she turned the corner and thought she was out of sight, her pace slowed to her usual superior glide and she went to her office, grabbed her purse, and left, cool as a cucumber."

The curse that flew out of Paige's mouth was more colorful than her usual vocabulary, and her hand instantly flew to her mouth.

Daisy, however, laughed uproariously. "*Yes!* Exactly! That is *exactly* what I thought! I was tempted to follow her and see if she went to Starbucks or to get a pedicure. Maybe I should keep a trench coat, hat, and dark glasses here, so she won't know it's me following her. What do you think?"

"I think you'd stick out like a sore thumb wearing that around town. Please don't."

"Fine. But I'm telling you, I'm going to catch her in the act and then maybe if someone else went to your father with how Ariel is manipulating everyone, he'll have to believe it."

"I'm not holding my breath. He's so over the top about having a grandchild that he'll probably forgive anything. Ariel could probably bankrupt the company and he'd forgive her."

"Paige…"

"I'm serious! You'd think she was giving birth to the king or something!"

"First grandchildren tend to bring that out in people."

"Yeah, well, it doesn't make it any easier for the rest of us," Paige said miserably. "Oh God. Maybe I *am* jealous! I sound jealous, don't I? Ugh. Why?"

"You're not jealous. You're tired of being taken for granted," Daisy said reassuringly. "You know what you need to do?"

"Quit and work on the other side of the country?"

Daisy considered that for a moment. "Let's say that's option number two. No, what you need to do is complete whatever task they've given you like a total professional. But *only* that task. Don't involve yourself in anything else that's going on—just focus on the job at hand. They did give you something specific, didn't they?"

Paige nodded but was almost afraid to admit what it was. She had gotten a glimpse of Daisy's crush on Dylan, and she had a feeling that once she said what her job was for the campaign, she was going to need a tranquilizer gun to calm her assistant down.

"So what is it? Are you in charge of the catering hall for the launch? Oh, did she assign you to solicitation calls for donations? No, no…I bet she has you working on ordering promotional materials, right? And probably with her face on it next to Literacy Now's logo!" Cracking herself up, Daisy took a minute to laugh. "Okay, come on. Out with it. What ridiculous task did they assign you? Name-tag maker? Celebrity dog walker? Come on…you have to tell me."

Bracing herself for what she was sure was going to be a full-on meltdown, she said, "I'm babysitting Dylan Anders."

Then she froze and waited for Daisy's response.

And waited.

And waited.

"Oh…my…*GOD*!" Daisy screeched. "Are you kidding me? Like…like…you get to hang out with him for like…the entire length of the campaign? That's three months! Three months! Do you realize how long that is?"

"Um…three months? Approximately ninety days?"

Daisy jumped up and paced a few steps away from the desk and then back again, slamming her hands on the surface. "You get *ninety days* with Dylan Anders to yourself! Can I help? Please, Paige! Let me help!"

If it were up to Paige, she'd let Daisy do it all, but that wasn't the way this worked. "I'm sure once we figure out how all this is going to go, I'll need your help, but as of right now, I'm still feeling a little clueless about what everyone thinks *I'm* supposed to do with him."

"I can think of a few things," Daisy murmured with a grin.

"Okay, let's just…get through the next week and figure out what the heck I'm supposed to *do* with Dylan, and then I promise to let you have some time to work with him. How does that sound?"

Rather than speak, Daisy squealed and then ran to hug Paige.

Yes, Daisy was a hugger.

There was a loud knock on her office door, and they both turned to see Dylan standing in the doorway.

A very *angry* looking Dylan.

Luckily Daisy chose to stay silent as she looked at Paige.

"Dylan," Paige said, forcing a smile on her face, "it's good to see you. Is it four o'clock already?"

He said nothing, but his eyes conveyed that he was as unhappy as she was. Maybe even more.

"Daisy? Could you get us some coffee, please?"

With a nod, Daisy quickly made her way out of the office—giving Dylan only a brief glance and a nervous smile.

Once she was gone, Dylan sauntered into the room, his eyes never leaving Paige's. When he stopped in front of her desk, she braced herself for what he had to say.

"You got assigned to be my handler," he spat. "Whose idea was it? Yours? Afraid I'm going to screw up your *precious* campaign?"

It was on the tip of her tongue to remind him how he was the one who came to her, not the other way around, but she didn't. That wasn't her style. She believed in being professional—no matter what.

"Why don't you have a seat?" Paige motioned for him to sit down, but he didn't budge. She, however, definitely needed to sit down. After a moment, she decided to try to calm him down. "I can't say whose idea it was. It came as a bit of a shock to me as well. However, I don't see it as a bad thing. I believe with me acting as your…guide…this whole thing will be relatively quick and painless for you."

Dylan raked a hand through his hair and moved a few steps away before sitting down, his elbows resting on his knees. "Look, I don't need a damn guide. Or a babysitter. Or an assistant. This isn't brain surgery! I need to film some promos, get some pictures taken, and speak at a couple of events. It's not a big deal, Paige."

She slouched a little in her seat, praying for patience. "I realize that. I honestly do. But the whole thing—the campaign and your part in it—is out of my hands." She held up her hands helplessly and realized how much it hurt to admit that. Especially to him.

He sat up straighter and looked at her in confusion. "What do you mean?"

With a sigh, she told him how her entire day had gone and how her father and Ariel had broken the news to her. "So you see, this isn't exactly how I envisioned things going either."

"But…I thought this was your campaign, your clients."

She nodded. "It was. *Was* being the operative word here."

He muttered a curse and then relaxed in his chair. "So now what?"

"Honestly, I have no idea. I just found out about it when Ariel dropped off her revised schedule. Daisy brought it to me a few minutes before you arrived, so I haven't looked at it yet."

"Care to look at it together?" he asked. "Seems to me it's going to affect us both."

He was right. It was. "Sure. Why not?" And before she could say another word, Dylan stood, picked up his chair, and came around to her side of the desk.

Not quite what I was expecting, she thought.

He sat close to her—almost too close—and once she opened the file, he leaned in closer.

Clearly, he has no concept of personal space, she mused. But then she caught a hint of his cologne again and had to fight the urge to move closer and inhale.

"What does this mean?" Dylan asked, and Paige realized she hadn't been paying attention to the schedule, whereas Dylan was already reading it.

A quick first glance showed that, for the most part, nothing about the campaign's timeline had changed and Paige breathed a sigh of relief. "Okay, so far nothing has changed," she said to him.

"That's good, I guess. Although being how I had no idea of the schedule, it doesn't mean a whole lot to me. I need to know what *my* schedule is going to look like with this and where I'll need to be and what I'll need to know," he explained, his eyes still scanning the paper in Paige's hand.

She was about to tell him when he would be starting when a side note caught her eye: "Have Paige write scripts for all participants." Unable to help herself, she muttered a curse and flung the paper aside.

"Problem?" Dylan asked with mild amusement.

Earlier, she had felt comfortable unleashing while Daisy was here—and for some reason, she felt that same ease with Dylan. Jumping up from her chair, Paige let loose.

"Like it's not enough that I did all the groundwork for this project, but I then get pushed aside for my sister, so she can take over, and then she *still* won't do any of the work! Now I have to write all the scripts for the people *she* chose! I had all of that done for the people—the authors—I wanted to have participate. Now I have to find out who else she went and contacted and figure out how to write up what they need to say! And that's on top of babysitting you!"

"Hey!" he cried, coming to his feet.

"Oh, knock it off," she snapped. "You were the one who wanted in on this so flipping bad. You thought you'd be cute and poke at me on Friday to get a place in this whole thing. Well, now you do! And this is what goes with it! So if you want to bail, there's the door!"

Wow, did it feel good to get *that* off her chest.

Her breath was ragged and her heart was hammering in her chest, and when she looked at the shocked expression on Dylan's face, she smiled.

Then started to laugh.

His expression went from shocked to annoyed in the blink of an eye. "You think this is funny?"

That made her laugh harder.

"There is nothing funny about this," he said firmly. "I think you've gone completely mental." He waved her off and started to walk around the desk, but Paige called out to him. Dylan turned and looked at her.

"I'm sorry, but… Oh God! You have no idea how much I needed to do that," she said, with a sigh of relief. "A while ago, I wanted to punch something, but I think this was just as effective."

"Yeah, you've gone mental," he said, shaking his head. "This isn't going to work." With a determined stride, he made his way to the door.

"Wait!" Paige called out, racing around the desk to block him from leaving. "Don't… You can't leave."

"But you just said—"

"I know what I said, but it was in the heat of the moment." When she saw she had his full attention, she went on. "I want you to be a part of this project, Dylan."

"Why? So you can have a part in it that isn't fetching coffee? Because from the way this whole thing sounds, it would be the next step down for you." With another rake through his hair, he let out a frustrated huff. "Look, it was obvious from the get-go you didn't want me for this, so I'm giving you an out. Who knows? With me gone, maybe your sister will do right by you. Or maybe you'll get to take on some different campaign. I think it's for the best if we let this go."

"No," she said firmly, crossing her arms across her chest.

"Excuse me?" he asked with a slight smirk.

"You heard me. No," she repeated. Paige realized how ridiculous she must have looked. Dylan was almost a foot taller than her, and here she was attempting not only to block his path, but to stand up to him as well.

His only response was to arch a dark brow at her.

"I know it seems crazy that I'm suddenly asking you to stay, but I think we can help each other."

No response.

"You'll get to take care of your…community service."

"It's not only about that!" he snapped irritably.

"No, no…I know. I know. Sorry," she said quickly. "But it is a contributing factor that we can't simply ignore, correct?"

He gave a curt nod.

"Okay. So we'll deal with it and you'll also get a chance to show everyone how you don't need a handler."

She was careful not to use the term *babysitter* again. "By the time this is done, you'll be well on your way to showing the world that you're a changed man."

Dylan studied her intently for a moment. "And what do you get out of this? I mean, you're seriously pissed about how this has all turned out and the role you've been relegated to. So what's in it for you?"

Good question.

"The people at Literacy Now are friends of mine." Or at least Paige had thought they were. "And no matter what, I want this campaign to be a success. And though my role has been…diminished, it doesn't mean I'm not going to work hard to see that everything runs smoothly and to help out wherever I can."

For a long moment, Dylan said nothing. Then he crossed his arms over his chest and leaned down toward her. "I'll agree under one condition."

Anything—at that moment, she would have agreed to anything but didn't want to come off as desperate. "Okay," she said with a calmness she wasn't quite feeling.

"I want you to admit—right here, right now—that you're pissed, and if given a chance, the person you'd punch is your sister."

Paige took a step back as her eyes went wide. "I don't see where that has anything to do with…well… anything!"

He shrugged.

"Why? Why would you want me to say that?"

"Because it's the truth. You know it. I know it. And I need to know that you're going to be honest with me and not blow smoke up my ass because you think it's your job to play nice all the time."

"I can assure you I've never blown smoke up anyone's...well...you know."

"Say *ass*."

Paige rolled her eyes. "Seriously? This is getting ridiculous."

He shrugged again.

When she realized he wasn't going to budge on this, her shoulders sagged with defeat. "Fine. I'm pissed. I'm beyond pissed. And if she were here right now, even though I wouldn't do it, I would fantasize about punching Ariel for taking this campaign away from me." Straightening, she did her best to strike a defiant pose. "Happy?"

"Almost. You missed one."

It was the smirk that got her—got her riled up and had her refusing to step away from the challenge.

"Ass," she said, doing her best not to smirk at him. "I've never blown smoke up anyone's ass. There. Can we move on now?"

His smirk grew into a full-blown smile and Paige had to stop herself from swooning.

The man had a killer smile—dimples and everything.

Dylan held out a hand to hers to seal the deal. "I believe we can."

"Seriously? You're going with the Sicilian defense?" Mick asked.

Dylan didn't even look up. "Yup."

"Can't we have a friendly game? Play for enjoyment?"

This time Dylan did look up from the chessboard. "This *is* enjoyment. The point of the game is to win and to use the proper strategy to do so. I know you don't like the Sicilian defense, and therefore, it gives me the advantage." He grinned. "And I'm enjoying it."

Mick laughed and studied the board. "Yeah, well…I think we need a new game to play. This is getting too predictable for you."

"Nonsense," Dylan countered. "Every game of chess is different. And what would we play instead of this?"

"Scrabble."

Dylan burst out laughing. "Not a chance, buddy. I can do this, I can play cards, I can even hold my own in Dungeons and Dragons, but don't make me spell. It's too much. And boring as hell."

"Not to someone who enjoys working with words," Mick said, reaching out and making his move.

"See? You never made that move before. Every time, it's different. And I'm perfectly happy with it."

"It wouldn't kill you to branch out and maybe play something someone else enjoys," Mick grumbled.

Looking up, Dylan studied his friend. "You don't enjoy this?"

"I do, I do…but you take this stuff way too seriously. I'm here to hang out and relax. There are times when a game of chess has you out for blood."

"And that's wrong why?"

"Um…because it's a game?"

Dylan rolled his eyes and then sat back and studied the board again. "Chutes and Ladders is a game. Chess is not."

Rather than continue to argue, Mick got up and walked to the wall of windows in Dylan's study. "So what's going on with the house? Did my Realtor call you?"

"He did," Dylan said distractedly. "We have multiple offers and haven't had even one showing."

"How did you manage that?"

"I told him I don't want gawkers. He can show it after I'm out."

Mick walked over. "Correct me if I'm wrong, but you're not going to move out until the house is sold sooo…"

Dylan shook his head. "I'm planning on being out at the end of the month."

"Why? What in the world are you thinking?" Mick asked as he sat down. "What's the rush?"

He shrugged. "I'm ready to be done with it. This place is way too big, and it doesn't hold any good memories for me."

"That's a bunch of bull. This place was your dream house when you bought it," Mick snapped. "Stop being so dramatic, Dylan. You don't need to go to such extremes."

"I think I do," Dylan replied mildly. "This house reminds me of how much of my life I wasted. Any place I find now will hold more significance for me." He paused. "Your move."

Mick sighed loudly and moved his pawn without looking. "Have you started looking?"

"Nope."

Another sigh. "Then how are you going to be out of here by the end of the month? Which, by the way, is only two weeks away."

"I know. I'm selling the place furnished and only taking the personal items. For now, they'll all go in storage. I'm moving into the Beverly. I've got a suite for a month."

"The Beverly? Why would you do that? The place is swarming with paparazzi!"

Dylan shrugged again. "I have nothing to hide, Mick, and honestly, I'm tired of avoiding them. I've lived like a choirboy since I got out of rehab so I'm yesterday's news. Trust me. It's not going to be an issue."

Mick didn't look convinced. "I don't want anyone hassling you. But that's not my real concern."

Looking up, Dylan waited for what Mick had to say. After a long minute, he sighed. "Get to the point, Mick. What's your concern?"

"The bar."

It would be pointless to look surprised. "And?"

"And…are you sure you're in a good enough place in your head where you can deal with having the temptation so close by?"

"Dude, I'm good. It doesn't matter where I live. If I wanted to drink, I could get a drink. I'm not chained to the furniture here. I still had bottles stashed around here that you never found."

Mick's face registered his surprise. And though they were normally brutally honest with one another, Dylan still wasn't ready to admit the one time he'd gone off the wagon after his stint in rehab.

"I appreciate your concern—I do. But I'm good. And if I get to a place where I'm not, then I promise to call you. Deal?"

Mick's response wasn't immediate, but when he did reply, it was with a nod and a shrug. "Yeah. Sure. Deal."

They played the next few moves in silence.

"So what's going on with this literacy thing? I saw

you're going to start filming some PSAs this week. You ready for it?"

Dylan thought of the script Paige had written for him and how she had coached him through how she wanted it read. He chuckled at the memory.

"What? What's so funny?"

"Paige Walters."

"The chick who's working with you?"

Dylan nodded. "Yeah. She's a bit uptight about this whole thing. Not just with me it seems, but with everyone. She's got a script for each participant, and as if that isn't enough, she has very specific ideas on how she wants us to read them—inflection and whatnot. It's wild."

"That's enough to get on your nerves, huh?"

He nodded again, but he didn't really agree. If he were honest, he'd admit that it was cute as hell. She was this tiny, little thing walking around in big boots and big glasses, and it seemed like she could do a dozen things at once. Everyone listened to her and wanted to please her—including himself—and she moved with all the confidence in the world—until her family showed up. Then it was like someone flipped a switch and she became this meek, quiet, and insecure girl.

It was both fascinating and frustrating to watch.

There had been quite a few times when he'd been tempted to ask Paige what her deal was—why she didn't think she was good enough for her family—but by the time they were alone again, he found he didn't want to upset her.

It was irritating to be so aware of other people's feelings.

"So what's your script?" Mick asked, interrupting his thoughts.

"I'm talking about how reading helped with life on

the road. You know, because with all the traveling and going to other countries, I had to know where I was going. She asked for a couple of stories where it was important for me to be able to read and navigate through the business aspect of the music business and not just play the bass, stuff like that."

Mick headed to refill their drinks and Dylan walked over to the French doors that led out to his yard. There was the pool, the hot tub, the deck—it was beautiful, but it left him feeling…nothing. He wasn't going to miss this place, no matter what Mick thought. The memory of drunken parties, of passing out on the lawn, of people vomiting all over the bushes… Yeah, he wasn't going to miss this place at all. It was time to start fresh and that meant a new house with new memories.

He thought of Riley and made a mental note to call him later. Riley Shaughnessy—the lead singer of their band Shaughnessy—had managed to avoid all of the pitfalls of the rock-and-roll lifestyle. He wasn't a drinker, he wasn't a partier, and he never did any drugs. And now he was married with a daughter and another baby on the way and still living in the house he had first purchased when they signed their second major record deal. Yeah, Riley was someone who had it all together, and Dylan should make an effort to get together with him and maybe get some advice on what he should be doing now.

If he asked Mick, Mick would say he should be careful, cautious, and take things one day at a time. Well, he was sick of that. It was what he'd been doing ever since he got out of rehab. It was time to start figuring out how to live now—clean and sober. Millions of people did it every day, so why was he so afraid of it?

"I always loved this yard," Mick said as he came out and handed Dylan his water. "This layout is a thing of beauty."

"Yeah, until there's a hundred people drinking, smoking, throwing up, and having sex all over it. Then it's a wasteland," Dylan murmured, looking around and still envisioning those days. He shuddered.

"It wasn't all bad, you know," Mick reminded him. "Not every party was a drunken orgy."

"Most of them were."

Mick shrugged. "Come on. We gonna finish this game or what?"

Dylan thought about it for a minute and then shook his head. "Nah. You weren't all that into it and my concentration is shot. We'll pick it up next time."

"Uh-uh. Fresh game next time. I know I was playing like crap. If you're going to subject me to another game, I should at least get the chance to play it without all the careless mistakes."

"Whatever," Dylan said with a chuckle.

"You know, you could always find someone else to play chess with," Mick said, feigning offense.

"Nah. I like how you pretend you're trying. It's fun to watch."

"Yeah. I'm a riot. But seriously, it wouldn't hurt my feelings if you found someone else to torture with this game for a while. Maybe one of those literacy people wouldn't mind a game or two while you're in between scripts," Mick said with a laugh.

And for some reason, Paige's face instantly came to mind. What types of games did she like to play? Strategy games like chess? Word games? Number games? He figured her to be more of that variety rather than something silly like Pictionary. He planned to ask her when he next saw her. He'd been learning a lot about her, mostly by observing her, but he had a feeling if he simply forced her to sit still once in a while, they could have a really good conversation.

The kind like they'd had that first day over coffee.

And suddenly, the thought of not playing chess with Mick again wasn't unappealing at all.

Chapter 4

TWO WEEKS.

They'd been in full-steam-ahead mode with the Literacy Now campaign, and Paige was on the verge of pulling her hair out.

She'd written all the scripts and then worked personally with each of the authors—yes, Ariel had allowed her to keep a few authors—and celebrities, but unfortunately, Ariel kept changing things without telling her. Not that it was anything big, but Paige was someone who was regimented and enjoyed having her list and crossing things off it—in order. So far, the only thing that had gone smoothly was the one thing she thought was going to mess her up the most.

Dylan.

"Hey, I grabbed a couple of sandwiches on my way here. I figured you hadn't had time to stop and eat yet."

Speak of the devil.

Turning, Paige gave him a smile of gratitude. "Thanks. I haven't."

Dylan looked around the studio space they were working in today to do the publicity photos of all the participants—alone and in a group. Paige had lost a lot of sleep trying to line up everyone's schedules so they would all be here at the same time for at least an hour.

No small task.

"I double-checked and then triple-checked with

everyone to confirm they'd be here and we're still missing about…"

"Four people," Dylan finished for her as he unwrapped her sandwich and handed it to her.

"Thanks." How did he know? How could he possibly walk in here and instantly figure out what was going on and what she needed? Rather than make herself crazy with yet another thing, she took a bite of the sandwich— turkey with bacon, lettuce, and tomato on whole wheat. Her favorite. After she finished chewing, she smiled at him. "You remembered."

He chuckled. "You've ordered it almost every day this week. I figured I couldn't go wrong ordering one for you."

"It's perfect. Thank you." She began to look around for where she'd put her bottle of water and found Dylan handing her one. A new one. A cold one. Her shoulders sagged as she looked at him again and accepted the drink. "I'm beginning to feel like you're here to assist me and not the other way around."

He shrugged. "What time did you get here this morning?"

Paige took another bite of her sandwich and looked away with a small shrug.

"Paige?"

"Seven," she mumbled.

"Seven? No one was scheduled to start until ten! Why would you get here so early? That wasn't on your schedule or your list of responsibilities, and you know it." His tone was light but firm, but she felt thoroughly admonished.

Clearly she had shared way too much over the past

few weeks. It wasn't as if he were shining a light in her face and interrogating her, but he had a way of getting her to talk while they were working together. And when she talked, he listened. Clearly.

They ate in silence as people milled around them. Paige couldn't help but feel anxious—this whole photo shoot wasn't going as planned and there were still several people missing. She needed to finish eating, make some calls, and—

"Hey, do you play cards?" Dylan asked.

She swallowed the last of her sandwich and looked at him in confusion. "Um…what?"

"Cards. Do you play cards? Like poker or solitaire or gin rummy?"

Did she? Paige had to think about it for a minute before saying, "No. I don't think I've ever played those."

Dylan's eyes went wide. "Really? What about board games? You into any of them?"

"You mean like Monopoly?"

He nodded. "Sure. Or checkers, Clue, Trivial Pursuit…"

"I've played all of those, but not in a long time."

He paused, took a drink of his iced tea, and then asked, "What about chess? Ever play?"

A slow smile spread across her face. "I used to play it all the time with my grandfather when I was little. He died when I was fourteen. No one else in the family was interested. Once he was gone, I didn't have anyone to challenge me."

Was it her imagination or was Dylan trying hard not to smile too?

"What? Why are you smiling like that?"

"Like what?"

"Like you're suppressing it," she said laughing softly. "This is a ridiculous conversation, isn't it?"

"The part about the chess or my smile?" he teased.

That had her laughing again. Dylan could be charming, and he had a way of making her feel…happy and way less serious than she normally was. "Come on. Something is clearly on your mind. So spill it."

"I was just thinking how you need a distraction for when things like this happen," he said simply.

"You mean lunch?"

Now it was his turn to laugh. "No, I mean when you see something going wrong because other people aren't doing their jobs and you want to jump in and fix things. You need something to do so you won't give in to the urge."

"And you think a board game is going to help with that?"

He shrugged. "Couldn't hurt."

Paige laughed as she shook her head. "You don't know me very well. This is who I am. I'm a fixer. I have a compulsive need to take care of things. If I see a problem, I fix it—or I try to." When he tried to comment, she held up a hand to stop him. "Let me put it this way—it's physically impossible for me to sit back and watch people struggle without stepping in. I can't."

Dylan looked at her with a mild expression. "If you're too scared to try…"

She huffed with annoyance. "I didn't say I was scared. I said I have work to do that can't be ignored."

Dylan took another drink of his tea and then leaned in close. "Let me ask you something—who's in charge of this photo shoot?"

"I am."

"Liar," he said softly but with a grin.

Another huff. "Okay, fine. Ariel is supposed to be here."

"And where is she?"

The last text Paige had received claimed that her sister was on her way. But that was…two hours ago.

Dammit.

"She got detained," she said, although why she was defending her sister, she didn't know.

"Detained or did she know you'd be here to take care of it?" Dylan challenged.

"Hey!" Paige snapped. "You don't know what you're talking about and I don't appreciate what you're implying."

With his hands held up in surrender, Dylan took a step back. "Sorry. My mistake. I'll sit over there with Stevie and Alan. Let me know when you're ready for me." And then he cleaned up his lunch mess and turned to walk away.

"Dylan…wait."

Looking over his shoulder at her, he waited.

"Sorry. I didn't mean to snap at you."

He smiled. For some reason, she was starting to enjoy seeing him smile. As much as she hated to admit it, Dylan Anders was becoming a friend with whom she enjoyed spending time. Paige no longer looked at their time together as a chore, but rather a perk. Their conversations were always fun and he was quite pleasant to look at.

Not that she went for the scruffy, rock-star type.

At least, she never had until now.

But Paige was far too intelligent to think someone like Dylan would give her a second look. He was being nice to her because he had to. Or felt like he had to. They had formed a friendship and that was that. During her Google searches, she'd found a plethora of pictures of Dylan with various models and other beautiful and glamorous women. Tall, thin, sexy women. If there was one thing Paige knew about herself, it was how she certainly didn't fit into *that* category.

So what if he remembered her favorite sandwich and made sure she had something to eat? He was being nice. Still…no one else around her seemed to care if she hadn't eaten. And so what if he was concerned about her stressing herself out and tried to find a helpful solution? He was probably bored and looking for something to do to pass the time and figured, as his official assistant/babysitter, she'd be open to entertaining him.

Only…it felt like more. Like he was a genuinely nice guy who put the needs of others before his own. Or was she seeing something that she wanted to see? True, it had been far too long since she'd been in a relationship or even went out on a date. Maybe she was a little… needy, in the male-companion territory.

And it didn't help that he was so attractive.

"Dammit," she muttered.

"You okay?" Dylan asked.

Crap! She hadn't meant to say anything out loud. "It's nothing," she said quickly. "I just hate that everyone isn't here yet. I should probably make some calls and see what's going on."

"You mean call your sister and let her know that she needs to call the talent?" he asked sweetly.

And if she hadn't found his smile so darn attractive, she'd want to slap it right off his face.

"No," she said with a hint of irritation. "We're on the clock and people need to get here now. I'm not starting a phone tree. Excuse me."

As she pulled out her phone to start making calls, Dylan gave a small shrug and walked over to where a couple of other musicians who were now part of the campaign were sitting.

Great. He had to have a sexy ass that looked amazing in a pair of faded jeans.

A-ma-zing.

Fairly grab-able.

"Ugh…I really need to stop thinking like this," she said with a weary sigh and startled when a voice answered on the other end of the phone.

"Margaret, hello! It's Paige Walters!" She went into her spiel and explained how they were all waiting for her and then had to stifle a groan when Margaret apologized profusely and swore she was on the way.

As did the other three people she called.

Across the room, she spotted Dylan laughing with a group of people. He looked good—comfortable, relaxed. His dark hair was mussed, and Paige made a mental note to talk to the hair and makeup people about leaving it alone.

It looked good on him.

What must it feel like to be *that* comfortable in your own skin? She knew from some of their conversations that he was just now starting to feel that way. The time in rehab and his new focus on his life turned things around for him, but still. Paige didn't have any vices—didn't have a need for therapy—and yet, she still always felt out of place. Okay, maybe not always, but certainly in some social settings.

Feeling inferior had been a lifelong thing. It didn't help that she had an extremely charismatic older sibling who seemed perfect at everything. Ariel had an outgoing personality and a sense of ease and grace in all that she did. Paige had learned at a young age that she lacked the talent and social skills—and the good looks—to compete. So she put her focus on academics, exceling in areas her sister hadn't.

Unfortunately, her sister also had a talent for laying on a good guilt trip.

It started with her asking Paige to cover for her when she'd break curfew or do the chores Ariel forgot about. It was a pattern that had started early on, and clearly it was still going on today. But how was she supposed to break it? Anytime she'd brought it to Ariel's attention, things got turned around and Paige ended up being the one to apologize!

Yet another of Ariel's talents.

Ugh.

Who knows? Maybe spending time with Dylan would be beneficial to her and the way she looked at herself. Maybe she could learn something from him, and when this campaign was over, she would believe in herself all the time and not only some of it.

So for now, she would be the friend.

The buddy.

The work babysitter.

And she'd pray those dimples and that smile stopped making her tummy flutter all the time.

When Dylan got home later that afternoon, he tried calling Riley, but his call went to voicemail. Feeling slightly unsettled, he called Matt Reed, the guitarist for Shaughnessy and another close friend.

"So…what are you doing, reading poetry and crap?"

Dylan rolled his eyes and let his head rest on the sofa cushions. "No, that's not what I'm doing. Weren't you listening at all?"

"I am, I totally am, but I'm still confused. This is a literacy thing, but you've yet to do anything that has to do with reading. So, what gives?"

Dylan explained the entire layout of the campaign, how they were in the staging part of it with taking publicity shots and shooting the promos. "Once all that is done, we'll have events to go to where we'll be speaking about and promoting the cause."

"Events? You mean like book clubs?" Matt asked with a chuckle.

"If you're gonna be a dick, then I'll say goodbye now," Dylan said, feeling irritated.

"All right, all right, I'm sorry," Matt said and then cleared his throat. "How are you feeling with all this? You've been holed up alone for a while. This has got to be weird for you."

"What do you mean?"

"For starters, this is the first social thing you've done in about six months," Matt began. "Then—and don't take this the wrong way—this is something that is so different from your usual thing. We never did publicity stuff like this alone. Well, Riley did some, but for the most part, we did everything as a group. Now you're out there solo. And for a fairly…normal cause. There is nothing rock-and-roll related about it."

"Nope." And it had been one of the things that appealed the most to Dylan. There was less of a chance for anyone to get on him about his past this way. True, Stevie Campbell and Alan Day were musicians—but they were more of the soft-rock scene. Nothing hard or partying about either of them. It was nice to talk shop with them earlier, but other than their craft, he had nothing in common with either of them.

"Are you going crazy yet? How much time do you have left?"

"It'll be three months when it's all said and done."

"And it will take care of your community service stuff?"

"Yup."

"Damn. It seems like a long time. Hopefully you'll meet some people who make it more tolerable."

"Well…the chick who's acting as my handler—"

"Oh God. You're not sleeping with her, are you?"

"What? No! Why would you even ask that?" Dylan croaked.

"Dude, that's totally your MO," Matt chuckled. "So what's the deal? Is she old? Fat? Married? No…wait, that one hasn't stopped you in the past."

"Shut up," Dylan murmured. Everything Matt was saying was true—there had been far too many years when Dylan hooked up with women he shouldn't have. But he was a different man now and hooking up with Paige—sleeping with Paige—was… Well, he wasn't going to allow himself to go there.

It was bad enough that his subconscious seemed to want to go there nightly. There had been several very… explicit and erotic dreams where Paige was the star. And in each and every one of them, he took great pleasure in taking those big glasses from her face—a face that was flush with excitement and her lips were red and glossy and making a perfect *O* because she was in awe of what they were doing.

Once the glasses were off, he found it was sexy to slowly remove the crazy layers of her wardrobe. Seriously, the woman wore layers of scarves, sweaters, tights, skirts, and large chunky jewelry. In his dreams, it was like opening up a present—taking each one of those items off her was a sensual experience. He almost groaned at the image that was now right in front of him and had to force himself to stop. She was off-limits and he wasn't going to go there with her.

No matter how much he wanted to.

It was hard work to make all these changes in himself, his life, and not sleeping with every available woman was part of it. He needed to show some self-control. And besides, Paige was barely tolerating him. She was heading up this campaign—no matter what anyone else at her agency thought. And sleeping with the boss, so to speak, was definitely not something he wanted to be known for. Especially not after he'd worked so hard to clean up his act.

So he didn't allow himself to even think of Paige as a woman, let alone an attractive one, when they were together. She wasn't his usual type, but it turned out his usual type wasn't particularly good for him.

Or maybe they were never really his type at all.

Right now, Paige Walters seemed more and more like the perfect woman for him. She was funny and attractive, and he loved hanging out and talking to her. Dylan loved how she wasn't afraid to eat what she wanted and how she owned up to her own shortcomings and mistakes. She was honest to a fault and took care of everyone around her.

Honestly, she was too good for him and he needed to remember that too.

"Enough about me," he said, realizing both he and Matt had gone quiet. "What's going on with you? How's Vivienne?"

"She's great," Matt said, and Dylan could hear the smile in his friend's voice. "We're heading to Paris next week to see her parents. It's a big step for her—this is the first time she's taking the trip willingly."

"She doesn't get along with her parents?"

"She does now. But for years, her trips to France tended to end with her feeling inferior to her brother and then being depressed for weeks. She and her mom finally started having a better relationship, and I'm hopeful this visit will be a good thing for all of them. Plus, you know, Paris. It will be nice to go there and not have to work."

"I'm sure. I know we've been there on tour but for the life of me, I don't remember it," Dylan admitted. "How messed up is that?"

"Very," Matt said and then chuckled. "I'll send pictures."

"Thanks," Dylan replied, laughing too. "So what else is going on? Things any better with your dad?"

Matt sighed loudly. "I'm trying, I really am. But

sometimes it's hard to get past the memories, you know? We're seeing a family counselor—can you believe it? Me and him go together three times a month, and on the fourth visit, his wife and daughter go with us."

"Why? I mean, they don't have anything to do with your issues with your father. Seems like if he needs help with his wife and kid, you could skip that week."

"I thought so too, but apparently this is to help us learn to come together as a family unit."

"Is it working?"

"Not yet," Matt said wearily. "Don't get me wrong. I like his wife. I adore the kid. But it's normally when I see him being this great guy with them that I tend to lose it."

"Sounds about right. What does the therapist say?"

"She says my lashing out is normal, but I need to find another way of expressing my emotions."

Dylan couldn't help but laugh. "Wow. How very textbook of her."

"I know, right?"

"So have you? Found another way of expressing your emotions?"

"Vivienne bought me a punching bag," Matt replied with a laugh. "When I get home from a session, I go right to the home gym and pound on it for a while. It's not the best solution, but it's something."

"Maybe I need to do that."

"Get a punching bag? Why? Who are you pissed at?"

Dylan laughed again. "I'm not pissed at anyone, but working out might be a good way to fill this downtime. I'm telling you, I would love to get together and jam with someone, anyone, but you're all the way in North

Carolina, Riley's busy, and… Wait. Has anyone heard from Julian?"

"I talked to him last week," Matt said. "For the first time in ages, he seemed like his old self. Like he finally saw through all of Dena's nonsense and he was ready to be done. I think it's safe to say the wedding is on hold indefinitely and it probably wouldn't take much to get him to come out and jam someplace."

"Oh man… I would love that. Would you and Viv be willing to fly out here for a week or something?"

"We've got the Paris trip first, but after that, I'm totally open to it. If you get a chance, talk to Riley. And maybe if both of you call Julian, we can get something together for around the middle of the month. What do you think?"

"I'm on it! Once we have a date, I'll let you know."

"Perfect!" Matt said happily. "All right, I've gotta go. Viv is making my favorite Mexican food for a late dinner, and it's almost ready. Take care of yourself, Dylan. And behave!"

Dylan said his goodbye with a laugh, and when he hung up, he was still smiling. Talking with his friends—his *real* friends—did that for him. And knowing he could look forward to seeing them all in a couple of weeks and playing music with them was enough to lift his spirits.

Not that they needed lifting, but he was getting bored.

He had always enjoyed music—listening to it, playing it, writing it. It came naturally to him. During his time in rehab, Dylan had sort of punished himself by not playing it. He didn't feel like he deserved to get any joy from anything. So when Mick had come to see him and brought Dylan's bass with him, Dylan had refused to play it—told Mick to take it back.

And that had been his attitude since.

But maybe it was time to change that.

Rising from the couch, Dylan made his way across the house, toward his music room. He had a collection of bass guitars and several acoustic guitars. He looked around the room and his fingers began to twitch.

Yeah. It was time.

Picking up an acoustic, he sat on one of the stools scattered around the room and began to tune it. It had been over six months since anyone had touched these instruments, so he was fairly certain every guitar in the room needed to be tuned, but for now, he'd stick to this one.

No need to get ahead of himself.

He wanted to play. Wanted to hear the music, feel the music...or simply just feel.

It took almost a half an hour to get the guitar to sound the way he wanted it to, but once he did and Dylan began to strum, it was as if he was transported to the greatest place in the world. Everything around him faded away as the music came to him. He didn't have to think about the notes, the chords, the movements—it was as natural to him as breathing.

Time stood still as he went from simply playing songs that were familiar to him to creating something new. Slow ballads, heavy rock, country tunes... His entire body rejoiced in the return of the music. Sweat beaded on his temples, his arms and hands began to cramp, and when he finally stopped, it felt as if he'd played a complete concert. A quick glance at the clock showed he just about had. Two hours had gone by, and he felt exhilarated.

Carefully putting the guitar in its stand, Dylan left the room and went to the kitchen to grab something cold to drink. As he downed a bottle of water, he went in search of his phone and found it in the living room. The light was flashing to let him know he had a text message. When he picked it up, he saw Paige's name and smiled.

He pulled up her message and read it.

And then read it again.

As if sensing his disbelief, the phone rang—almost falling from his hands—and her name called out to him.

"If you don't want to do it, I'll completely understand," she said instead of greeting him.

"I don't understand what this means," he said. "This wasn't on the schedule, right?"

"It wasn't. Ariel decided she wanted to kick things off with an impromptu get-together. Something low-key."

Dylan chuckled. "The Beverly Hills Hotel is *not* low-key. But…it will be convenient."

"How so?"

"I'll be moving in there at the end of the week."

"You will? Why?"

"My house is up for sale and I don't want to be here while there are people coming through to look at it. We already have offers, but I won't let anyone come in and look while I'm living here."

"Dylan, how are you handling all of it? Are you packing up? Do you have another house lined up?"

He explained his theory and why he was moving into a hotel for a month. "I still don't know what kind of house I want. All I know is I'm ready for a change."

"So this party would be a major inconvenience with its timing. Don't worry about it. I'm sure—"

"Paige, it won't be an inconvenience. I'll be living in the same hotel as the party. I'm sure I'll be able to come downstairs and socialize for an evening. Who knows? It might be fun."

She made a sound that Dylan would have to say sounded like a snort, but he couldn't be sure. Either way, it was enough to signify her disbelief.

"C'mon, Paige, admit it. It might be fun."

"It's a waste of time and money!" she cried. "We could be using those funds for something else to help the foundation! We don't need a ridiculous cocktail party! I swear, it's like she totally doesn't understand what the point of this campaign is!"

"If the client didn't want it, I'm sure they'd say something," Dylan pointed out.

"I think they're dazzled by the celebrity guest list," she muttered. "I thought I knew these people well, but they are easily swayed by the thought of rubbing elbows with the rich and famous."

"And you're not?" he said, poking her because he knew she wasn't, but he liked getting her riled up a bit.

"Of course not! How could you even ask that? I'm more concerned with raising money for reading programs. I don't need to have crab puffs with...with... Elton John! That's not going to give me a reading program at the local library."

"Elton's going to be there?"

"No, he's not going to be there! I was making a point. Something like this is frivolous and not necessary and—"

"I think you're wrong," he said lightly and sat and waited for her outrage.

"Excuse me?" He could almost picture those big eyes going wide.

"Look, here's what this is about—you have a cocktail party and you invite a ton of people who have money. You introduce them to the cause, and if they are not directly involved with the campaign, you give them enough of a push to convince them to donate. So if you think about it, it's a great idea. With any luck, you'll cover the cost of the party and have a sizeable donation to make to Literacy Now. See? Not frivolous."

There was silence on the other end of the phone, and there wasn't a doubt in his mind that she was racking her brain for some comeback.

"Either way, count me in. I'll be moving in Friday night, and the party is Saturday night, so I'll have time to come."

"Oh…well…good. That's great," she said, but there was something in her voice…a hesitation. She sounded uncertain about something.

"Was there something else you needed, Paige?"

"Um…"

"Because it sounds like you've got something else on your mind."

"Fine. Please don't get mad at me for this."

Dylan let out a weary sigh. All his good vibes from playing music seemed to fade away. Someone was still concerned about him and what he'd do in a public setting. "It's all right. I know what you're going to say. You're going to have to stand guard and make sure I don't do anything to make a scene or make a spectacle of myself, right?"

"Um…sort of. Just…there was some concern about you being in that setting and how it might be…rough for you, that's all. So it's not that anyone's afraid of what you'll do to embarrass anyone or anything like that. It's truly concern for your well-being. I swear, Dylan."

Well, that wasn't so bad, he guessed. Still not great—people thinking he still couldn't control himself yet—but there were worse things in life, he guessed.

"It's okay, Paige. Really. It's not a big deal." He paused. "So I guess you're stuck with me as your date," he said playfully.

"*Date?* What? I mean… No. No! It's not like that. I swear. I don't expect you to *date* me! I mean, that would be crazy. Insane! You don't date women like me…*pfft*… That's just… I'm certainly no supermodel or anything so…really… It's no big deal."

Okay. Wow. That was *not* the reaction he had expected from the normally cool and collected Paige. Should he comment on it?

She cleared her throat and went completely quiet, and Dylan figured by bringing any more attention to her little…outburst, he'd embarrass her. So he let it go.

"I appreciate everyone's concern and I'll plan on seeing you Saturday night, okay?"

"Sure," she replied, sounding relieved.

"We don't have anything else planned for this week, do we?"

"No. It was the photo shoot today. And I want to thank you for all you did."

"Me? I don't think I did anything except smile for the camera."

Paige laughed softly. "You were prompt, you brought

me lunch, and you kept everyone talking and engaged in between shoots. So thank you. You were a big help."

Well, damn. That was probably the first time anyone had ever thanked him for acting…normal. The thought of it made him smile. "I'm glad I could help. And don't hesitate to ask for help at any of these other… stops. I really don't mind. I'd rather be useful than just stand around."

"I appreciate it, and again, thanks." She paused. "So…um…I guess that's it."

"I guess so." Funny, he felt reluctant to end the conversation.

"Yeah."

Hmm… "What are you doing tonight? Anything exciting? Not working late, I hope."

She laughed again. "No. Not working. I'm home with my feet up and playing Scrabble on the computer."

"Really? People do that?" he teased.

"Well, I do. You got me thinking about board games today, and since you obviously can't play them alone, I got on my computer to see what I could find. And you're right. It's very relaxing."

"Glad I could help. I think there's virtual chess. You know…if you're interested."

"Really? I'll have to look that up."

Dylan couldn't help but smile at her excitement. "So you and your grandfather used to play, huh?"

"All the time. We used to have the best conversations during our games. It was our special time together." She let out a wistful sigh. "I miss him so much, and even though it's been, like, fourteen years, I still remember how much those games meant to me."

"Like I said earlier, it's a great memory to have."

"Mmm," she said, and it sounded far sexier than it should have.

"I should probably go. I'm starving, and I need to find something to eat."

"You haven't had dinner yet?"

"Nope. I was tuning and playing guitar and lost track of time." He looked at the clock and saw it was almost eight. Not terribly late, but it seemed like lunch was a lifetime ago.

"Well...go find something and I'll see you on Saturday night."

"Yeah, okay. Great. I'll see you then."

"Have a good night, Dylan," she said.

"You too."

～～～

Three days later, Dylan tossed his jacket on the hotel room bed and sighed.

He'd done it.

He'd walked away from the home he'd owned for the past eight years.

He kept waiting to feel...something. The Realtor had done a final walk-through with him and kept saying things like "I'm sure you're going to miss this" and "This must be hard for you," but in truth, he wasn't and it wasn't. The house was the last major tie he had to his life prior to rehab.

There was still the band and Mick, but the house held the most bad memories for him. From this point on, he knew Riley, Matt, Julian, and Mick would be there to encourage him to stay the course. And it felt damn good.

As he walked around, he noted how it was going to be strange going from living full-time in a 7,500-square-foot house to an 800-square-foot hotel room. Lucky for him, Shaughnessy had spent so much time on the road that hotel living wasn't going be a total shock. It wasn't ideal, but it also wasn't permanent. He'd lucked out in scoring one of the recently refurbished suites. It was modern with a hint of vintage glamor, which he found he liked.

The furniture was oak and had touches of mohair and leather, and the room offered an amazing view of LA. He moved from the living room into the bedroom and knew he'd made the right choice. A standard room would have been fine, but with the two-room setup, he would have plenty of space to relax. He ran a hand over the king-size bed and smiled. The rest of the furnishings were nice to look at, and he was sure they were comfortable, but his main requirement had been a king-size bed. He enjoyed sprawling out, and should he decide to invite someone up to join him for the night, he knew they'd appreciate the extra space.

Paige's face immediately came to mind, and he cursed himself. Maybe he needed to find someone to hook up with—and soon. He had to stop envisioning Paige in these scenarios because that wasn't going to happen. It couldn't. And the sooner he distracted himself from *that* fantasy, the better.

He kept on moving and checked out the luxurious marble bathroom. There was a shower and a Jacuzzi.

And there were images of Paige naked in both of them.

"Dammit," he hissed.

Yeah, he definitely needed to find a distraction because this was starting to get out of hand. Hopefully at the cocktail party tomorrow night, he'd be able to find someone he was attracted to and could get over this drought he was in. Memories of his last failed attempt at getting laid played in his mind, and more than anything, it pissed him off.

"I used to be able to have sex with little more than the crook of a finger," he murmured as he walked out of the bathroom. "It shouldn't be this hard."

Speaking of hard… Yeah. The image of Paige in the shower was instantly replaced with the image of her in his bed. Walking quickly, he went out to the living room, where it wasn't hard to imagine her bent over the sofa.

His cell phone rang and he reached for it like a life-line. "Hello!"

"Hey, buddy! You sound a little frantic. You okay?"

It was Riley. Thank God. If ever there was someone to put him on level ground, it was Riley Shaughnessy. Sitting down on the sofa, Dylan kicked off his shoes and relaxed. "I'm good. I'm good. The phone startled me. I moved into the Beverly today and was checking the room out."

"Right. Mick told me you were doing that. You know you could have come and stayed with us, Dylan. We have a guest room. The door's always open here."

"And I appreciate it, but I know you and Savannah are busy with your own things and your daughter. Also, I figured Savannah might not appreciate another kid under her roof."

Riley laughed. "Maybe. But I want you to know if

you get tired of hotel living, you're more than welcome here."

"Thanks, man. I appreciate it. Really. So what's going on?"

"Not much. I got your message the other day and finally had some time to sit down and call you. How's the community-service gig going?"

Dylan told him all about what he'd been up to and about the party tomorrow night.

"Cocktail party, huh?" Riley asked. "You sure you're ready for that?"

If anyone else had asked, Dylan probably would have been offended. But Riley knew him almost better than anyone else. "In my mind I am," he answered honestly. "But I'm never going to know until I try. The good thing is it's right here in the hotel, so if I'm uncomfortable, I can leave and go to my suite. And Paige knows my situation, so she won't be put-off if I bail in the middle of it."

"So you're dating the campaign chick? Do you think that's smart?"

He sighed and raked a hand through his hair. "I'm not dating Paige. She's sort of been assigned to keep an eye on me so I don't screw up anything. Apparently my reputation has some people nervous. So she's more like…a handler."

"Ah. So…nothing's going on between the two of you?"

"Why do people keep asking me that?"

Riley laughed. "Because it's what you used to do! You dated our wardrobe chick, the PR chick, the intern from Mick's office—"

"Thank God he never found out about that," Dylan said.

"Please. Of course he found out about it. Why do you think we were suddenly doing those pop-up shows in the Midwest?"

Dylan sat straight up. "Are you kidding me? *That*'s why we were sent out on that damn tour?"

Riley laughed harder. "Man, you seriously didn't know? We all wanted to kick your ass for getting us into that!"

"I had no frigging idea. I really thought Mick didn't know!"

"That girl was something like his best friend's daughter, dude! You're lucky he didn't string you up by the balls for it."

Dylan groaned. "It was only a couple of hookups."

"It was enough for him to find out and for her to start blabbing how you were dating."

"I don't even remember her name," he murmured. "How crappy is that?"

"Very, but in your defense, it was at a time when you were partying particularly hard."

He sighed. "Why didn't anyone stop me? Why didn't anyone smack me in the head and tell me what a mess I was making of my life?"

Riley was quiet for a moment. "We all tried, Dylan. At one time or another, we all tried. You didn't want to listen. There were times when the three of us and Mick would sit and talk about forcing you into rehab or at least doing an intervention, but…" He paused and sighed. "We should have. You have no idea how much it killed me to know that if we had stepped in sooner, things could have been different. You still would have gone to rehab, but you would have been spared the accident and the charges that went with it."

"Believe me, I wish I could have avoided that too, but it had to happen. I think that was what it took to make me open my eyes. I am thankful every day I didn't kill anyone."

"We all are."

"You know what the hardest part of all this is?" he asked, going somber.

"What?"

"I made such an ass of myself that I've got this reputation now. No one's going to let me forget how I was this party boy douchebag. People look at me differently. I need a handler so I don't make a scene places. I hate it. I deserve it, don't get me wrong, but I hate it."

"It's going to get better over time, Dylan. This is all so…new. And you're just now going out and interacting with people again in public. You have to expect a certain amount of hesitation from them. Everyone's waiting to see if you changed. So this is your chance to prove them wrong. Show them you've changed, that you're not going to make a scene—you're *not* that party boy douchebag anymore. Once they see you've reformed, they'll move on. If you ask me, this campaign was perfect timing for you."

"I don't know about that, but it's certainly not as bad as I thought it would be."

"Well, that's something at least."

"I guess." Dylan realized Riley was right. This cocktail party was the perfect opportunity for him to prove how much he had changed. And if it all went well, he wouldn't need a handler the next time around. He wouldn't need Paige to…

Damn. Next time, there'd be no excuse for her to act as his date.

Something to think about at a later time.

Shaking his head to clear it, he put his feet up on the coffee table and said, "So I talked to Matt the other day, and we're thinking of getting together the middle of next month and jamming. He said he'd fly over, and he thinks Julian might be up for it too. Nothing official, just the four of us hanging out and playing music for fun, like the old days. You in?"

"Are you kidding me? I've been praying for this to happen!"

"Why haven't you said anything?"

"I was waiting for you to be ready," Riley replied. "I didn't want to push, and I knew you had other things to deal with and didn't want you to feel pressured or anything."

"I appreciate that. I picked up a guitar for the first time a few days ago."

"Really? You haven't played?"

"Uh-uh. Not since before the accident."

"Wow."

"I know. It was sort of my own form of penance. I didn't think I deserved to play."

"Wow... I don't know what to say."

Dylan shrugged even though Riley couldn't see him. "But I have to say, once I picked up a guitar and started playing?"

"It was pretty damn great, right? When I was struggling with the songs for my album, I avoided playing—especially when Savannah and I first met and she was interviewing me. Then one day, she handed the guitar to me and demanded that I play. Once I started? Oh...

man…it was such an incredible rush."

"Yes!" Dylan cried. "It was. I played for two hours straight, and after that, I started tuning each guitar up one at a time."

"How many do you have now?" Riley asked with a chuckle.

"About twenty-five."

Riley let out a low whistle. "Where are they? You can't possible have them all with you at the Beverly."

"No. Most of them are in storage. I picked four of them and brought them with me. Although, it's not like I can't get to the others if I wanted them. These four just happen to be favorites, and I think they'll work fine to keep me going for a while. I can't believe how much I missed it."

"It feels great to do it again, I'm sure. And now you'll be in good shape when we all get together in a few weeks."

"I can't wait. You have no idea. I feel like I'm finally ready to engage in life again."

"We missed you, buddy. Really. And you're doing okay? Feeling good?" Riley asked.

"I am. I'll admit I'm a little freaked out about this party tomorrow night. I wasn't at first, but once other people started voicing their concerns, it got me thinking. What if I'm not ready? What if people tell me I can handle one drink and I believe them?"

"Damn. I have no idea, Dylan. I wish I did. Only you know your limits, but I would imagine you're not supposed to drink at all. Am I right?"

"Yup. My counselor told me there might come a time when I can handle being in social situations without being tempted but...I don't know. I don't think I'm there yet."

"So maybe this isn't a great idea for you to go."

"No. I have to. I'm going to have to take that first step eventually. And I think Paige is the perfect person to have with me to keep me in line."

Riley laughed softly. "So...Paige. Why? What's she like?"

Dylan didn't even have to think about it. His mind instantly knew what to say. "She's amazing—she's serious and hardworking. She's no-nonsense and isn't afraid to speak her mind. She knows all about me, and she was brutally honest about not liking me when we first met."

"And now?"

"Now? Now I think we're becoming friends. She works too hard, and I'm trying to get her to relax, and she's been keeping me in line."

"Have you needed to be kept in line?" Riley teased.

"Nah...but it's cute how she thinks she has to hover sometimes. And we haven't done a whole lot yet. But I catch her doing it—hovering, watching me, like she's afraid I'm going to whip out a bottle of vodka and start jumping on the furniture or something."

Riley laughed out loud. "She sounds like exactly what you need."

"Yeah...she is," Dylan said wistfully, and immediately an image of her leaning over him came to mind— leaning over him and wanting to kiss him. That was a favorite image. She'd be a little bossy—he bet she liked being in control in the bedroom too—and he'd gladly let her if given a chance.

"Oh...no," Riley whined.

"What? What's the matter?"

"You're going to sleep with her, aren't you?"

"No! Dammit, Riley. I already told you I'm not."

"Yeah, but I can hear it in your voice. You're thinking about it."

Why deny it? "Okay, fine. I'm thinking about it, but I'm not going to act on it. I know how important it is not to screw up right now or give the press anything to worry about—or our PR people."

"And how do you plan on doing that? If the two of you are working together for the next month or so, how are you going to keep from letting that happen? No offense, but you don't have the best history in this particular category."

"Hey! I know I used to be that way, but I'm more in control now! And the way I plan on dealing with it is finding...someone else to distract me. God! I hate saying it like that because it still makes me sound like a jerk."

"Okay, okay, I get it. I'm not trying to beat up on you, I swear. But I know you. And I can tell you're into this woman."

"It doesn't matter. It can't happen. I won't let it. And it's a moot point. Paige Walters is not the type of woman who would slum with someone like me," Dylan said, and it hit him that it was probably true.

"Why? What's wrong with you?"

"Let's put it this way: her family is very...conservative. Hell, Paige is conservative. She took one look at my tats and cringed. I imagine her dating a...lawyer or an accountant. Some intellectual. Not a tatted rock star fresh out of rehab. She goes to book clubs, not concerts."

He stopped when he realized how defensive he was starting to sound.

"And on top of that, she's not like anyone I ever dated."

"You mean besides her having a brain?" Riley joked.

"Very funny," Dylan deadpanned. "No, she's just… She's different. Like she's more hipster than high fashion. She's so small next to me and…" He muttered a curse. "I'm thinking way too much about this, aren't I?"

"A bit."

"It's all right. It's proximity. I'll go to this party, and my focus will be on making a good impression on everyone. I can't get distracted by…Paige. I'll mingle. I'll do the whole social chitchat thing and move on. I'm getting good at keeping things under control these days. This shouldn't be any different."

On the other end of the phone, Riley sighed with relief. "Okay, so…you're good. Who knows? Maybe you'll meet someone tomorrow night at the party and… get distracted. Not the worst plan in the world."

No, it wasn't.

And Dylan knew it was what he needed to do.

It just wasn't what he wanted to do.

Or *who* he wanted to do.

Chapter 5

Paige was running around the ballroom checking, double-checking, and triple-checking that everything was in order. Not that this was her event, but she knew how things could go wrong and thought it would be helpful if she checked the place cards and made sure all the brochures and literature were available.

It was a thankless job, but somebody had to do it.

Actually, Ariel's assistant should have been doing it, but Paige hadn't seen her around yet, and there was no point in waiting when she could handle it herself.

She spoke to the event coordinator and to the catering manager, and made sure the hors d'oeuvres would be passed around and not just placed on tables. Then she spoke to the bartenders to discuss how they would handle people who were drinking too much. Granted, that one was none of her business, but she was concerned. There was no way she wanted any drunken spectacles for this party.

And ironically, it wasn't Dylan who came to mind.

No one specifically did, but with open bars, things could get out of control.

When she felt everything was in order, and to her liking, she decided to freshen up. Grabbing her purse from a nearby table, she was about to turn and go when Ariel stepped into the room.

Which was shocking since the event wasn't due to start for almost an hour.

"Thank God I found you. It looks like I'm in time," her sister said as she breezed toward Paige.

"Why? What's the matter? Everything is under control here. I've talked to the caterer, the waitstaff—"

Ariel waved her off. "Please. That's not important."

"Not important?" Paige cried. "Are you crazy? Events like this don't run themselves, Ariel! You need to follow up with these things!" She rolled her eyes in frustration. "Honestly, how could you not—"

"Okay, stop talking," Ariel said firmly, grasping Paige by the shoulders. "The staff here is top-notch and doesn't need you or me or anyone to babysit them."

Now she was confused. "Then...then what's the matter? Why are you here so early? Is something wrong?"

Ariel nodded solemnly. "Definitely."

Paige braced herself. Was it their father? Had something happened to him? Their mother? Oh God! Had there been an accident? "Ariel, just tell me! What's going on?"

Before Ariel could respond, three women came into the room and made a beeline for them. They stopped next to Ariel.

Paige suddenly got suspicious.

"Everything is set up, Mrs. Blake," one of the women said. Paige looked at them and they reminded her of the snooty saleswomen from *Pretty Woman*—completely the type of people Ariel would hang out with. But when they all started eyeing her, Paige knew exactly what this was.

"Paige," her sister began. "This is an important event,

and I knew you weren't going to be properly prepared for it. So…surprise!" she said with a smile. "Here's your personal style squad! They have a room set up with dresses and shoes and…proper accessories."

Paige frowned and looked at herself. She wore a standard black cocktail dress and…okay, the shoes were more sensible than stiletto, but they were comfortable! "There's nothing wrong with what I'm wearing, Ariel. I appreciate you wanting to help but…"

But Ariel wasn't listening. She took Paige gently by the elbow and started walking her toward the door, with her squad trailing behind her, murmuring about what they had to work with.

"They're going to do your hair and makeup," Ariel went on. "If we had more time, I'd insist on a manicure and pedicure but…" She sighed dramatically. "We'll do what we can."

Paige stepped out of her grasp. "No, we won't do what we can!" she snapped. "I don't need a manicure or pedicure! I don't need my hair and makeup done. How many times do we have to keep going around and around about this? I'm not you! I don't need to look and act and dress like you!"

With a long-suffering sigh, Ariel looked at her hench-men. "Do you see what I'm talking about? It's like she doesn't even care that she's dressed like one of the wait-staff. Girls, please. Help me convince Paige how much better she'll look *and* feel when you're done."

Everyone started talking at once and it wasn't until they were in the elevator that Paige realized she'd been walking with them.

Dammit.

Turning, she tried to tell her sister one more time she didn't need or want this, but Ariel was standing on the other side of the elevator doors as they were closing.

Double dammit!

"Now don't worry," glamor gal number one was saying. At some point, Paige was sure they'd introduced themselves, but she hadn't been listening. "Your hair is in great shape but needs to be styled. We're not going to cut it or anything, just use some rollers and irons to make it fabulous."

Glamor gal number two stepped in front of her. "Are these glasses a necessity or do you have contacts?"

"Um…I have contacts. I was wearing them earlier, but they were bothering me so…I took them out."

"Oh, they're going to need to go back in," she said. "We're going to make your eyes look amazing, and we don't want them hidden by these dark glasses."

Paige groaned. "Fine."

Then it was number three's turn. "I have a dozen dresses with me for you to try on. They've all been approved by your sister, but you need to try each on so we can see which one looks and fits the best."

"But what if I don't like the one you pick?" Paige asked nervously and then watched as her squad looked at her as if she were crazy.

"Sweetheart, trust us when we say we know what's best for you," number three said with a smile that didn't quite reach her eyes. "And if this is the style of…outfit you normally wear," she went on, motioning to Paige's current dress, "I don't doubt you'll have issues with what we picked. But like I said, we know what works and what doesn't. And this dress you're wearing? It doesn't."

The elevator doors opened and rather than fight it, Paige let herself be led along. It was pointless to argue.

She only hoped she wasn't going to fall and make a fool out of herself when they tried to pass her off as some sophisticated debutante.

Dylan had texted Paige that he was heading down, but she hadn't responded. He knew she was probably busy running around making sure everything was in order, so he wasn't too concerned. He'd checked his reflection about a dozen times before leaving the suite. It had been a while since he'd dressed in anything except a T-shirt and jeans. Now, dressed in black slacks, a proper button-down shirt, and dress shoes, he felt…awkward.

Everything fit him perfectly, but he still felt as if he were a kid playing dress-up.

And he hated it.

In the elevator, he reminded himself how he didn't have to stay long and how everyone would be dressed similarly.

That was the chant he kept playing all the way to the ballroom.

Stepping through the doors, he saw there was already a good amount of people present. Clearly, he had managed to be fashionably late and commended himself. He made it ten feet into the room before he started scanning for Paige.

Off in a corner, he spotted her father talking to a group of people. The stylish woman next to him was obviously his wife. He saw how Ariel favored their mother but couldn't quite see who Paige resembled. As he tried to imagine the Walters family standing together, he would almost say that Paige didn't look like any of them.

She was just…Paige.

Speaking of…where was she?

Scanning the room, he spotted Ariel, several of the other artists who were part of the campaign, and a couple of other familiar faces from the entertainment world and the media, but still no sign of Paige.

A waiter approached and offered him a glass of champagne, but Dylan instantly declined. He'd get to the bar and get a club soda or a bottle of water eventually, but right now he wanted to find out where Paige was. Was it possible she wasn't here yet? That didn't seem like her at all.

"Dylan! Hi!"

Turning, he saw Daisy walking toward him. She smiled brightly but seemed a bit shy about approaching.

"Hey, Daisy," he said, smiling at her. "How are you?"

She giggled softly. "I'm fine, thanks. And you?"

He nodded. "I'm doing well, thanks for asking. Um… have you seen Paige? I can't find her."

"Really?" Daisy asked, seeming confused. "She was by the door a minute ago." She looked past him toward the entry and nodded. "Yup. There she is. You must have walked right by her."

Dylan turned around and looked toward the door, but he didn't see Paige. He spotted a staff member talking to one of the—

Ho-ly… Words escaped him.

He blinked hard and then focused again and swore his eyes were deceiving him.

"She looks great, huh?" Daisy said from beside him.

"But don't tell her that. When I said it earlier she nearly bit my head off."

"Wait, she… What?" He turned his head to look at Daisy and found her nodding.

"It's true. She got ambushed by Ariel and her glam squad or something like that, and they gave her a makeover. I think she looks amazing, but she doesn't want to hear that. Maybe her Spanx are a little too snug."

"Her… What the hell are Spanx?" he asked, but at this point, he didn't care. He wanted to go over and talk to her.

He needed a minute to…get his head in check.

The dress she was wearing looked like it was made for her. It showcased all her curves. With all her layered dressing, Dylan never would have imagined she was hiding a body like this. All lush curves and a tiny waist and… Wow. He felt himself starting to sweat. He was already struggling with the erotic dreams of her where he had no idea what was underneath her layered wardrobe. But now that he'd seen her like this?

Yeah…he'd be wise never to close his eyes again.

"That burgundy color looks amazing on her. That's what I told her," Daisy was saying beside him. "It brings out her eyes. And that's another thing—her contacts! She never wears them because she says they're a pain, but look at her face without those glasses! Her eyes are naturally huge. All this time I thought they were getting magnified from the glasses, but they're not. Go figure. And look at her hair…it's like something out of a shampoo commercial! Why does she wear it in a ponytail if it can look like that?"

"I gotta go," he murmured and made his way toward

Paige, feeling as if some invisible force was pulling him forward.

His eyes scanned her from head to toe and the stilettos on her feet were the stuff of fantasies—super-high, super-skinny heels and tiny straps and... Dylan groaned. He needed to focus on something else before he reached her; otherwise, everyone would know what kind of thoughts he was having. Seriously, he was already getting hard, and the closer he got, the worse it was getting.

Baseball stats.

Guitar tuning.

Chess.

All these things were innocuous thoughts, and yet somehow, his mind had managed to turn them dirty.

Baseball had him thinking of all the bases he'd like to reach with her.

Guitar tuning had him imagining playing her the way he'd play a guitar.

And naked chess.

He was screwed.

"So, if someone could make sure we have some of the Literacy Now cards on the serving trays, I think it would be very helpful," he overheard Paige saying. When she spotted him, she smiled nervously. "Excuse me."

Paige stepped away from the uniformed hotel employee she'd been speaking to and slowly made her way toward him. He couldn't help but smile because she looked like Bambi had when he was learning to walk. Walking in stilettos was clearly not her thing and when she reached him, she instantly hooked her arm through his.

"You okay?" he asked, studying her face.

Her eyes—which were done up in a smoky look—slowly met his. "If you promise to let me hold on to you for the rest of the night, I should be." She straightened and looked around the room. "What are the odds of me being able to kick these shoes off and sit for the rest of the night?"

"Slim to none," he said, grinning. "Not because it isn't allowed, but because it will make you crazy to sit here and watch what's going on and not be able to fix things or supervise."

"I know," she murmured. "Dammit."

The pout on her face was adorable and sexy at the same time, and with her curvy body pressed against his, Dylan knew he needed to find a distraction. Fast.

"Everything looks great," he said, taking his eyes off her and looking around the room. Honestly, the room looked like your average, run-of-the-mill banquet rooms, but he figured it would be rude to mention it. "And everyone is smiling so…good job."

She scoffed beside him. "It looks nothing like what I had planned."

Okay, letting her bitch would also work for keeping him distracted so… "What would you have done differently?" He began to stroll slowly around the room, keeping to the perimeter so no one else could hear her words.

"I had envisioned themes," she said quietly. "One section of the room would be done up in science fiction decor, another section would have a more romantic setting. A Victorian look would be over there," she went on, pointing to a far corner with a sigh. "I pictured costumed characters walking around talking about literature and it all being a little more…"

"Cultured?"

Paige looked up at him with a sad smile. "Exactly." Shrugging, they kept walking. "This is all fine but…this looks like every cocktail party at every hotel I've ever been to. There's nothing here other than the banners to let you know what the event is for."

Dylan never paid much attention to parties like this having a theme—well, unless it was a costume party or something—but after listening to Paige's description of what she'd planned, he was disappointed it wasn't happening.

He leaned down a bit as they walked—even in her stilettos, he towered over her—and said, "For what it's worth, I think your party would have kicked this party's ass."

She laughed. "I'm sure there's no need for anything like that, but thanks."

For the next hour, they mingled. Paige introduced him to so many people that his head began to spin. For the life of him, he couldn't believe she could keep track of all the people they were talking to—authors, investors, publishers, librarians, booksellers, on and on it went. The only thing that kept him focused on anything was her arm looped through his.

Still.

That in and of itself was odd.

Actually, the entire evening was odd.

This was the first time Dylan had attended something social sober. It felt weird and unsettling, and he was thankful for Paige's distraction; otherwise, he was pretty sure he'd be having a panic attack by now. He had no idea how long he was supposed to mingle. Another hour? Two? Until it ended? Considering Paige hadn't let go of him, he figured he was locked in until the end of the night. And the thought wasn't all that unpleasant.

Go figure.

"Have you ever considered writing a book?"

Dylan blinked a few times before he realized this particular group of people were all looking at him expectantly.

"Um…what?"

Paige's arm tightened around his. "Thomas was wondering if you'd ever considered writing a biography."

His eyes went wide as he looked at her and then at the small group that had surrounded them. "Seriously? Who would want to read about my life?"

"I would imagine a lot of people," Thomas—who was an editor with a prominent publishing house—replied. "People are fascinated by the rock-and-roll lifestyle, and you've led a very colorful life, Mr. Anders. And now here you are all cleaned up after hitting rock bottom. Your story could be very inspirational."

"Somehow I doubt that," Dylan murmured.

"Trust me. The majority of your story would be sensationalized—the sex, the drugs, the name-dropping. It's what the people want. The fact that you cleaned up after a stint in rehab for almost killing those people…"

"None of their injuries were life threatening," he countered defensively.

"Okay, okay, okay," Paige interrupted with a smile. "Thomas, I'm sure if you have a card you could give to Dylan, he'd be more than happy to talk to you about this in a more appropriate setting."

Thomas pulled out a card and handed it to Dylan. "I'd

love to talk to you about it, Dylan. I can already see the cover in my mind—the bad-boy rock star back-to-back with the cleaned-up choirboy. People will eat it up!"

It suddenly felt too hot in the room, his suit too tight. With his free hand, Dylan tugged at his collar a bit and cleared his throat before sliding the business card into his pocket. "Thanks. I'll think about it."

"You'll have to excuse us," Paige said with her smile still in place. "We're getting ready to do our presentation. Enjoy your night." She led him away and it took every ounce of strength not to pull free and tell her how there was no way he would consider doing a book like Thomas had described.

Ever.

But he didn't. Instead he walked silently beside her, knowing he was only doing it because she feared falling and breaking her ankles in those damn shoes. As they walked up to the front of the room where her father, sister, and Daisy were standing, he wondered if she did need to do a presentation. He'd thought she was getting them away from what was becoming an awkward situation.

"Oh, good, you're here," her father said, taking Paige's hands in his and kissing her cheek. Paige had to disengage from Dylan's arm to make that happen and Dylan found he missed the feel of her immediately. He gave Dylan a mild stare before saying, "We're getting ready to hit the stage."

"I'm ready for it," Paige said with confidence. "I spent all last night perfecting my pitch, and I think…"

"Um, Paige…sweetheart…Ariel is doing the presentation," her father said, and Dylan noted how the man at least had the decency to look uncomfortable.

"What?" she said, her tone hushed and…hurt. "But…I wrote… I had planned…"

"Paige, Ariel's heading up the campaign, and it's only right that she do the presentation," Robert went on. "We're all going to be up onstage with her—me, you, and all the members of PRW who are involved in the project—but Ariel is the only one speaking. I thought you knew that."

She didn't say a word. She simply nodded, and Dylan had a feeling he was the only one to notice the quiet sniff.

Dammit.

As if on cue, they all turned and started to make their way to the stage, but Dylan reached out and touched Paige's arm. She turned, and her eyes were the slightest bit shiny with unshed tears.

He cursed slow and profane. "Are you all right?"

She nodded. "I'm fine. Thank you."

"You don't have to go up there, you know," he said. "We can leave right now. You can kick off your shoes and we'll sprint out of here if that's what you want."

She looked at him oddly. "I…I can't."

For a minute, he thought she was going to agree with him. He let out a weary sigh. "Dammit, Paige, that was… It was bullshit!"

She immediately shushed him and moved in close. "You need to keep it down," she hissed. "People are starting to stare."

It didn't matter to him but he played along. With his head bent low, he tucked a finger under her chin and forced her to look at him. "I don't care what people are looking at, okay? What happened here? What I just witnessed? That was wrong on so many levels. Why do you put up with it?"

"It's my job, Dylan," she said with resignation. "It's what I do. Even when I don't want to. I do what I'm told and…and…make the best of it."

And that's when it hit him—he was part of her job. She was told to babysit him, and she was. Maybe they weren't becoming friends like he thought they were, maybe she was just doing her job.

Great.

Now he was even more pissed than he had been a minute ago.

"I need to go," she said quietly, and when she turned to walk away, he let her.

Around the room, people were taking seats at their tables. Dylan had no idea if he even had a table—hadn't bothered to check—and right now he didn't care to find out. He wanted to leave. He'd put in an appearance, and he should be free to go. Eight months ago, he would have walked over to the open bar and had a field day, but now he wasn't sure what he was supposed to do.

Knowing he couldn't stay standing in front of the stage, he turned and made his way toward the back of the room. He had no idea what he'd do there, but it was better than standing here like an idiot. The lights dimmed a little as Ariel and company weaved around the tables and took the stage. Dylan made it to the back wall and found a spot where he could watch Paige. She stood at the end of the line of eight people—far away from her father and sister.

Ariel started speaking, and Dylan instantly zoned out. He knew her type—polished and sophisticated but shallow. It was obvious she wasn't passionate about this cause like Paige was; she knew how to schmooze and get more funding for it. Not a bad business tactic, but he loathed the way she went about doing it.

Stepping on her own sister.

In his book, that was beyond low.

He watched as Robert Walters beamed with pride as his daughter spoke, and it made Dylan wonder if he would have looked the same if it were Paige at the podium. Would he be standing there with a smile, or would he be more stoic? Why these were his thoughts, he had no idea, but it was a good way to kill time— figuring out the dynamics of the clearly dysfunctional Walters family.

She droned on and on in all her polished glory, and when Dylan looked at his watch and saw only fifteen minutes had gone by, he began to wonder if the rest of the room was as bored as he was.

"Ugh, don't you hate these things?"

Dylan turned and found a beautiful woman leaning against the wall beside him. He gave her a small smile and then hesitated. Right now, he wasn't looking to make any more small talk and was simply biding his time until Paige was done with whatever it was she was doing up on the stage with her family. The woman sighed, and he wondered if he should at least acknowledge her comment.

As if reading his mind, she smiled and held out her hand. "Morgan Lewis," she said. "We met last year in New York. My boyfriend, Steve, plays drums with Supersonic. You jammed with them on a couple of their tour dates."

His mind was fuzzy on that, but he shook her hand and smiled. "Right. How are you?"

"Bored," she said with a small pout. Dylan noticed the glass of champagne in her hand and wished he had a bottle of water or some club soda right about now. "I know this is a good cause and all, but would it kill them to put on some decent music and maybe have a bigger variety at the bar?"

Yeah, the last time she had seen him, he would have been thinking the same thing. But it wasn't something he was looking to get into right now, so he opted to focus on why they were both here.

"So you're here to support Literacy Now?" he asked.

Beside him, Morgan let out a delicate—and slightly tipsy—laugh. "Hardly. I read *Vogue* when I'm bored but other than that…"

"Then why are you here?"

She looked at him for a moment as if he'd suddenly started speaking Greek. "It's a celebrity event. The press is here. It's good exposure." She paused and looked around. "Steve's around here someplace. I think he went out to the hotel bar to get us something better to drink."

"Is the press here? I didn't notice them," Dylan said mildly, and turned his attention to the stage.

"C'mon, let's go find Steve," Morgan said, hooking her arm through his and giving a small tug. "We'll go grab something to drink at the hotel bar because this one sucks, and then we'll go out and be seen. You haven't been around in so long, I'm sure you're dying to get out and party! With one phone call, Steve can get the guys together and we can hit a club or two and put on an impromptu show."

Was this woman for real? Did she have any idea why he hadn't been around?

"Um…look, Morgan, I'm not interested in…"

Then she turned her body and effectively blocked his view of the stage as she pressed up against him from head to toe. Her breasts were pressed up snuggly against him as they spilled over the top of her strapless cocktail dress and Dylan felt…

Nothing.

And that pissed him off too.

Even if he had no interest in this woman personally, as a man, shouldn't he feel at least some appreciation for the female form? A stirring of arousal for her effort?

"Please, Dylan," she purred, running one perfectly manicured finger along his jaw. "We had so much fun in New York. Don't you want to have fun with me again? Steve won't mind." And somehow, she pressed in closer, her breath hot against his ear even though she wasn't whispering. "It can be our little secret."

He was about to respond when the whole room erupted in applause. Putting some distance between them, Dylan began to clap—thankful for something to do rather than acknowledge what Morgan had just said. All around them, people started to get up and walk around, and he saw that Paige was no longer onstage with her colleagues.

Where in the world was she?

Craning his neck to see beyond Morgan, Dylan tried to remember if Paige had seen where he'd walked off to.

And then he remembered… *"It's my job. It's what I do."*

Right.

"So what do you say, Dylan? We'll grab Steve and blow this lame party."

"What are we blowing?" Dylan turned at the sound of a male voice and found Steve Bladen standing beside them with a big grin on his face. "Dylan! Holy shit, man! It's good to see you!"

With no other choice, Dylan shook his hand and then had to stand there while the guy rambled on and on and on about how much fun they'd had together last year. Even if Dylan could have remembered, he highly doubted it was quite as spectacular as Steve was making it sound.

Just when he thought he'd lose his mind listening to the story, Steve switched gears. "So what do you say? Me, you, Morgan? I've got a limo outside. Let's go have some fun like we used to."

There was a soft gasp, and he knew that it didn't belong to Morgan.

Could this night be any worse? Paige asked herself as she tried to hide her horrified reaction to what she'd overheard.

She was gone for all of ten minutes and Dylan was making plans to go out and party like he used to.

Unbelievable.

And yet…believable.

She looked at the woman standing beside him in her tight, strapless gown and wanted to scream at the unfairness of it all. Just because Dylan had been the epitome of a gentleman all night with her didn't change the fact that under the right circumstances—or in this case, the questionable ones—he was still a man. Still a bad-boy rock star who slept with supermodels.

Looking at herself, Paige loathed her forced choice of apparel even more. With a stammered "excuse me," she turned to walk away.

But the stupid heels did her in.

She felt her ankle turn in an almost unnatural way and she knew she was going down and willed herself not to cry.

Strong arms came around her immediately and prevented her from face-planting on the carpet. All the breath whooshed out of her as Paige found herself pressed against Dylan's chest.

Even though all she wanted to do was cling to him and linger, she gave Dylan a shove to put some distance between them.

"Hey," he said softly. "You okay?"

Honestly? She wasn't. Her ankle was killing her, and she was embarrassed and annoyed at her sister's presentation and had hoped she could lean on Dylan while she cried about how unfair it all was.

Seeing him with this bedazzled, blond nightmare and one of his cronies, Paige realized Dylan was only nice to her because he had to be. She was the key to his staying on this campaign and completing his community service. Nothing more.

And *that* bothered her.

More than she had thought it would.

She had been seeing them as becoming friends. She enjoyed talking to him and spending time with him and in all those times together, she had started to forget who he was.

Witnessing this little encounter brought it all back. And she hated it.

"I'm fine," she lied with a mirthless laugh. "I knew these shoes would do me in."

Dylan gave her a smile—one she usually liked looking at—and Paige had to force herself to look away. Clearing her throat, she went on, "So I'm going to throw in the towel and kick them off and call it a night. I appreciate you coming and supporting the cause."

He frowned at her. "You're leaving?"

She let out a sigh. "I wasn't needed here, was I? I mean, I didn't have to give a presentation, and I was left out of the speech altogether so…" She shrugged. "Now if you'll excuse me, it sounds like you have plans and I think I need some ice."

He reached for her—she knew he did—but with her head held high, she walked away. Every step hurt like crazy, but she didn't stop. With her eyes focused on the exit, she did the one thing she'd never done before.

She shirked her responsibilities and didn't care.

It was a first for her. She took her position seriously and knew how important it was to present the happy family–united front image. Well, not tonight! Tonight she was going to kick off her shoes as soon as she found a quiet spot outside of the banquet room and drive herself home barefoot.

Click-clack-click-clack—her heels made that annoying sound with every step she took. People were out in the halls and she smiled but kept up her determined stride until she made it to the lobby. There she found an upholstered bench against the wall—which luckily was bookended by large potted plants—and gently took the shoes off. Her right ankle was already starting to swell, and she knew driving was going to be painful.

"I have to get home and then I can ice it and everything will be all right," she said to herself. Gingerly, she got to her feet and instantly winced.

She managed to walk all of two steps when Dylan stepped in front of her. She gasped and looked up at his face.

His very angry face.

"What the hell is the matter with you?" he demanded.

"Me?" she cried. "What are you talking about?"

"You just walked out of the event you planned! People were calling after you and you didn't even slow down!"

Had they? She hadn't noticed.

"I was done," she said simply. "I'm tired, and now my ankle hurts, and as I said a few minutes ago, I wasn't needed. I didn't think it was a big deal to leave."

The look Dylan gave her showed he didn't believe her one bit. "Really?" he asked sarcastically. "Paige, if there is one thing I've learned about you, it's that everything is a big deal to you—especially this literacy thing. So don't bullshit me, okay? If you're pissed about your sister stealing your thunder, then say so. I'm not gonna argue with you on that one. I think it was a rotten thing for her to do."

Part of her melted a little at his words, but she already knew he was on her side where that was concerned. And rather than feel good about it, she forced herself to remember that he had plans of his own—with people who were more suited for someone like him.

"Don't you have a limo waiting for you?" she asked mildly.

"A limo?" he repeated. "Why would I have a limo? I have a room upstairs."

Right. Because why wait to party in a limo when he could have a party of his own in three minutes in the privacy of his suite.

God, how she hated this!

"Yeah, okay. Whatever," she murmured and went to move around him. "I need to go." In the back of her mind, Paige was prepared to make a glorious exit with her dignity intact.

Her ankle, however, had other plans.

One step. It took one stupid step to make her cry out in pain.

Before she knew it, Dylan scooped her up in his arms and made his way toward the elevator. "Wait! What are you doing?" she demanded, wiggling against him. "My car is that way!" Pointing at the entrance to the hotel for emphasis, she tried to get out of his grasp. "I need to get my valet ticket and…"

The elevator dinged its arrival.

Dylan stepped inside and hit a button, and Paige hit him in the shoulder.

"Ow! Seriously, what the hell, Paige? What's gotten into you?"

"I am not going up to your room, Dylan!"

"Why not?" he shouted at her.

"Because I'm not into partying with your friends or threesomes, that's why!"

You could have heard a pin drop.

Slowly, Dylan lowered her to her feet, and this time she was prepared and babied her ankle when her foot hit the carpet.

"Um…excuse me?" he asked, his voice low and gruff.

Hands on her hips, she knew she would emerge victorious here. "I don't party." There. She'd said it.

He nodded. "Um…yeah. I get that. But what was that other…um…thing you mentioned?"

"Threesomes. I'm not into them."

"And…who's having a threesome?"

She snorted with disgust. "Right. Because the blond with the limo isn't up here, right? You left her and her… her…offer to come chase after me? Somehow I doubt it."

He didn't say a word. For the life of her, she seriously thought he'd argue with her. That he'd demand to know why she would think that or he'd tell her she was crazy because no man could turn down an offer to go out on the town with a supermodel.

But he didn't.

When the elevator came to a stop, he wrapped an arm around her waist and gently led her from it and down the hall toward his room. She wanted to argue that she didn't want to go, but she was in pain and wanted some ice and maybe some ibuprofen.

He slid the key card into the slot and then opened the door and helped her inside. Paige braced herself to see a naked woman on the bed, and had to admit, she was confused when she didn't see the blond from downstairs.

Or anyone.

She was about to comment on it when Dylan helped her onto the couch and then arranged some throw pillows for her to put her foot up on. Then he walked over to the phone, and she heard him call the front desk. Her head was pounding as she let it roll back on the sofa. She closed her eyes and wanted to die of embarrassment.

No supermodel.

No party.

No threesome.

And she'd made a complete fool of herself in front of him.

Great.

Her craptastic night was complete.

She could hear Dylan moving around in the suite but couldn't bring herself to open her eyes to see what he was doing. He was quiet—like he was in stealth mode—and yet all she could do was pray she was having a nightmare and eventually she'd wake up.

A few minutes later there was a soft knock on the door, and she braced herself for what was coming. Was it room service? Concierge? The supermodel?

Dylan's soft footsteps walked across the room, and she heard him thank whoever was at the door and then… she opened her eyes and turned her head and stared.

"Paige, this is Dr. Solanki. She's the hotel's concierge doctor. She's here to look at your ankle."

He'd called for a doctor? Seriously?

"Um…I'm sure it's fine," Paige said nervously, hating how now she'd have to add showing her fear of doctors to her repertoire of embarrassments for the evening. "I just twisted it. A little ice and some ibuprofen and it will be fine. Really." And then to try to prove her point, she stood.

And cried out.

Dammit, why didn't she learn?

"Okay, okay, let's take a look," the doctor said as she stepped forward. Paige had to admit, she didn't seem all *that* intimidating—she looked close to Paige's age and had big, brown eyes and a calm voice. All in all, very different from Paige's own family physician—old and grouchy, like Yosemite Sam.

For the next several minutes, Paige answered questions about how she twisted it, what hurt and what didn't as the doctor gently moved her foot this way and that. When she finally stood, she looked down at Paige and smiled.

"You twisted it pretty good, but I agree with your earlier observation—ice it, ibuprofen, and rest. And you should stay off it for at least twenty-four hours."

"Thank you," both Dylan and Paige said at the same time. Paige looked at him but noticed he wasn't smiling—probably trying to figure out how to get her home if she wasn't supposed to walk.

With a wave and a wish for a good night, Dr. Solanki left as room service appeared. She noticed Dylan accepting the two buckets of ice and what looked like a bag or pack to put it in. When he closed the door, he walked into the suite and went about fixing her an ice pack before coming over and putting it on her foot for her.

All without a word.

Then he handed her a bottle of water and a couple of ibuprofen tablets.

Without a word.

Okay, what was she supposed to say? She'd jumped to conclusions and said some stupid things and acted like a brat. Maybe she should just…

Dylan was setting up a chessboard on the sofa and then sat. He made the first move and then waited.

This was it? He wasn't going to talk? They were supposed to play chess? Fine. She'd play along—literally and figuratively.

She moved.

Then Dylan moved.

And she moved again.

The silence was maddening.

"Okay, I'm sorry," she finally blurted out. "I... shouldn't have accused you of bringing me up here for... well...you know. It was ridiculous." When she finally forced herself to look at him, she saw sadness in his eyes.

Wait...sad? Why?

"I know you would never do that with me," she went on. "Especially not with me. But that doesn't give me the right to pass judgment. So...I'm sorry."

Dylan's expression went from sad to angry and she was even more confused than she'd been five seconds ago.

"What did you mean by that?" he asked, his voice deadly calm, but Paige could tell his teeth were clenched.

"By...by what?"

"Especially not with you. What was that supposed to mean?"

Groaning, her head fell on the couch. Seriously? Hadn't she been through enough tonight? With a sigh of resignation, she faced him—and the music. "Look, I'm not blind, Dylan. I know who I am and what I look like and what kind of man I attract. I'm certainly not a supermodel, and I have never invited anyone to get naked in a limo."

"Jesus, Paige."

"No...no...it's okay. I'm okay with it. Really. I told you when we first met that I had looked you up online, so I know the kind of women you...you're...well, that you spend time with. So the thought of you bringing me up here to...you know...was crazy on my part. And stupid. And ridiculous," she added because she couldn't make herself stop talking. "And…"

Dylan pinched the bridge of his nose and let out a very long breath before he looked at her. "In the spirit of honesty, let me start by agreeing with you—you're crazy."

She couldn't help the gasp that came out.

"But not for the reasons you seem to think," he quickly added. "That woman you saw talking to me downstairs? She's been dating that guy, Steve, who was standing there with us. If memory serves, they've been together for years. The offer was to go out and party, yes. But it was also to go out and jam somewhere. That's it."

The eye roll she gave him also couldn't be helped.

"Yeah, yeah, yeah…believe what you want, but I'm telling you the truth. When Morgan came up to me and introduced herself…" He shrugged. "There was nothing she was going to offer, her or Steve, that held any appeal to me. That part of my life is over and… I don't know. I'm not willing to tempt fate and put myself in situations like that. At least not yet."

"Dylan, come on. I'm not a moron. Drinking aside, you had to at least have some interest in hanging out with them. He's a fellow musician, she's gorgeous, and…"

He shook his head. "And shallow and vain and someone who likes being in the tabloids. Like I said, not interested."

Who was Paige to argue with that? He sounded pretty earnest, so she didn't have a choice but to believe him.

"However," he said, interrupting her thoughts, "the reason I think you're crazy is because you're not seeing what everyone else is seeing where you're concerned."

She frowned at him. "Excuse me?"

He nodded. "You are this amazing woman—you're smart and funny and talented…"

Oh God, here it comes, she thought. The whole "you're a good friend" speech.

"And you're beautiful."

Wait…what?

When her wide eyes stared at him, Dylan nodded again. "It's true, Paige. You are a beautiful woman. Why don't you see that?"

And then it hit her, the whole glam-squad-makeover thing.

Stupid beauty fairies. She'd like to kick their well-toned asses right about now.

"I get it," she said. "This whole get-up tonight… Yeah. Everyone thought I looked great. But you know what? I hate it. This isn't a dress I would ever wear, and I think we can both agree on why I shouldn't wear stilettos. And all this makeup? I feel like I'm wearing a mask! So great, everyone thought I looked beautiful tonight, and that pisses me off!" she cried.

And then felt herself almost starting to cry.

"Hey, hey, hey," he said soothingly, wiping away the stray tear rolling down her cheek. "That's not what I meant, Paige. It wasn't only about tonight."

"Right," she scoffed. "You, Dylan Anders, who's dated some of the most glamorous women in the world, finds me attractive. I'm sure."

"Why is that so hard for you to believe?" he asked, and she could tell he was seriously confused by her reaction.

"You know what? It's nothing. Never mind." She

looked down at the chessboard. "I believe it's your move."

Honestly, she thought he'd put up more of a fight. But he didn't. Instead, for the next thirty minutes, they played chess.

In total silence.

Until he clearly couldn't take it anymore.

"Why can't you accept that you're beautiful even when you don't have all this?" He waved to indicate her dress and hair and makeup.

"Why can't we let this go?"

"Because it's ridiculous," he countered.

"Exactly! Which is why we need to move on." She made her move and immediately realized she'd made it possible for Dylan to win.

But he wasn't looking at the board; he was looking at her. "It's ridiculous because for such a smart woman, you're being obtuse."

"Obtuse?" she parroted. "You're calling me obtuse?"

"I am."

She needed to call his bluff and shut him up. And remarkably, her suggestion was out before she had a chance to think about it. "Kiss me."

Dylan's eyes went wide and his back straightened. "What?"

Paige gave him a knowing smirk. "Kiss me. If I'm so beautiful…if I'm *so* attractive, prove it. Kiss me."

"I'm not going to kiss you, Paige."

And darn it, she didn't want to be disappointed, but she was. It was a stupid idea and yet…she'd wanted him to kiss her—even if it was just to prove a point.

Rather than show how upset she was, she continued

with her point. Whatever it was. "Exactly. Because you don't find me attractive. And that's why you wouldn't bring me up here for...you know."

"Oh, for crying out loud, Paige, it's threesome! You can say *threesome*. You shouted it at me in the elevator."

"I don't need to say...it," she replied. "It's not important."

"Then why do you keep bringing it up?" he said with a grin.

Great. Now he wanted to discuss threesomes with her? Why wasn't this ice working? Why couldn't she go home?

"I'm done bringing it up," she said after a long moment. "Actually, I'd like to go home." Flexing her foot, she couldn't help but wince.

"You know you can't drive like that."

"I don't have a choice. Although I guess I can call for a cab or an Uber or something."

"Just...stay here tonight. I'm sure by the morning your foot will feel better."

Stay here? In his room? Was he serious? Which is exactly what she asked him.

"I'm a bit wired from the party. It was the first time I've gone to something like that since rehab. It felt weird, and my mind's been racing, so I'm probably not going to sleep tonight. You can take the bed. I'm going to end up watching TV all night anyway."

If she were honest, she'd tell him she was exhausted and didn't have the energy to deal with cabs or Uber or even getting from point A to point B.

But she didn't.

"I shouldn't, Dylan. I think tonight has been weird

for us both. And besides, the thought of sleeping in this ridiculous dress is enough to make me want to cry." That part was the truth. She was so Spanx-ed into the ridiculous thing that breathing hadn't been easy all night.

He stood and walked into the bedroom. Two minutes later he came back. "There's a shirt and a robe on the bed, and I pulled the comforter down for you. Get comfortable and I'll refresh this ice pack for you."

"Dylan…"

"Don't argue. For once. Please."

A small nod was her only response. Dylan helped her to her feet and to the bedroom. He left her sitting at the foot of the bed and then closed the door behind him to give her some privacy.

She hated how much of a gentleman he could be at times.

Peeling the dress off was a combination of pain and pleasure. It felt good to breathe again, but she had to wrestle her way out of it more than she cared to admit. And knowing she'd have to put it on tomorrow to get home was already making her want to scream. Once it was off, she tossed it onto a chair and reached for the shirt Dylan had taken out for her—it was a simple black T-shirt. She smiled because it was almost exactly like what she wore at home. Slipping it over her head, she smiled at how it smelled like him.

It was like winning a sad second place prize in a competition she didn't realize she wanted to participate in.

It took her a few minutes to wash all the makeup off and try to do something with her hair. She finger-combed it and shook it out and she looked like an '80s video-vixen reject.

Ugh.

Stupid mirrors.

Limping over to the bed, she climbed in and sighed at how glorious it felt. The sheets were incredibly soft, and the mattress was the perfect level of firmness, and there were enough pillows to make her feel right at home.

If she'd been at home, she would have showered to wash the night off her, but her foot would have protested like it was now. Which was a shame since that was one of the most decadent bathrooms she had ever seen. Maybe if she was feeling better in the morning…

Dylan knocked and she called out for him to come in.

"I wasn't sure how long—" he stopped when he looked at her and Paige figured he was trying to hide how horrified he was by her makeup-free appearance.

Might as well finish the night with a bang, she thought.

She arched a brow at him and waited for whatever it was he had to say.

Clearing his throat, Dylan walked over to the bed. He didn't make eye contact with her but went about his task of propping her foot up and putting the ice pack on it. "I don't think you should sleep with this on it all night, but you should let it stay on for as long as you can." He straightened and walked into the bathroom. Two towels in hand, he came out. He placed one on the pillow under her foot and the other on the floor beside the bed. "You can…um…you can just drop that when you're done."

She figured he meant the ice pack, but it was humorous watching him.

Then he left the room and came back with a fresh bottle of water and the bottle of ibuprofen. "You know, in case you wake up and need some more in the middle of the night." He turned his back to her and looked around the room. "There's a remote for the TV on the table next to the bed, and if you're hungry or need anything, you can holler for me or call room service or whatever and—"

"Dylan?"

"Hmm?"

She rolled her eyes because he didn't turn around. "You know you're proving my point, right?"

Now he turned. "What point?"

"That I'm not attractive," she said and hated how it was clearly her who couldn't let this go. "I took off my makeup, and you can't even look at me."

In a million years, she never could have predicted Dylan's reaction to her words.

He moved like a ninja and had his hands braced on the mattress on either side of her as he was nose-to-nose with her. "I have been trying my hardest to be a good guy here, Paige. I am many things, but I'm not a liar." He reached up with one hand and cupped her jaw—and he wasn't exactly gentle. "Whether you want to believe it or not is on you, but I think you're beautiful. When I walked in here, all I could think was how you take my breath away. Most women need all that…crap on their face to make them look good, but to me, you look so much better without it."

She swallowed hard, unable to believe what she was hearing.

Dylan's thumb caressed her cheek. "You don't need all that because you, Paige, are naturally beautiful."

She swallowed hard again. "Then why…?"

"Why wouldn't I kiss you?" he whispered.

She nodded, unable to look away from his heated gaze.

"Because for the first time in my life I'm trying to get my shit together. And kissing you would be reverting to who I used to be. I was the guy who slept with PR people and assistants and women I shouldn't." He paused and rested his forehead against hers. "I know if I give in and kiss you, it won't stop there. And I'll pursue you until you agree to sleep with me. And then when it all falls apart—like it always does—everyone will look at me and see that I'm the same screwup I always was."

"Dylan…" He placed a finger over her lips, and she almost groaned.

"So it's not that I don't find you attractive," he said, his voice low and possessive and a little bit thrilling. He straightened and took one of her hands in his and placed it over the front of his pants, over his very impressive erection. "I do. But the last thing I want to do is drag you into the mess that my life is."

"But…your life's not like that anymore," she argued softly.

He inhaled deeply, and Paige realized she was still touching him. "Trust me," he said sadly. "It is."

Unable to help herself, she gently rubbed him and let out a breathy sigh.

Dylan squeezed her hand ever so slightly before taking a step back. "You're already stuck working with me. And even though I know we've come to be friends, the truth of the matter is I'm not someone you'd normally spend time with."

"That's not…"

"It is true, Paige. You know it and I know it." There was no condemnation in his tone. Just a sad disappointment. "It's one thing for me to have to deal with people passing judgment or reminding me of the mistakes I made. I'm sure there are some women out there who wouldn't mind dealing with it for the sake of using me for their own gain. But that's not you."

Now he was starting to piss her off. She knew she was uptight about a lot of things and her recent behavior certainly didn't help her case, but it didn't mean she was so rigid or such a snob that she'd...she'd... What? What was she thinking? At first, it was a kiss to prove a point, but now it was more.

A lot more.

Like, *Why can't I be someone Dylan Anders can sleep with and then walk away?*

Wait...was that something she wanted?

Looking up at him—the vulnerability in his eyes, the sexy way his dress shirt was opened at the collar and the sleeves were rolled up...and that wasn't even considering the whole erection thing. Right. Who was she kidding? That was like the giant, shiny, red bow on the whole package.

All her life, Paige played things by the rules, always wanting to be safe, and where had it gotten her? She was a nobody at work, no one took her seriously as a leader and, dammit, she was tired of being forced to follow. Right now she wanted to take the lead and be brave and break the rules.

All of them.

With Dylan.

"What if I said I wouldn't mind dealing with all of

it?" she asked, praying she sounded confident and not at all nervous.

The intense look on his face told her she'd struck a nerve and it made her bold.

"What if I said I want you to kiss me and...you wouldn't have to pursue me to convince me to sleep with you?" She let out a nervous laugh. "I'm already in your bed."

He stood as still as stone.

"Dylan, I..."

But she never got to finish because he turned and walked out the door, gently closing it behind him.

Chapter 6

SHE WAS MADDENING.

A week later, Dylan found himself hiding out behind a green screen and praying he could have five minutes to get himself together. He was sweating, his heart was racing, and he was hard as a rock. Not that that particular effect was new—he'd been in a heightened state of arousal since the cocktail party.

He'd done the right thing by not kissing Paige. He knew that.

But apparently, Paige didn't agree.

Over the course of his life—particularly from the age of fifteen on—Dylan had been pursued by a lot of women. Something about playing in a rock band seemed to make women wild. He'd been pursued by groupies, models, actresses; he'd come home to find naked women in his bed; and on the road, he'd find them in his hotel room and numerous other places. They were obvious in their pursuit, brazen.

Not Paige.

It was a touch that was innocent enough but lingered.

It was a throaty laugh at something funny he said.

It was the way her wardrobe seemed to get a lot less layered and a lot more...sexy. But not in an obvious way. She still wore her sassy, little skirts with tights and boots, but gone were the scarves and sweaters and instead were silky blouses or clingy tees. Gone were the clips or bands to hold her hair back; now it was loose and curly and smelled so damn good that being near her made his mouth water.

He was seriously losing it.

To anyone observing them, nothing was out of the ordinary. Paige was handling everything for the campaign that she had to—and a lot that she didn't have to—and she kept everyone in line. Every promotional appointment—photo shoots, speaking engagements, group interviews about the campaign—was run with military precision, and she wasn't showing him any preferential treatment.

At least not to someone who wasn't aware of what had transpired between them.

For his part, he tried to keep everything as normal as possible. He brought her lunch when he was getting some for himself; he made sure he was on time for things or lent a hand where it was needed. But when she thanked him, her eyes seemed to...well, they seemed to be saying a lot more than *thank you*.

And it was such a turn-on that it was making him crazy.

Oh, and then there was the morning after.

Hell, he wished it was *that* kind of morning after, but it wasn't. Either way, Dylan had congratulated himself for leaving the bedroom that night without doing anything more than letting her touch his hard-on. All night long, he thought about that simple touch and how he should be given a medal for walking away and staying on the living-room side of the door. And how did she thank him? By getting up bright and early and walking across the living room in nothing but his damn shirt.

She was all legs and mussed up hair and sleepy eyes, and when she smiled at him, he had to sit on his hands to keep from reaching out for her.

A call to the concierge desk and she had new clothes delivered to the room so she wouldn't have to put her dress or heels on. And wouldn't you know it, the simple, black yoga pants and Beverly Hills Hotel shirt and hot-pink flip-flops looked sexier than her cocktail party ensemble.

Peeking around the screen, he looked at her and frowned. She was talking to her father and… Wait. Was that Mick?

Leaving the security of his hiding spot, he stalked over to where the three of them were. "What's going on?"

Mick held up a tabloid newspaper, and Dylan took it and read.

DYLAN ANDERS OFF THE WAGON! WILD
NIGHT OUT WITH SUPERSONIC! HAS HE
RETURNED TO HIS PARTYING WAYS?

"What the hell?" he cried. "What is this about?"

Roberts Walters looked at him. "If you'd read beyond the headline, you'll see they're talking about your little…excursion Saturday night after the launch party."

As much as he didn't want to, Dylan forced himself to read the story. Not one word of it was true. According to their "source"—whom he knew was Morgan— Dylan had hit the hotel bar with Morgan and Steve and then drove around LA drinking and partying until the wee hours of the morning. The article ended with: "Shaughnessy's bad boy is back!"

"It's a lie," Dylan said defiantly, shoving the paper at Mick. "None of that happened."

"Dylan—"

"No," he interrupted. "None of this happened!"

"So you're saying you didn't see these people at the party?" Robert asked with more than a hint of disbelief. "Because there's a picture of the three of you right there."

"Yeah, I saw them and I talked to them for a few minutes, but I did not leave with them."

"Dylan," Mick said solemnly. "I'm not going to lie—this isn't good. You're not supposed to be drinking and, well, the rest of it…"

"There is no rest of it!" Dylan shouted. "Nothing in this article beyond talking to Morgan and Steve is true!"

"It's your word against theirs," Robert said. "And the Literacy Now people are not amused. This is not the publicity they wanted." He paused. "I think it's best if—"

"Wait!" Paige cried. "Dylan's telling you this article is false and libelous. Why is he being punished for this?"

Mick looked at her and gave her a small smile. "It's their word against his, and unfortunately, more people are going to believe theirs. Especially with the picture."

"But…why? I mean, all that picture shows is three people talking. And from a distance. How is that enough to condemn him?" Paige asked.

"I don't like it either," Mick said slowly. "But still, with Dylan's history, the press is going to believe this. They have no reason not to. And he's got his community service he needs to finish, and we can't have this turning into a big thing. We need to find him something else to fulfill his commitment."

"As I said," Robert began patiently, "our people with Literacy Now feel—"

"Dylan wasn't with Morgan and Steve!" Paige said with frustration.

"Paige, sweetheart," her father said and then patted her on the arm, "I understand that you feel bad. After all, he's been your responsibility—"

"Okay, that's enough," she snapped before Dylan had a chance to respond. "I was with Dylan Saturday night. All night. So I *know* he wasn't with those people or doing any of the things they implied and that this story is a lie."

All three men looked at her like she was crazy. Dylan wasn't sure if he was grateful or pissed off.

Robert cleared his throat, and Mick studied his shoes, and Dylan just…waited.

"They're lying, and as a PR firm, I am confident we can clear this whole thing up quickly and quietly without it becoming some media circus," she went on. "Dylan is not the same person that article described. You ask anyone at the event, Father. He was by my side the entire night except for when I was up on the stage. When I went to find him, he was talking to the two of them, but we left together. It sounds to me like they were being spiteful because he turned down an offer to get some publicity with them. I'll bet if you checked with the hotel's security cameras you'd find that they left on their own. And you'll also see…" Paige paused and moved closer to Dylan. "You'll see Dylan carrying me to the elevators and that I didn't leave until the next morning."

Yeah, Dylan was pretty sure Robert Walters was going to lose his shit if the bulging vein in his forehead was anything to go by.

"I see," was all he said.

Dylan cursed himself. He had done everything he could to keep something like this from happening and yet it had anyway. And what was worse, it was uglier because of the circumstances. He'd have loved to get his hands on Steve and strangle him for putting him and Paige in this predicament.

Paige let out a sigh. "So now what?" But she didn't wait for an answer. "I say we pull the tapes to confirm our story. We don't need to offer an excuse or an explanation as to why those two chose to sell out someone they claim to be a friend. Let the press draw their own conclusions." She shrugged. "Seems to me the best thing to do is not make a big deal out of this and not give them the attention they crave."

Dylan nearly choked trying to hide a laugh.

"I'll handle it, Paige," her father said. "However…"

Here it comes, Dylan thought.

"To make this look a lot less…scandalous, we're going to say that you and Mr. Anders are involved romantically and have been for some time—even before the campaign."

"Fine," she said.

"No," Dylan said at the same time.

Paige turned and looked at him. "Dylan, this will solve everything. You won't have to look for another way to do your community service. It will be a public acknowledgment that you're not drinking again and that you're not the man this article," she said with disdain, "painted you to be."

"But it's not right, Paige. This is exactly the kind of thing I mentioned to you the other night. You shouldn't have to deal with this."

"And yet I already am," she said with a smile.

A sweet smile.

One of those smiles that meant more than what it appeared to.

"Look, Dylan," Mick chimed in, "they're right. It's all in your favor and would be a great boost to the image we want people to start having of you. From now till the end of the campaign, you and Paige play the part of a happy couple. You're already spending a lot of time together, so it's not like you have to do anything different."

He had a point, Dylan thought. "I... I don't like this," he sighed. "Paige shouldn't have to pay for something she didn't do."

"Like Mick said," Paige explained, "we're already spending a lot of time together. No big deal. Nothing has to change."

It was the impish grin and gleam in her eye that told him she had more on her mind than what she was sharing.

Although, if they were playing the part of a happy couple in public, he'd have an excuse to touch her too and share heated looks. He couldn't act on them—wouldn't allow himself to—but for a couple of hours a day, he could torture himself and pretend he was good enough for her.

Every night since she'd slept in his bed, he'd smelled her on his pillow—she was becoming an obsession.

Yeah, he was seriously losing it.

And he wasn't sure if this new turn of events was the solution or a potentially new problem.

Within minutes, Robert said his goodbye and, along with Mick, promised that this whole situation would be resolved within twenty-four hours. Both he and Paige thanked them and watched them leave. When she turned and smiled at him, he had his answer.

This was a new problem.

And if he thought the last week had been an issue, it was nothing compared to the rest of the day.

She smiled.

He smiled.

She touched.

He touched.

Big mistake.

It was one thing to be touched; it was quite another to be the one touching.

Dylan already knew what her skin felt like from when he'd caressed her cheek, but her hands were incredibly soft and so was her wrist. He discovered that her pulse beat like wild whenever he got close to her and found himself reaching out and caressing the sweet spot on her neck that he wanted to taste more than anything.

"That's it for today," she said sometime later.

He shook his head to clear it. "Um…what?"

"We're done here for today. You did great with your PSA." Paige flipped through the pages in her planner. "And it looks like we are good until Tuesday. We have a meeting with the local library council to discuss scheduling for appearances. We don't want to bring everyone involved to every event, so we have to coordinate everyone's schedules and scatter you all out." She looked up at him. "Does that make sense?"

"So you mean while I'm talking at a library in Culver City, someone else will be talking that day or that week in Hollywood?"

She smiled. "Exactly. I'm going to need a copy of your schedule to take with me."

"I thought I was going with you?" Wasn't that the plan? Hadn't she been saying "we"?

"You could... Then you'd get first choice on dates and locations. But I don't want it to look like I'm playing favorites with my boyfriend."

She said it all a little distractedly, and Dylan wondered if she realized the slip.

He stepped in close and lowered his head, so his lips were a whisper away from her ear. "But you're supposed to show everyone that I am your favorite, remember?" His tongue came out and swiped at the shell of her ear, and her soft intake of breath told him this was a spot he wanted to explore again.

"Dylan..."

"Good night, Paige! Good night, Dylan!" The camera crew headed for the door, and within minutes, they had the place to themselves.

Bad idea! Bad idea!

Looking around, he confirmed that everyone else was gone. When had that happened?

"So," Paige said as she leaned in closer to him, "would you like to get something to eat? Some dinner?"

It was her tone.

Alarm bells rang in his head, and he knew he had no one to blame but himself. It was safe—sort of—to play around with an audience. It took on a whole other meaning when they were alone, and licking her ear while they were alone was not playing. Taking a step back, he stuck his hands in his pocket and let out a huff of frustration.

"Thanks, but...I've got plans," he said.

She blinked at him as if she didn't understand what he was saying.

"So Tuesday, right? I can have my schedule to you beforehand. I'll email it to you and then…" He shrugged. "I think we don't have to see each other until Thursday at that luncheon thing, right?" He knew he sounded like an idiot, but it was going to be hard enough pretending with her for two more months—no need to go out of his way to torture himself when escape was close by.

With a shrug of her own, Paige turned her back on him and looked over her calendar. "Um…yeah. Thursday. You need to be there by noon. You have the address." Then she began to gather her things and if he wasn't mistaken, she was talking to herself about all the things she had to do between now and then. He'd have said she was talking to him, but her voice was so low he couldn't hear more than every fifth word.

Cautiously, he stepped closer.

"Like I don't know what *that* is about," she was murmuring, and Dylan realized that staying was only prolonging the inevitable.

"Well, I guess I should go," he said as he started backing away toward the door. The studio space didn't belong to PRW, so he knew they weren't responsible for locking up. He also knew there were offices down the hall and she'd be okay here by herself. Right now, he was more concerned with his own sanity. If he stayed, there was a really good chance of him taking her behind the green screen and kissing her and doing a hell of a lot more than licking her ear.

"I'll see you Thursday," he called out.

No response.

Sighing, he turned and continued to walk toward the door and instantly stopped when she called his name.

So close.

Turning, he saw her walking toward him. He couldn't read her expression—was she upset? Mad? What?

"Paige...I..."

"Shut up," she said, her voice authoritative and...

He couldn't finish the thought because she cupped a hand around his neck and pulled him down and kissed him.

For the love of it... She had done everything except offer a naked limo ride and Dylan still hadn't made a move!

A girl could only wait so long.

And boy, oh boy, was it worth the wait.

Every inch of him was hard and muscled and felt so good wrapped around her. She wanted to climb him like a tree. Coupled with the softness of his lips and gentleness of his caress, Dylan Anders was every naughty fantasy she'd ever had—and all he'd done was kiss her!

Paige's hands anchored in his hair as she went from being the one controlling the kiss to the one being controlled. Dylan's kiss went from wow to *ohmygod* in less than a second. He kissed, he tasted, he devoured, and Paige was more than willing to be devoured.

For hours at a time.

When his lips left hers to lick the shell of her ear— she really liked that—and her throat, she let her head fall back as she fought to catch her breath.

"Come home with me," she panted. "Please. Please, Dylan."

He bit her gently and then soothed that tender spot with his talented tongue and she was certain they were on the same page. She ran a quick checklist in her head: Bed made? Check. Bedroom clean? Check. Legs shaved? Check. If she could just get him to the car…

Dylan lifted his head, and she could feel his entire body practically vibrating. Good. She wanted—no, *needed* him like that. Turned on and unable to say no. Playing the seductress was so not her thing, and she had never been sexually aggressive, but everything about this man brought that out in her.

"Paige," he said breathlessly.

"Yes?" *This was it!*

"I… We can't do this."

Say what?

"What do you mean we can't do this? We already are doing this!" It was pointless to pretend she wasn't pissed off. There was only so much a girl on the verge of climbing a man could take!

Dylan took a step away. And then another. And another. He raked a hand through his hair, making it stand on end, and even *that* managed to look sexy on him!

The bastard!

"Look, I think lines are getting blurred," he began. "We talked about this, Paige. I told you why we can't get involved."

"And you know that, to the world, it's going to look like that already. I don't see why we can't take advantage of this situation. It's obvious we're attracted to each other. I don't see what the big deal is!"

He studied her for a long moment and Paige wanted to walk up to him and shake him.

But she didn't.

"Because you deserve better than this," he said, his voice void of emotion. "You deserve better than a fake relationship with someone like me. Trust me."

"Dylan…wait…"

But he didn't. He turned and walked away, and Paige watched him go.

There was a part of her that said to run after him and make him see that he was wrong. But the logical, regular part of her told her to respect his wishes and let it go.

With a weary sigh, she collected her things and made her way out of the studio. She stopped at the front office and thanked the receptionist on her way out. As the warm afternoon sun hit her face, Paige reached in her bag for her sunglasses and slipped them on.

And then stood on the sidewalk and contemplated what to do next.

She didn't have errands to run, and she didn't want to go into the office. She could drive around the city, but traffic was always a nightmare, so that wouldn't be a relaxing endeavor either. Pulling out her phone, she checked the time. Three o'clock. There was always… Nothing. There was nothing she wanted to do. No hot yoga, no Zumba, no spinning class. Then she laughed at herself because it had easily been six months since she'd been to the gym, so why even consider those activities?

"Because I have way too much pent-up energy and need to do something with it," she murmured and walked to her car. Inside, she started the car, turned on the air, and still tried to think of what to do. She didn't want to go home. Home was where she had hoped to be with Dylan right now.

Dylan.

Why did he have to be so difficult? Why did he have to choose to be a good guy with her? Why couldn't he just hold on to those bad-boy morals a little bit longer?

Who was she kidding? She liked Dylan exactly the way he was. Thinking back to their first meeting, she realized how much her feelings for him had transformed. His looks were always something she admired, but the more she got to know him, the more she saw beyond the sexy rock-star looks and saw a man with a kind heart who still struggled with far too many demons. And who could blame him? That tabloid story about him had to be painful for him. Here he was doing everything he could to change his public image, and on his first real outing, someone had to take him down.

Paige silently prayed there was video of Morgan's drunken walk from the hotel with another man. Though the footage of her and Dylan going into the elevator would be more than enough proof that he hadn't done any of the things he'd been accused of, she wanted to inflict some pain on Morgan too.

Wow. Who was she all of a sudden? She had never been a spiteful or vindictive woman. And she'd never been one to stand up for herself or for…

She'd stood up for Dylan.

Her heart kicked hard in her chest. Yes, she had stood up for him to her father and his manager, to defend him—his character. The look on her father's face had been one flash of disbelief before he'd schooled his reaction and kept it strictly professional. Talking to her father about her sex life had never come up and should have been a pretty big roadblock to admitting she was with Dylan.

But it hadn't.

Today she had broken through so many of her own obstacles, so why was she quitting now? Why, when she was so close to having what she wanted from Dylan, had she let him walk away?

"Because he doesn't want me," she said, banging her head on the seat. "Well, he does. But not enough to take the risk."

A soft gasp came out as the thought took hold.

He's afraid.

And who could blame him? Look at what had happened with Morgan, and she had a feeling Dylan didn't have a whole lot of reason to trust anyone right now. Hadn't she just said he was fighting his own demons? What if intimacy, sex, relationships were part of those demons? Why couldn't she be the one to show him there were still good people in the world and how it was okay to take a risk?

"Sure, one stupid confession in front of Dad and all of a sudden I'm the poster girl for taking risks?" she said with a snort. And then she thought about it. "Why *can't* I be that poster girl?"

And that was exactly what she was going to be.

Brave.

Bold.

And hopefully…very satisfied.

It took her an hour to get to the hotel; she made one stop for a quick wardrobe change, and traffic had been a complete pain. Then she had circled the block three times to give herself one last pep talk.

You can do this.

She wanted Dylan. She wanted to help Dylan. But more than anything, she needed Dylan.

You can do this.

Pulling the car up to the valet, she grabbed her ticket, climbed out, and walked determinedly into the lobby. While her immediate thought was to go right up to his room, she realized she was thoroughly unprepared. With a quick look around, she spotted the gift shop and ran in for a few necessities—breath mints and condoms. She paid and slipped the bag into her purse before heading to the concierge desk. There she told them exactly what she needed and gave them Dylan's room number and asked for it to be brought up in an hour.

That was enough time, wasn't it?

"Make that two hours," she said with a shy smile and was thrilled when the woman behind the desk simply smiled and nodded.

Feeling confident, she strode to the elevators and was fortunate enough to have one arrive seemingly just for her.

Three minutes later, she was standing at Dylan's door.

She knocked and held her breath.

He pulled open the door and the ability to speak simply deserted her. His shirt was open, his shoes were off, and his hair was still a glorious mess.

He was the sexiest thing she'd ever seen.

"Don't say a word," she said when he went to speak. "I heard everything you said earlier and I remember everything you said to me last Saturday night. I'm not asking you for some sort of long-term commitment. I'm not even asking you for a serious relationship. All I know is that when I'm with you…I feel…everything. You make me feel so much, Dylan. I look at you and I'm not seeing the celebrity with a troubled past—I'm seeing you. The man. The one who plays chess and brings me turkey sandwiches. The one who went food shopping with me and held me up while I walked around in those ridiculous shoes. That's the man I see. The one I want."

She saw him swallow hard as he stood in the doorway and she stepped in close, pressing her body against his.

"You can tell me to leave. You can tell me it's all a mistake." She leaned in and kissed his chest. His magnificent, tattooed chest. "But tell it to me later. Please."

He let out an audible groan as he hauled her into the suite and slammed the door shut.

Thank God! she thought.

Relief, pure and simple, swamped him.

The entire drive to the hotel had him questioning everything: Was leaving the right choice? Was he wrong for walking away from something that could be incredible because of previous bad decisions? How long was he supposed to keep punishing himself? Wasn't he entitled to some happiness? And now that Paige was here and in his arms and wrapped around him like she was afraid to let go, he had his answer.

Yes.

Yes, dammit. He deserved to have a little happiness. He had to admit, the sight of her standing in his doorway had floored him. From everything he had learned about Paige over the past month, she had not seemed like someone who actively went after what she wanted. She accepted other people's decisions and went on with her life—even if she didn't agree with it. After all, she certainly didn't fight for her position at work where their campaign was concerned. So that could only mean one thing:

She *really* wanted him.

Reaching down, he cupped her ass and lifted her. Those wonderfully sexy legs of hers wrapped around him, and he had to fight the urge to take her against the wall. Although...

"Bed," she said, lifting her lips from his. Lips that were wet and red and swollen from the force of their kisses. "I've been dreaming about being in that bed with you."

Her honesty was probably the biggest turn-on of all.

Turning with her still in his arms, he strode to the bedroom and lowered her onto the bed. He meant to stand up, to strip his shirt off, but Paige was having none of that. Her legs tightened, effectively holding him to her, and he had to admit the position had promise.

"Take your shirt off," she said as she began pushing it off his shoulders. "I want to kiss and lick and touch all your tattoos." Then she let out a sexy giggle as she looked up and met his eyes. "I can't believe I just said that out loud."

This girl.

Because she was turning him inside out, he was willing to do whatever she wanted, give her whatever she wanted.

This time, when he went to pull away, she let him. Dylan quickly stripped off his shirt and sent it flying. Paige's hands were on his chest before the garment even hit the floor. Her hands were smooth and hot and felt so good that he groaned with pleasure. When was the last time anything had felt this good? When was the last time he had gotten this turned on by the touch of a woman's hand? His eyes closed and his head fell back while he allowed her to explore him.

He was straddling her, and all he could think of was how much he wanted to reverse their positions. While he had been more than willing to let Paige take the lead so far, he just... He needed to do this. Now.

In the blink of an eye, he slid his hands under her back and rolled them until she was the one straddling him. Her swishy little skirt bunched up, and he had to fight to keep his hands from sliding underneath it. Instead, he looked at her, met her heated gaze, and said, "Now you can kiss and lick and touch all you want."

And holy hell did she.

Her hands roamed his torso, his arms, and then rested on his chest. Her lips—God, those soft, wet lips!— kissed the trail her hands had set. Dylan reached out and anchored his hands into her hair because now that he had her here, there was no way he was ready to let her go.

It had been too long—too damn long—since he'd been so consumed with need, with want. And if he allowed himself to think back, Dylan knew it had been years since anything sexual had felt remotely like this. Back then, his senses had been dulled by alcohol. But this? What was happening right now in this very

PG-rated encounter was better than any porn he'd ever seen.

And that took his mind to a whole other level.

"Paige?" he asked huskily.

She lifted her head from his chest and looked at him, her expression dazed.

"What are you wearing under this skirt?"

A slow smile played at her lips and he watched as her hands lowered to the hem of the garment and then slowly slid it up. And...

"Those are... I mean...they're not..."

Running her hand over her thighs as she lifted her skirt ever so much higher, she let out a sexy little moan. "They're thigh-high stockings."

His mouth seriously began to water. "Were you... Do you normally...?"

"I bought them on my way here," she said softly.

He tore his eyes from the sight of her thighs and looked up at her. "You did?"

She nodded. "I was thinking...well, hoping..."

Dylan reached up and cupped her cheek. "What? What were you hoping for, Paige?"

"I hoped you'd like them. That you'd see them and... not want me to leave."

He inhaled deeply. "Baby, I don't want you to leave. And it has nothing to do with these sexy stockings."

Her shoulders relaxed, and she smiled at him, the relief on her face was obvious. "So you like them?"

He grinned as he nodded. "Oh, I like them all right. I like them a lot. And...I think I want you to keep them on for a while."

A breathy little "oh" was her only response.

"Promise me something," he said gently, his tone going serious.

"Anything."

"Promise me you'll wear these when we're working, like at a public appearance or maybe at a meeting. The thought of you having these on under your skirt and knowing I can reach out and touch you…"

She hissed out a breath and ground herself against him.

So fucking sexy.

And then he did it—he reached out and touched her, and it was better than he imagined. "Yeah. I want to know I can touch this soft skin of your thighs and no one will know but me."

"Dylan," she panted, still wiggling, still grinding.

"Tell me, Paige. Tell me what you want. Tell me."

"I want you to stop talking and touch me. Everywhere. Now. Please."

His hands inched higher and touched the soft lace of her panties. "Well…since you said please…"

He didn't stop talking. In fact, his words got dirtier and his hands got way more involved. And judging by the way she cried out his name, Dylan knew he was giving her exactly what she wanted.

———

If this was what it was like to go after what you wanted, Paige was seriously rethinking how she currently was living her life.

When she'd shown up at Dylan's room, she wasn't sure how it was all going to play out. Turns out, it was better than anything she could have ever imagined. Never before in her life had she been more thankful than she was right now that she had gone after what she wanted.

Turning her head, she looked over at Dylan and had to suppress a proud grin.

He was on his back—his body slick with sweat, and he was still trying to catch his breath.

Yeah. She'd done that to him.

As soon as he had pulled her into his suite, Paige knew she was out of her element. The men she had slept with in the past were far more…reserved where sex was concerned. It had always been pleasant but not passionate. Dylan's hands and lips and body oozed passion.

And she wanted it again.

Tentatively, she reached out and touched his hand.

"If this is part of your evil plan to kill me so I'm out of the campaign, I give up," he said breathlessly, and Paige couldn't help but laugh.

Laughing while in bed after sex? Who was she?

"First of all, killing you would be a bad thing."

"Don't look good in orange?"

She swatted playfully at his arm. "No…I mean, I don't look good in orange, but that's not the reason."

"You enjoy your freedom?"

His playful side was something she loved about him. Scooting closer, she placed her hand on his stomach and waited for him to face her. "I enjoy you."

There must have been a million thoughts going through his brain because she could see in his eyes that he wanted to say something but didn't. It was okay. She wasn't fishing for compliments. She wanted to let him know how she felt.

"Dylan," she began softly. "This has been the greatest

afternoon for me. Maybe I should have respected your wishes and kept my distance and kept things professional between us, but…"

Reaching out, he placed a finger over her lips. "I'm glad you didn't listen to me. All week, I've been going crazy." He paused. "Actually, that's not true."

Her heart sank.

Oh God. What if this was like…pity sex? Pulling her hand from his body, Paige immediately began to think of how she was going to get up and get dressed and leave while she had a trace of her dignity still intact.

Grabbing her hand back, Dylan held it against his chest, over his heart. "Paige, you've been making me crazy—in a good way—almost since we met," he said solemnly. "I meant what I said to you last week—you deserve so much more than I can give you. You deserve a man who doesn't have so much baggage and who isn't so…"

Paige climbed over him and forced him to look at her. "Everyone has baggage, Dylan. Everyone. I'm a mess too, you know."

He gave a mirthless laugh. "Paige, you aren't a mess. You're a little uptight and structured, but you certainly aren't a mess."

She rolled her eyes. "Oh, please. I let everyone walk all over me—especially my family. I have daddy issues, I have petty jealousy issues with my sister, and I'm a bit neurotic about making sure I keep it together all the time, and it's starting to make me crazy."

"And that's why the last thing you need in your life is someone like me. I'm always going to be someone who draws attention for the wrong reasons. People don't forget the bad stuff you do, and I did a lot of it. And it doesn't matter how long I stay clean and sober—it's always going to be how people refer to me: 'former bad boy' or 'former alcoholic.' My counselor in rehab told me it's a title I shouldn't shy away from. Getting over my addiction is a big accomplishment so if I can say former, that's a good thing."

"It is," she said encouragingly.

But he shook his head. "I want to move on from that. I want to be recognized for my music, for who I am now. I don't want to keep looking back or having my past thrown back at me."

Sighing, she leaned down and hugged him. "I don't know what to say. I've never been in that position to the same degree."

Dylan shifted and lifted her up so he could see her face. "What do you mean to the same degree?"

It was easier to climb off him. Shifting, she pulled the sheet up to cover herself. She knew it was crazy considering everything they had just done, but right now, she needed a little bit of a shield.

"I work for my father. I've always worked for my father. And he made me start out at the bottom and work my way up to where I am now."

"Did he do that with Ariel?"

She nodded. "Not as much. She was promoted much faster than I was, but it was because she presented a more polished image. She always has." Another sigh. "I was awkward and shy, and I didn't mind doing the grunt work behind the scenes. After a while, I almost blended into the background. And it was fine. Really. Then people started talking like I must be the idiot daughter if my father was too embarrassed to let me work up on the executive floor."

"People said that?" he asked incredulously.

"Oh yeah. I overheard it, and I guess my dad did too because a week later, I got promoted. The first campaign I got assigned to, I was given the task of putting together the PowerPoint presentation. I was a whiz at that sort of thing, and it meant I was still behind the scenes while being part of the executive team."

"So what happened?"

"I was left out of a crucial meeting with the client. And when we did our presentation, half of the information was wrong. My father was mortified and he let me know how disappointed he was in front of everyone. It was a couple of years ago, and I still have people asking me if I remembered to go to all the meetings and are always double-checking my work before any clients see it."

She hung her head as she finished speaking, too ashamed for Dylan to see her.

His hand twisted in her long hair with a gentle tug. "Hey," he said softly, and Paige had no choice but to look at him. "I'm sorry. I hate that you have to deal with that."

She shrugged. "I'm used to it. I hate it though. It was one time, and it wasn't my fault that I was excluded from the meeting and not given the updated information. But whenever I bring that up, I'm told I'm making excuses."

Dylan was quiet for a moment. "That's why you do it, don't you? That's why you take on so much and make sure everything goes smoothly. You're trying to prove yourself."

Busted. And all she could do was nod.

He cursed under his breath and sat up. "When will it be enough? When are you going to see that you're good enough? That you're talented and freaking great at your job? Are you waiting for your father to say 'good job'? Will that make you relax?"

"Honestly, I don't know!" she cried. "I can't remember him ever saying those words to me where this job is concerned. He used to say it to me regarding school and my grades, but not once has he said it at work."

"Does he say it to your sister?"

It was like someone kicked her in the stomach. Of course he said it to Ariel. She was like his mini-me, for crying out loud! She sighed loudly. This was not the conversation she wanted to have after what they had just shared.

She lowered the sheet, exposing her breasts to his gaze once again. Then she stretched and noticed Dylan's whole demeanor instantly changed.

He had her pinned beneath him a second later. "Nice distraction method," he said gruffly.

Feeling playful, she rubbed her breasts against his chest. "Glad you liked it. I never tried it before. I may need practice with perfecting it."

He chuckled. "Baby, you don't need practice for anything. You're already perfect."

And damn if that didn't make her heart squeeze a little.

"Oh yeah?"

He nodded. "Yeah."

Slowly, she repeated the motion and gave him a sexy grin. "That had nothing to do with distractions. That was all for pleasure. I like pressing up against you. I like how warm your skin is."

Dylan lowered his head to her shoulder and kissed her there. "Yours is warm too. And soft. And so damn sweet."

She let out a small moan as she raked her hands through his hair.

A knock at the door had them both going still. "Ignore it," he said before he went back to trailing kisses from one breast to the other.

She remembered her order with the concierge. How was it possible two hours had gone by already? "You should answer it."

Dylan lifted his head. "Seriously? You want me to get up now and answer the door?"

She nodded. "It could be important."

"It could also be nobody. Or housekeeping. I don't need fresh towels. Trust me." More kisses. And another knock at the door.

"Room service!" a voice called out.

That had Dylan jumping up. "Room service? They must have the wrong room. Wait here." Grabbing his jeans, he was slipping them on when Paige called out to him.

"They don't have the wrong room," she said with another catlike stretch. "I placed an order before I came up here."

He arched a dark brow at her. "Really?"

"Mm-hmm. Now go let them in and hurry back." Paige watched as he left the room and closed the door behind him for her privacy. Part of her was feeling self-conscious and like she should crawl under the blankets, but her new inner vixen told her to stay exactly where she was because Dylan would be back any minute.

And he was.

The bedroom door opened, and he walked in carrying a silver tray.

"Care to explain this?" he asked with amusement.

"I would have thought it was obvious." Rolling onto her side, she rested her head in her hand. "I figured we'd be hungry right about now, so a little snack was in order."

He nodded. "Strawberries and cream. Excellent choice."

"And I knew I was going to crave something sweet."

"That explains the cake pops."

"And if you'll give me a few minutes, the last item will make complete sense."

Ten minutes later, Paige sighed as she rested her back against Dylan's chest.

"Um…I'm not sure what I'm supposed to be doing here," he said with more than a little uncertainty.

"You're supposed to relax and enjoy this. Doesn't it feel amazing?"

"I guess."

This time her sigh wasn't one of pleasure but mild annoyance. "You've never taken a bubble bath? Seriously?"

"Maybe when I was five. But in case you haven't noticed, I'm a guy. Guy's don't take bubble baths."

She rolled her eyes. "Yes, they do."

"Not real ones," he murmured.

"So you're going to sit there and tell me the hot water doesn't feel good? That the jasmine and vanilla don't smell amazing?" Carefully she turned around and stretched out on top of him. "And that being naked with me in the tub isn't fun?"

"Baby, having you naked anywhere is fun. This seems like a lot of work when we're both going to get up and go back to the bed."

Paige playfully splashed him. "Come on," she said with a small laugh. "How can you not be enjoying this? When I was here Friday, all I wanted to do was come in here and test this tub out. This entire bathroom is amazing."

"That's what you were thinking of while you were here? Taking a bath?" he asked with mock offense.

She laughed again. "Well…it wasn't *all* I thought about. But it certainly played a big part in my fantasies."

Dylan's eyes lit up. "Oh, yeah? Tell me. Were they naughty fantasies? Did you need to take a bath because you were so dirty?" he asked lecherously.

Now she cracked up. "You are such a perv! Knock it off!"

Dylan laughed with her and hugged her close. With a kiss on the top of her head, he shifted them around until they were in their original position. "Okay, so a bubble bath was part of your fantasy, huh?"

Paige nodded. "It was. I'm a bit of a sucker for a soaking tub. I had one when we were growing up, but my condo doesn't have one. I dream of owning a house someday with a spa-like bathroom."

Behind her, Dylan was quiet.

"Of course, that's a long way off. Real estate in California is ridiculous. As it is, my condo payments are sucking my will to live." Then she shrugged. "Still, a girl can dream."

She snuggled a little more against him and was rewarded with his wonderful hands coming up and cupping her breasts. She let out a soft sigh, resting her head on his shoulder.

"The bathroom I had in my house was twice the size of this one," Dylan said gruffly. "Maybe even three times. The tub was huge and the shower could fit four people easily."

She didn't want to think about how he could know that.

"And I can't remember ever using the tub. It was a great selling point for the house, but it was never something that was on my radar."

"Do you miss it? The house, not the bathroom," she quickly added.

Dylan laughed softly. "No. It was... I don't know. It was the first thing I bought when Shaughnessy made it big. I didn't need it because we were on the road so much, but I thought it was something I should have. Looking back, I realize how ridiculous it was."

"I don't think that's true," she reasoned. "There's nothing wrong with buying a home."

"That's it though—it wasn't a home. It was a house. It was a status symbol. It was far too big for one person, especially one who was never around."

His voice sounded...odd. Not sad, not detached, but...odd. Turning her head slightly, she looked up at him. "Is that why you decided to sell it?"

"No. It held too many bad memories of who I used to be. I didn't want that sort of thing around my neck like a constant reminder."

"Dylan, you do realize that not everything about you and the way you used to be was bad, right?"

The look on his face was one of complete disbelief. "You didn't know me before, Paige. You have no idea—"

She held up one hand to cut him off. "No, I didn't know you before, but it doesn't mean anything. I've done my homework where you're concerned, and let me tell you, you're wrong about how you view yourself."

He started to push her away to stand up, but she maneuvered around so she was straddling his lap again. "Hear me out," she began. "You are an incredibly gifted musician. I've heard the music you did with Shaughnessy and I've heard the music you played with other groups. Anyone who talks about your musical skill does it with awe. When the band went on hiatus, you were in high demand. Why? Not because you drank, Dylan, but because you are an amazing bass player!"

"Paige—"

"You grew up in South Carolina as an only child. Your parents are always quoted sharing stories of how you've been playing music since you were a small child—piano, guitar, harmonica, anything you could get your hands on. You played music at church, at parties, and for some of their work functions."

His eyes went wide, but he stayed silent.

"Your dad's a bank manager and your mom is an administrative assistant at the middle school in your hometown. Every year, you donate money to the music department at her school and you've even gone and talked to the students about the importance of music in their lives. And you did all that long before you went into rehab, so you can't use that as an excuse."

"I haven't gone back since though," he said with a hint of defense.

"But you will," she countered smugly. "It's part of who you are. You'll go back when you're ready, and you'll have an even more important message to share with those kids."

"Right. Because it's important to talk to them about how I screwed up my life."

"As a matter of fact, it is," she said firmly. "Dylan, not everyone gets a chance to turn their life around. Most people don't think it's possible. You can show them that it is. You can give them hope."

She could see the range of emotions in his eyes—the anger, the disbelief, the annoyance, and…the vulnerability. Deep down, she knew he wanted to believe her, to believe that he was someone who deserved to be happy and be an inspiration.

To overcome his past.

This totally wasn't the conversation she envisioned them having while naked in the bathtub. And besides, she felt like she'd pushed him enough for the time being.

It was time to take it down a notch in the conversation department and ratchet it up in another.

Slowly, she bent her head and kissed his jaw.

"Paige…"

Then she licked her way down his neck and then up again. She bit his earlobe and heard his soft hiss, and when his hand came up and splayed across her lower back, effectively holding her to him, she knew they were on the same page. Dylan's head slowly fell back and he seemed more than happy to let her have her way with him.

Funny how she was beginning to enjoy doing that as well.

He was addictive—the taste of him, the texture of his skin. It was like she couldn't get enough. And as she continued to explore him, Paige knew she needed to take advantage of this time together.

Because her homework on Dylan not only showed her that he had some great qualities—it also showed that he had a short attention span.

Chapter 7

It took a lot to impress someone as cynical as Dylan, and yet in the past week, the Walters family managed to do that.

The Tuesday after Paige had shown up at his hotel room found him looking at an article online that effectively proved Morgan Lewis had lied. The media was now attacking her for lying about Dylan while he was trying to get his life back on track, and he felt only a minimal amount of pity for her.

Suddenly he was trending on social media, with people cheering him on and talking about how sorry they were that people were trolling him and trying to defame him. He was getting calls from outlets looking to interview him and get his spin on the whole thing. Both Robert Walters and Mick advised him not to respond, to let the professionals handle it.

So yeah, he was impressed with the way PRW had handled this whole situation.

Then there was Paige. That same day, he had been sitting next to her at a conference room table listening to… He had no idea. He was too distracted by the woman sitting beside him. She was dressed as she usually was, except now he knew what she had on underneath. And when she crossed her legs, he saw the top of the thigh-high tights she was wearing and caught a glimpse of that soft skin he loved to touch.

Knowing how Paige was a stickler about business, he had debated about whether to test the waters with her in this particular area.

Boy was he glad he had!

At the first touch of his finger on her knee, she had uncrossed her legs—slowly and in a way that no one would have noticed. When his hand traveled higher and inched under her skirt, she'd spread her legs a bit to give him more to explore.

He still had no idea how she'd kept from letting everyone in the room know what he was doing to her because he was ready to start panting from the images in his mind. She was sexy and intriguing, and she managed to surprise him more and more every day.

They worked together, they went out in public together, had been photographed doing all those things, and it didn't seem to faze her in any way, shape, or form. She smiled when she was supposed to and posed when they needed to and then went on with whatever it was they had been doing without complaint.

It was…weird. In the past, women he dated tended to either love or hate the camera. Okay, most of them loved it and would become blatantly pissed off if they felt they weren't getting enough attention from the paparazzi. But not Paige. It was such a nonissue with her that it almost made him want to make an issue of it to find out how she really felt.

Now that was weird, right?

Either way, he was impressed with her because she fit seamlessly into his crazy world, and got him out and enjoying life again. It was amazing how one carefully placed comment to the press could change everything! He no longer felt he had to hide out in his hotel room or punish himself by living in solitary confinement. He was playing music every day and starting to write some new stuff that he couldn't wait to share with the band when they got together to jam next week.

After talking with both Matt and Riley, they decided on a weekend sort of thing in North Carolina, at Matt's new place. He and Vivienne had moved into a house they had renovated to fit both of their needs and, according to Matt, it included a state-of-the-art studio. It meant being out of town, but after checking his schedule, he saw there wasn't anything planned for him with the campaign, and he was free of any commitments.

Convincing Paige to let go of some of hers, however, required some convincing.

Why it was so important to him for her to come away with him for the weekend he couldn't say. Obviously, Vivienne was going to be there and Riley mentioned Savannah was going with him as well. Julian and Dena were once again on the outs, so he was going to be flying solo for the weekend but didn't seem bothered by the fact that the girls were going to be with them.

Plus, Dylan wanted to see how Paige interacted with the band—with his life.

Right now, things were kind of safe. He was in a good place in the public eye, and he didn't have anything going on other than the work with Literacy Now. What he wanted to know was how she would see him when he was working apart from her and if she clicked with the guys and their wives.

"I don't understand," she had said when he first

brought up the trip. "You want me to go with you to… hang out with Matt's and Riley's wives? Why?"

He shrugged. "For starters, I thought it would be nice to get away for the weekend. I know it's not anything glamorous but…"

"You know I don't care about that stuff, right?" she quickly interrupted. "You know I'm not spending time with you so you can spend money on me and show off, right?"

Clearly, he'd struck a nerve, but he put it aside. Taking her hand in his, he caressed her wrist. "Paige, I know you're not like that and I didn't mean to imply you were. This is important to me. I've missed seeing them and they're all in good places in their lives right now, happy, and…I am too. And I have you to thank for that. So I had hoped you'd want to go with me and see how I am with the guys."

She smiled slowly and sweetly, and even blushed. "I don't want to distract you while you're there. You only have a weekend, and it's been so long since you've been together. I don't want to be in the way and…" She paused. "You know what? Never mind."

"No, no, no. Come on. Finish what you were going to say," he urged.

Looking up with him behind those big glasses, he could see her insecurity. A heavy sigh preceded her words. "I don't want to be there and then not see you the entire time because you're playing with the band. Savannah and Vivienne know each other. I'm sure they've become friends, and I'm not…I'm not comfortable being dropped in a group of strangers. Especially not for an entire weekend. I'm sorry."

That night, he'd let it go. He didn't comment on what she'd shared, but he also knew he'd bring it back up and turn her to his way of thinking.

Which he was starting right now.

The knock on his door told him she was here. No matter how many times he tried to give her the room key, she declined. Part of him respected that, but it really ticked off another side of him. He let her in and greeted her with a kiss that was borderline erotic, and when he felt her melt against him, he knew their night was off to a great start.

"Wow," she sighed when he lifted his head. "I really like when you do that."

He couldn't help but smile as he stroked her cheek. "That's good because I really like doing it."

He let her go and led her into the living room. He'd ordered room service, and all her favorite snacks were laid out on the coffee table. He watched as her eyes went wide when she spotted them.

"Oh my goodness! What have you done?" she asked with awe.

"Well, I didn't feel like going out tonight. I thought we might stay in, watch a movie and relax."

The smile she rewarded him with told him he'd made the right decision. "That is perfect. I had the worst day and…let's just say this is exactly what I needed." Then she reached down and snagged a devil's food cake pop.

And when she moaned, he wondered if he could possibly wait to take her to bed or if it would be okay to strip her and take her against the couch.

"I know that look," she said with a laugh. "Don't even think about interrupting snack time!"

"Who, me?" he asked innocently.

"Yes, you. If you're going to put out cake pops and cookies and…" She gasped. "Nachos! You got nachos! You'll have to wait your turn, buddy. The first orgasm tonight will be compliments of the queso."

He couldn't help it—he cracked up. He loved how this girl was not shy about her food and could put him in his place so perfectly. Hell, he'd gladly let the food serve as foreplay, because he knew when he did finally get her stripped down, it would be that much sweeter because of the anticipation.

She sat and Dylan walked over to the minibar and grabbed them each something to drink. He had water but he knew Paige preferred to have a cola with her nachos.

A man knew when to pay attention, and Dylan learned early on that food was to Paige what flowers were to some women. So he made notes of all her favorite combinations, and this was one of them.

He handed her the drink and sat beside her and helped himself to some of the nachos. "So why was your day so bad? What happened?"

"There's a new client at PRW. He's an artist looking for a firm to get him some exposure for his work. I don't think he needs PR as much as he needs an agent, but my father is trying to think of how we can do both for him, and it was exhausting to listen to. For the first time in my history with the firm, I did not want to be assigned a project."

"So how did you get out of it?"

Delicately, she licked some excess cheese from her lips and grinned at him. "I told him I was going to be traveling with you and didn't have the time."

Bingo! And just like that, he knew she was on board. There was no way she'd lie to her father about something like this, so Dylan was now freed up for the rest of the night. Seduction would be for seduction sake and no ulterior motives.

Then he felt guilty for having them in the first place.

Clearing his throat, he asked, "So you've reconsidered going with me?" Dylan needed her to be clear on this—that she was serious and not just using him for an excuse.

Paige nodded. "The more I thought about it the more I knew I'd regret not going with you. I'm excited about you getting to see your friends and playing and...I have to admit, the fangirl in me wants to meet them."

He grinned. "I thought you said when we met that you weren't really a fan?"

Her blush was instantaneous. "Well...once I started... you know...researching who you were, I started listening to the music and I got hooked."

Sitting back a bit, Dylan stretched his arms along the back of the sofa as his chest puffed out with pride. "Damn right you got hooked. We're awesome."

She giggled and moved closer to him, so she could put her head on his shoulder. "Yes, you are. I was highly impressed."

"Do you have a favorite song?"

"Oh, no you don't. We are not going to spend the night with me praising your music and telling you how great you are. No way."

"You may not realize it," he said in a low, seductive voice as he cupped her cheek, "but you're going to do that anyway—just not about my music."

The gasp that escaped her lips was so soft and so quiet and yet so damn potent that he had to kiss her.

One of the things he was coming to learn about Paige was that she loved kissing. Like seriously loved it. No sooner had his lips touched hers than she was crawling into his lap—and that was completely fine with him. He loved having her there. It wasn't the fast and frantic kiss like they'd shared when she first arrived, but it wasn't any less erotic. Tongues dueling and all wet, hot need.

"Paige," he said gruffly, kissing her throat, "if I promise to reheat the nachos, can we—"

"Yes!" she panted, rubbing up against him. "Oh God, yes."

They sighed in unison when he reached under her skirt and found bare thighs and tiny panties.

This girl…

Flying first class was a treat.

Having a limo pick them up at the airport was wonderful.

Sitting at a table with four of the biggest rock stars in the world was enough to make her want to throw up.

How is this my life? she wondered, and not for the first time. *How did this become my reality?*

Paige grew up in a wealthy and privileged home, but not where she was rubbing elbows with celebrities like this. There had been events PRW had worked on where there was a celebrity clientele, but she never interacted with them socially. And now, as she sat for dinner at

Matty Reed's house, it all hit her and was making her feel…well…sick.

"Breathe," Dylan whispered in her ear.

"What?"

He chuckled, low and deep and sexy in her ear. "I can tell you're tense and starting to freak out, but you need to breathe."

Doing as she was told, Paige took several deep, cleansing breaths and tried to relax.

"Good girl."

There was talking going on all around them, and she turned to Dylan and gave him a weak smile. "I'm so nervous."

"Don't be. Everyone here is a friend. Remember that. You don't have to think of something witty to say to impress them. Just be yourself, okay?"

She nodded but didn't feel any better than she had a minute ago.

"You're not breathing again," he said softly.

"I've heard a lot of great things about PRW, Paige," Riley said, and all other conversation stopped while everyone looked at her. Her stomach churned and she was thankful for Dylan's hand on her knee. The gentle squeeze reminded her to breathe. "How long have you been with them?"

Paige gave the basic history of the company her father started and how she'd been working in various positions there since she was a child. "I'm finally on the executive floor," she added with a smile.

"My sister is doing PR work," Riley went on. "She lives up in Washington State, with her husband. He's an artist. She runs a gallery in Seattle but does work with several other artists and sets up events and gallery showings for them. She's solo for now, but I know she'd love to branch out a bit."

"What type of art does her husband do?" Paige asked.

"He's a wood sculptor, and brilliant with it, actually," Riley went on.

"That's putting it mildly," Savannah added. "I'm telling you, I first met Ben about five years ago—I interviewed him for a magazine. He was a young punk, but the things he could do with a slab of wood were amazing."

"So you introduced them?" Paige asked.

"Indirectly," Savannah said with a grin. "He needed help on a project, a coffee table book he was doing, and we sent Darcy to help him. Then they got snowed in together and…the rest is history."

"That's so romantic," Paige said and hated the girly sigh that came out before she could stop it.

"Darcy's helping me get my photos into galleries," Vivienne chimed in with a proud smile. Paige was in awe of her beauty and grace and to hear she was an artist too was just… Wow!

"I didn't know you were looking to do that," Dylan commented. "Good for you!"

Vivienne thanked him. "Matt inspired me to do it. To me, it was a hobby, but he kept telling me my pictures were good enough to sell. So when we got together with Riley and Savannah about six months ago, when his whole family was celebrating—which baby was it?" she asked Savannah.

"That was Aidan and Zoe's baby," Savannah replied. "The first junior in the bunch!"

"That's right," Vivienne said. "And so sweet!"

"Aren't all babies sweet?" Matt asked with a grin.

"Trust me," Riley said, "not all the time!"

"Speaking from experience?" Dylan asked as he picked up his glass of water with a grin.

"I love my baby girl more than I ever thought possible, but there were times when she was an infant that I swore she was possessed or something. She would scream and cry and…" He shuddered, and Savannah swatted at him playfully.

"Stop! She was a wonderful baby!"

Riley smiled sweetly at his wife but gave all of them a look that said he was the one in the right in that discussion.

"Anyway," Vivienne said, "we went to the baby's christening and I met Darcy. We got to talking and she said she'd love to help me. Her sister-in-law Brooke paints, and Darcy has helped her get her paintings into galleries and boutiques up and down the southern part of the East Coast." She shrugged and picked up her glass of wine. "She's doing the same for me."

"Plus," Matt interjected, "because a lot of Vivienne's photos are of food from her blog and magazine, Darcy managed to get some of her pictures into a couple of restaurants too."

Everyone extended their congratulations, and conversations started up on various topics, and Paige finally felt herself relax. She watched Riley and Savannah and then looked over at Matt and Vivienne and was a bit envious of the two couples. It was obvious how in love they were, how happy, and Paige had to wonder if she would ever have that for herself. Probably not with Dylan, but…

"You okay?" he asked, leaning in close again.

"I am. Why?"

"You sighed, and it sounded like a sad one. So I wanted to make sure you were all right."

Nodding, she leaned over and kissed him on the cheek. "I'm fine. Just observing the dynamics here at the table, and I always get a little…"

Dare she admit this to Dylan?

"A little what?"

She shrugged. "I don't know…a little envious. Some people make it look so easy to be with someone, to be in love and just…click. Does that make sense?"

For a minute, all he did was stare at her, and she mentally kicked herself for bringing the subject up when they weren't alone.

He nodded and looked about ready to speak when—

"So am I the only one here who is freaking psyched beyond belief that we're going to jam?" Riley asked the group, and everyone laughed, including Dylan.

The moment was lost and she could only hope when they were alone later, they'd both forget she'd even brought it up.

———⁓———

It was two in the morning when she felt the bed shift and dip as Dylan slid under the sheets beside her. They were staying in the guesthouse on Matt and Vivienne's property, and it was lovely and private and, thankfully, only a short walk from the main house. Very convenient after she seemed to eat her weight in cakes and dessert while sitting and talking with the girls when the boys went to jam.

It didn't seem possible that you couldn't hear the

music but…that was exactly the case. Vivienne had explained how important it was for the space to be soundproofed because she worked from home, and Matt and gone to extremes to make that happen for her.

For all Paige's worries about being forced to hang out for hours on end with people she didn't know and how it made her uncomfortable, it was all for nothing. Both Savannah and Vivienne were incredibly nice, and she couldn't remember the last time she had hung out and laughed with friends like this.

Friends.

It had been a great night.

Now, as Dylan moved in close and wrapped his arms around her, she felt completely at peace. She had slept—not well, but she had slept—but she had also kept watching the clock and wondering when he was going to join her.

"Did you have fun?" she asked softly.

Kissing her temple, he replied, "I did. It was amazing. It's like I'd been playing in a fog for so long and this? This was like the thrill I used to get when I was a teenager playing with whoever I could find to jam with." He hugged her close. "Thank you for coming here with me."

She looked over her shoulder at him. "You're welcome, but…I had nothing to do with how tonight went. You went and played music with people you know and love and are comfortable with. It must have been like coming home."

"It was. It really was," he said. "But…having you here makes it even better. And I don't just mean here in the bed, although that is spectacular," he added as he kissed and nipped at her bare shoulder.

Sighing, she rubbed her bare bottom against him. "Oh, stop. If I weren't here, you'd probably be having a lot more fun."

He did some rubbing of his own and then let his hands join in, cupping her breasts. "More fun than this? I don't think that's even possible."

"You'd probably still be jamming instead of feeling like you had to come over here with me." God, could she sound any more pathetic? Why did she have to—

Dylan rolled her onto her back and beneath him in the blink of an eye. "First of all, I'm here in this bed right now because I want to be, not because I feel like I have to be. Second, we jammed for four hours. I'm exhausted. My arms were killing me and I could barely keep my eyes open. We all left the studio like the walking dead. I was thankful all I had to do was cross the yard. Riley still had to drive home."

"I hope he's okay."

"He's fine. He's only ten minutes away and he texted all of us when he got there."

And then something hit her and she started to laugh. Only a giggle at first, but then a full-blown laugh. Dylan leaned over and looked at her like she was crazy.

"Um…what's so funny?"

"It's just…" Another round of laughter came out before she could contain it. "It's a little funny because from the fan perspective, we look at rock stars as guys who would play 24/7 if they had the chance. They're alpha men who go about their business in the most masculine way possible." She shifted beneath him a little. "It struck me as funny how you guys were tired and dragging and then texting one another that you got home safely. It all seems very…normal. Not at all fitting with the rock-star image I had, that's for sure."

Then she started to laugh again and Dylan joined her. After a few minutes, he rested his forehead against hers. "We can't be in rock-star mode all the time. And even alpha men have to be safe and get their rest."

"Mmm…I guess you're right."

He placed a gentle kiss on the tip of her nose. "I should totally get some rest."

Disappointment hit her, but she knew he was right. They'd been up since before dawn to catch their flight, and with the time difference and all the traveling and then all the jamming, she knew he had to be exhausted. Wrapping her arms around his shoulders, she pulled him in for a hug, loving how hard and warm and wonderful his body felt on top of hers. She loved the weight of him, the muscles and the—

"But first, I'm going to do what I've been dreaming of all day," he said, interrupting her musings.

Anticipation immediately replaced the disappointment. Wrapping her legs around him slowly, she locked her ankles at his lower back. "And what's that?" she asked breathlessly.

"I'm going to touch every inch of you and taste every inch of you and then exhaust every inch of you," he said, and Paige could only moan and press up against him in invitation. "Does that sound all right with you?"

Her only answer was to pull his head to hers and kiss him.

Life got busier as soon as they touched down in LA.

Ariel's pregnancy and morning sickness meant she was out of the office more than she was in. Robert had asked Paige to step back in on the Literacy Now campaign as the head, and as such, she found there were many ways her sister had dropped the ball.

Typical.

Lucky for her, she and Daisy were used to this sort of thing and knew how to handle a crisis without freaking out too much. Paige knew she was extremely fortunate to have such a helpful assistant and was relieved she could hand off so many of the smaller tasks to her without worrying about them getting done.

In what seemed like a stroke of luck, Dylan was finally feeling comfortable going out and doing things on his own as well—not only on the work for the campaign, but also looking at other ventures in the music industry. While the weekend with Shaughnessy had been great, none of them were ready to commit to going back into the studio just yet. Riley and Savannah were enjoying their time with their daughter and were expecting another; Matt and Vivienne had moved into their new home, and she was embarking on this new career path with her gallery showings. And Julian? Well, he had been a bit of a mystery to her the entire weekend. He was pleasant enough and cordial but very quiet.

He seemed sad to her. Like really, really sad. When he played—the guys had invited Paige and Savannah and Vivienne to listen to them jam for a couple of hours—he played with a focus she'd never seen before. It was like the drums were an extension of himself, and he took it all very seriously. According to Dylan, Julian was an extremely gifted songwriter and drummer and cowrote most of Shaughnessy's music with Riley. On top of that, he had a near-genius IQ.

All of that added together still didn't equal the sadness she saw in his eyes.

Another bit of information she'd gotten from the girls was his on-again, off-again relationship with his girlfriend, Dena. They were supposed to get married several times in the past five years but never made it down the aisle. When Paige mentioned it to Dylan, he'd rolled his eyes and told her how he and the guys wished Julian would kick Dena to the curb and be done with her. But they didn't think it was ever going to happen.

It wasn't something Paige could begin to understand, but it didn't stop her heart from hurting for him.

So with a band project off the table for now, Dylan felt he needed to do something creative to keep this momentum going. He was working on music he would use for Shaughnessy at a later date, but he'd been meeting with Mick and some of the executives at their record label about doing some studio work with other groups. It wasn't his favorite thing to do, but for right now, he was having fun with it.

And on top of all that, whenever they went out and got stopped by the paparazzi, it was in a positive way. It was crazy how all the negativity toward him just... stopped. It was as if that one incident with Morgan had brought to the spotlight how unfair people could be. She knew the tabloids were fickle, and it could all change at any time, but for now, she was thankful things were leveling out for him.

Their new schedules, however, meant they weren't spending as much time together. Dylan was always asking her to come to the hotel and stay over, but some nights she wanted to go home and crash after a mentally exhausting day. And it wasn't as if she was against having him spend the night at her place, but whenever he showed up there, he never actually did spend the night. She attributed it to the fact that she had to get up so early and he tended to sleep in. He mentioned how he wasn't really a morning person and didn't feel right staying in her house, her bed, after she left for work, so it was easier to just not spend the night. Now it felt like they were drifting apart.

To his credit, Dylan had stayed with her longer than he ever had with any other woman. She knew this because of all the information she'd found out about him when they first met. She hated how she had that kind of data on him, but while her heart was slowly breaking, she could at least cling to the fact that he cared about her enough to stick around for a little longer than was his usual.

"Paige?" Daisy called out as she stuck her head into the office. "Dylan's here to see you. Can I send him in, or can I keep him out there and stare at him for a while?"

That made her laugh softly. Daisy never held anything back, and for the past couple of weeks, especially since the news broke of Paige and Dylan being involved, she had been asking all kinds of questions about him. Maybe Paige should make him wait to see what Daisy would do, but she missed him too.

And who knew how much longer she'd have him to herself?

With a chuckle, she shook her head. "You can send him in."

"Well darn," Daisy muttered with a small laugh of her own. "Fine."

A minute later, Dylan walked into her office and quietly shut the door behind him. "Hey, beautiful."

"Hey, you," she said as she got up from her chair and walked around the desk toward him. It was crazy and maybe stupid, but she loved to kiss him and be kissed by him. Some days it was the equivalent of a cup of coffee.

Or a cake pop.

Up on her tiptoes she went, looping her arms around his shoulders as her lips met his. It was sweet and slow and so delicious that she couldn't help but melt against him with a happy, little sigh. When she lifted her head a minute later, she was smiling.

"Other than giving me the strength to finish this day, what brings you here today?" she asked with a sassy grin. They hadn't talked about him stopping by, and as far as she knew, he had plans to do some recordings today.

They both made their way to sit, and once she was seated, Dylan spoke. "I have a proposition for you."

All kinds of dirty thoughts ran through her mind—the first being if she locked the office door, could they be quiet enough not to alert Daisy to what they were doing?

"A proposition?" she asked in a sultry voice.

For a minute, it looked like he blushed. "Baby, if I thought we could be quiet about it, I'd be propositioning you all over that desk."

"But…"

"But I know how loud we can be," he said with a wink. Slouching in a way that only Dylan could make sexy, he grinned at her. "Recordings got canceled for today, and I figured I'd take you to lunch."

And that had her grinning like an idiot.

There were so many ways Dylan surprised her, but none more than when he did something spontaneous and sweet like this. Putting dirty-girl Paige aside for the moment, she straightened in her seat. "I would love that. Thank you for thinking of me."

"I'm always thinking of you," he said, his voice solemn and serious.

Standing, Paige grabbed her purse from her bottom drawer.

"How much time do you have? I was thinking of trying this new Italian place a buddy of mine invested in. It's across town, so you know traffic will be a bitch, but if you're not in a rush…"

"I'm not, believe me. I need to step away from the office for a little while. I'm beginning to think…"

The sound of the door opening stopped their conversation.

"Ariel," Paige said with a forced smile. "I didn't realize you were coming in today. How are you feeling?"

"Much better," she said with her usual grace and charm. "My doctor gave me something to help with all this morning sickness and I'm starting to feel human again."

"Oh. That's great. So you don't think you should be at home and resting? Maybe it's work that's not helping with the sickness."

With a small shake of her head, Ariel turned to Dylan. "It's good to see you," she began. "And you were on my list of people to call today."

Dylan looked at Paige and then to Ariel. "I was?"

She nodded. "I was wondering if you'd consider lending your…celebrity…to the cause."

Dylan looked over at Paige again and then to Ariel.

"Ariel," Paige said, "what are you talking about?"

"Well, I think we're doing well with the PSAs and all, but I feel like we're building up to this big event that's not very big."

"The fund-raiser is going to be big, Ariel," Paige argued lightly. "We have five hundred people coming who are all big contributors to the arts. I know we're going to—"

"Be bored," Ariel finished for her. "We're going to be bored. And what good is it to have a rock star on board if we're not utilizing him to his fullest potential?"

A trickle of unease began to work its way down Paige's spine. "Excuse me?" she asked through gritted teeth.

"You have him talking to people and groups and on camera for commercials and in print ads, but it's not a very rock-star thing to do. Why isn't he playing music? Why aren't we letting him play music?" she asked with a little more emphasis.

"Ariel, maybe we can talk about this—"

"Gah, Paige! I'm telling you, this is an amazing opportunity! No one's going to question why Dylan's doing it since you're 'dating,'" she said using air quotes. "It would look weird if he didn't play!"

"I don't think it would look weird," Paige murmured. "We've got a band booked. They do a wide range of music, so we can have dancing as well as soft music during dinner. I don't think it's necessary—"

"Well, I do, and I was talking to Dad earlier—"

"You've talked to Dad about this already?"

She nodded. "And we thought it might be fun and great publicity for Dylan and his band to perform at the fund-raiser."

For a minute, Paige wasn't sure what her reaction should be. Excitement? Sure. The thought of getting the kind of publicity from having the first live performance from Shaughnessy in years would be a huge boost to the campaign and the bottom line. Disappointed? A little. After all, it was yet another change to her original plans where this campaign was concerned.

"I came in here to get your opinion, but with Dylan here, it's even better," Ariel said. "If you have time, Dylan, I would love to sit and talk to you about it."

Dylan looked uncertainly between Paige and Ariel. "Um…I was getting ready to take Paige to lunch."

"This won't take too long, I promise," Ariel said with a big smile. She reached out and touched Dylan's arm. "I already have things mapped out and would love your input on how to make it all happen."

He looked at Paige, and she could see the indecision in his eyes. "Paige?"

She let out a quiet sigh. "I've got a few things to finish up here, so why don't you talk with Ariel, and when you're done, we'll go eat. Okay?" She forced a smile, and she had a feeling Dylan knew she was faking it.

"Um…sure. Okay," he said and then turned to Ariel. "This won't take long, right? Maybe thirty minutes?"

"Thirty minutes tops," Ariel agreed and then led him from the office, chatting the entire time about her vision for the show.

When the door closed behind them, Paige did something she had never done before.

She picked up her coffee mug and threw it against the wall in frustration.

There was a war waging within him.

As Dylan made his way toward Paige's office, he knew he'd screwed up.

But for a good reason.

Ariel and Robert Walters had offered him—and Shaughnessy—a chance to get some free publicity while contributing to a good cause. It was something that interested him greatly, and he knew if he pitched the idea to the guys, they'd be on board too. It should be a win-win.

Then he remembered the look on Paige's face when he'd left her office.

The disappointment.

The sad acceptance.

And this time, her family wasn't the only one to blame.

He had put that look there right along with Ariel.

He looked at his watch and cursed. Ninety minutes. He'd been gone for ninety minutes, and he could only hope she was still here and hadn't gone off to lunch without him. Honestly, he had lost track of time once Robert had started his pitch for all the benefits of having Shaughnessy and a few other bands play a public concert to raise awareness for literacy. It wasn't that it was such a new or different idea—actually it was pretty unoriginal—but at his current point in life, it was exactly what he wanted and needed.

Turning the corner to Paige's office, he saw her door was slightly ajar. He knocked lightly and heard Daisy call him in. When he stepped inside, he looked around and didn't see Paige but did spot her assistant picking something up off the floor.

"Need a hand?" he asked and immediately went over and crouched to help her. He picked up several small pieces of porcelain and looked at Daisy. "What broke?"

"A mug," she said but didn't look at him.

Dylan looked around and tried to figure out how a mug would get dropped and shatter this far from Paige's desk. "Um…"

Beside him, Daisy finished picking up the scattered debris, stood, and tossed it in the trash can by Paige's desk—all still without looking at him.

"Is Paige here?"

"No."

He sighed and tossed the few miniscule pieces of shattered mug in the trash before raking a hand through his hair. "Do you know where she went?"

"Out."

So he really had screwed up. "Look, I'm not sure what happened here but…"

Then she turned toward him, and Dylan had to admit, he took a step back because she looked fierce. "But what?" she snapped. "But you think it's okay to hurt Paige's feelings and then come waltzing back here and expect her to be waiting for you?"

"Daisy, I—"

"I have worked with Paige for a long time and believe me, she gets angry, but she's always in control of it. It never gets the better of her. This was the first time she ever did anything even remotely…violent. And why? Because of you! You and Ariel!"

"I didn't think it would be an issue," he said defensively. "I thought it was all fine and good because it was for the campaign! I thought she was okay with it!"

Liar, liar, liar...

"Well, she wasn't," Daisy said with a small pout.

"Come on, Daisy. Where is she? I need to talk to her."

She studied him for a moment. "I don't think she wants to talk to you right now."

"I'm sure she doesn't, but I need to make this right with her."

"Can I ask you something?"

"Sure."

"This whole thing that's going on with you and Paige—it's a way of keeping the bad press reports away, right?"

He let out an aggravated sigh. "That's how it started but—"

"Do you care about her at all? Or is all this about you and your reputation?"

Damn. She may have seemed like a chattering airhead most of the time, but she certainly didn't pull any punches when she needed to. "Not that it's any of your business, but I care about Paige. A lot. That's why I need to know where she is so I can talk to her."

Ten minutes later, Dylan was in his car, speeding out of the parking garage. Once he'd gotten Paige's whereabouts out of Daisy, the woman had continued to chatter at him about how he better make things right. He was trying to, dammit! Right now he wished he knew what to say and how to say it. He'd never had this kind of situation before, this kind of relationship, where he cared enough to want to make things right.

And now that he did, it had him feeling so sick and twisted up inside, he wasn't sure he liked it.

He hadn't wanted to talk to Ariel, if he was being honest with himself. He knew it was going to rub Paige the wrong way even if it was for the right reasons. He should have simply suggested they make an appointment to talk after his lunch with Paige.

Yeah, that thought hit him about thirty seconds after he'd walked out with Ariel. Unfortunately, the woman talked almost as much as Daisy did, and he couldn't get a word in edgewise for far too long. Then her father had joined in. Dylan had to wonder how Paige managed to have conversations with either one of them because they never seemed to shut up!

There were plenty of things Dylan had learned to accept about himself over the course of his life. First, he was a screwup. Most of the time it was by his own choice. It had started as a way to get some attention from his parents and then it became a way to get attention period. He was a classic case of the child who lashed out for all the wrong reasons. His parents weren't bad; they weren't abusive; they just weren't overly attentive. And to a guy who clearly enjoyed being in the spotlight, he took matters into his own hands to get them to see him.

But he was digressing.

Second, he was a bit self-absorbed. He was great at homing in on his own feelings, but he sucked at paying attention to the feelings of others. It was different with Paige. In any other circumstance, he would have known he'd handled things okay. This whole thing today had taken him by surprise.

Which brought him to the third thing about himself—

he was not good at thinking on his feet. It didn't seem to matter what the situation—if he had to make a snap decision, he always made the wrong one. The major difference with today's encounter was that he'd hurt Paige's feelings—not by missing lunch or not putting her first, but by not putting her before anything having to do with her family was a major misstep on his part.

It was funny, he mused, how family issues were the root of so many problems—it was something he and Paige shared. Not on the same level or for the same reason, but…

Only, it was the same level.

It was all about attention.

They both felt they didn't get the attention from their families that they deserved. Dylan chose to be rebellious while Paige just…accepted it.

Dammit.

Why hadn't he made that connection before? While he'd sympathized with her over the way her family treated her, he never truly related to it. Until now. Maybe that would work in his favor; maybe it wouldn't. All he could do was hope she'd listen to him when he got to her.

Fortunately, the universe was on his side, because for the first time ever, he made it through the city without hitting one traffic light. He turned onto her block and was relieved to see her car in her driveway. Daisy said Paige was going home, but in the back of his mind, Dylan had begun to wonder if she had maybe decided to go somewhere else to blow off steam.

Like batting cages or a gun range.

The image of her doing either of those things put a

smile on his face, and he had to force himself to push it aside until they were done talking.

At her door, he knocked.

No answer.

He rang the bell.

No answer.

After the third try, he turned to check the back when she opened the door.

Bathrobe on. Hair in a towel.

He hung his head and shook it. She'd been in the shower. Not ignoring him.

With a lopsided grin, he faced her. "Hey."

Holding the towel to her head, she responded, "Hey."

No makeup and in a robe that looked like it was two sizes too big for her and all he could think of was how beautiful she was. "Can I come in?"

Nodding, Paige stepped aside and motioned for him to come inside. Dylan walked straight to the living room and waited for her. She followed—eventually. It seemed to take her way longer than it should have. She didn't come close to him. She didn't kiss him hello, and dammit, that one hurt almost more than anything.

"I'm sorry," he said and realized he sounded louder and more defensive than he should have. He took a deep breath and let it out. "I'm sorry," he said, calmer this time.

With a shrug, Paige adjusted the towel on her head and then turned and walked into the kitchen. She got herself a bottle of water and came back.

Without one for him.

"We should have gone to lunch," he said as he began to pace. "I never should have left with your sister to talk about anything. It was wrong and I'm sorry."

"Okay," she said with a shrug as she sat down on the sofa.

Stopping, he looked at her and knew it was anything but. This was her MO. This was how she handled things. For whatever reason, she felt she deserved this crappy treatment, and that wasn't okay with him.

With a muttered curse, he walked over and crouched down in front of her, resting his hands on the sofa on either side of her. "No, it's not okay," he said, his voice a near growl. "I know you're mad at me, Paige. I know I messed up. I also know you threw a mug across the room because you were mad. So don't sit here and go meek on me. Tell me what you're thinking."

She didn't have her glasses on and yet her eyes looked just as big. There was so much emotion in them, so much he knew she wanted to say—he needed her to let it out.

But she didn't.

"Tell me I'm a jerk," he prompted.

Nothing.

"Tell me I'm a selfish bastard."

Nothing.

Then, he knew how to get her to speak up. Suppressing a grin, he said, "Tell me I'm a complete and total…ass." Now he did grin. "I dare you."

His gaze instantly went to her lips, which twitched ever so slightly. Then he looked up as she rolled her eyes.

Leaning in closer, he lowered his voice in a way he knew she loved. "Come on, Paige, say it."

"You're ridiculous," she whispered, but she was starting to smile more.

Dylan shook his head. "Uh-uh…you know the rules. You have to say it."

With one brow arched at him, she said, "Fine. You're a complete and total…ass."

"That's my girl," he said and gave her a quick kiss on the lips before he stood. Grabbing one of her hands, he pulled her to her feet. "Now go dry your hair so we can talk."

"We can talk while my hair is wet—"

"No, we can't," he countered. "Because it's distracting. I want to take the towel off your head and smell your shampoo and be a total perv with you. But that would not be appropriate right now." He gave her a gentle push in the direction of her bedroom and then gave her a light smack on her ass.

Paige let out a little screech and looked at him over her shoulder. "Maybe I wouldn't mind you being a total perv right now."

It was tempting—to put off having an uncomfortable conversation in favor of having Paige naked in bed was beyond appealing. "Paige…"

She walked into her bedroom, which was right off the living room, and Dylan figured they were on the same page again.

Then the hair towel flew out the door.

Yeah, he was tempted to follow her and watch as she dried her hair.

Then her robe flew out the door and…well…he was only a man.

——~~——

"This wasn't why I came here."

"I know. But I always wanted to test the makeup-sex theory."

Dylan laughed. Seriously, this girl was beyond perfect. He rolled onto his side and admired her—in her totally naked glory. He caressed the soft skin of her arm. "I'm serious, Paige. I messed up and I'm sorry. I wasn't thinking. The thought of playing again with the guys jumped to the forefront of everything, and…and it shouldn't have."

Turning her head, she looked at him. "Yes, it should."

"Excuse me?" Clearly he hadn't heard her correctly.

"Dylan, your music and the band are important to you. You're finally at a point where you're ready to take on that part of your life again. I get it. I'm not mad because you want to play."

"O-kay…"

"I'm upset because you came to the office and surprised me, and then as soon as something else came along, you…forgot about me," she said sadly, her voice so soft he almost didn't hear her.

He cupped her cheek. "Baby, I swear, I never forgot you. Ever. The whole time I was in there, I was wishing I were with you and cursing myself for not going to lunch. Then they both kept talking and talking and talking—"

"My dad was there too?"

"Um…"

She gave a delicate snort of disbelief. "It's okay, Dylan. I figured they'd go at you together. It's what they do. Like a little team."

"For what it's worth, Paige, the only draw is having an excuse to play with the guys. What your dad and Ariel pitched wasn't creative or exciting or all that big." He paused. "Look, in the last two months I've noticed a lot of things. I think your dad is brilliant in some areas…"

"I know."

"But not all areas," he finished. "I think what he did to get the press off my back was pure genius, but he didn't do it alone. He had you and Mick to guide him. I think your sister is a good spokesperson for the firm but she has no friggin' clue how to do anything on her own. She's great with jumping in and taking credit, but beyond that, she's useless."

He breathed a sigh of relief when she didn't argue.

"I think you, Paige, are the driving force in that company and you scare them."

"Me?"

He nodded. "Yeah, you. The entire time they pitched, it was obvious they were going to throw this at you to take over and make happen. Not because they think they're better or because they've got other things to do, but because they have no idea how to make it work. Your dad's getting older, Paige. If you ask me, he'd probably love to retire or at least cut back. He's probably tired, and it's hard to keep up with all the marketing trends—that's a young man's game. And your sister? She's lazy."

"That's great and all, but it still leaves me doing all the work and not getting any of the recognition."

"And you want that? The recognition?"

Paige was silent for a moment. "Everyone wants their hard work to be acknowledged, Dylan. I'm only human."

"I get it. I do." Here was his opening. "It hit me on the drive over here how alike we are." Pausing, he waited for her to comment, but when she continued to look at him, he went on. "Everyone wants their parents' approval. I know I did."

"Dylan, I've read a ton of articles where your parents are quoted saying how proud they are of you."

"They are and I know that. Now," he added. "But when I was younger, they were very detached. I got whatever I wanted and they never said no to me. When I wanted to take guitar lessons, I did. When I wanted to join the soccer team, they bought me everything I needed. When I wanted to take karate, they signed me up. And they went to my games and to my recitals and all that, but they never said they were proud of me or even 'good job.' It was like they couldn't speak the words out loud. To them, their presence relayed all those things and I was wrong to expect both—the words and their being there."

"Well, that's…odd," she said carefully.

"I know. And so I started to lash out and started doing things to get a rise out of them. I pierced my ear when I was fifteen. Got my first tattoo at sixteen—illegally, by the way. I was drinking by that time too and was sneaking in and out at all hours of the night and the most they said was how I needed to be careful, so I wouldn't hurt anyone. Not myself—anyone," he added for emphasis.

He rolled onto his back and stared up at the ceiling. "I drank more, stayed out more, and yet every Sunday we went to church together, and every night we sat down to dinner together, and nobody talked about how I was getting more and more out of control." This was all the stuff he came to realize while in rehab, but it felt good to share it with Paige. "I don't blame them for how far gone I got—that's all on me. But I do blame them for not caring enough to leave their comfort zones and confront me on my behavior. If they had even once told me I was a disappointment or how they were worried about me,

I might have listened. I'll never know for sure, but I'd like to think I would."

Paige took one of his hands and brought it to her lips and kissed it. "Can I say something?"

"Anything."

"Maybe it's not the kids you should be talking to."

He turned his head and looked at her. "What do you mean?"

"I mean, it might be beneficial to talk to parent groups about this sort of thing, teaching them how to speak to their kids and how to make a difference. Like you just said, you'll never know exactly what would have made a difference, but I bet there are parents out there who'd find it helpful. You could potentially save someone's life. Or even save an entire family."

His throat felt tight, and he forced himself to look away. "Maybe. I guess it's something to think about."

"I'm glad you shared this with me, Dylan," she said softly.

And then he did look at her again. "I wanted you to know that I get it. That I understand. You want that acknowledgment from your dad, from your parents, and they won't do it. My path led to destruction in a very obvious and public way. You not dealing with this and accepting their treatment has you internalizing it all, and it's slowly killing you, Paige. I see it in your eyes and on your face every time they do something like they did today. Like what I did today. You can't let people get away with it."

"I didn't internalize it today. I threw that mug," she said and gave him a sassy smile. "And I have to admit it felt really good."

Rolling to his side, he gave her a loud, smacking kiss on the cheek. "That could get to be an expensive and messy form of therapy." He stood and reached for his boxer briefs and slipped them on. He noticed the look of uncertainty on Paige's face as he looked at her. "I know it's not lunch but I really do want to take you out. How about an early dinner?"

"Italian? Because I've been craving some eggplant rollatini and spaghetti all afternoon," she replied as she climbed off the bed.

Dylan watched as she walked, gloriously naked, out to the living room to retrieve her robe. When she came into the room and passed her mirror, she frowned.

"What? What's the matter?"

Paige ran a hand over her hair. "This is never going to be right. I'm going to jump in and grab a quick shower to wet it and freshen up."

With lightning speed, Dylan whipped his briefs off. "You're probably exhausted and weak from missing lunch. I should join you and make sure you don't faint in the shower."

Her only response was to giggle and shake her head at him.

Following her into the bathroom, he watched as she started the water and felt like the luckiest man alive when she turned and held out her hand to him and pulled him under the steamy spray.

Chapter 8

LOOKING BACK, PAIGE COULD SAY WITH GREAT CERTAINTY that things changed between her and Dylan the day he came and apologized for skipping out on their lunch date.

And not for the better.

Two weeks later, Paige felt the strain and knew he was feeling it too.

Their work schedules were crazy even though Ariel was back at work. Somehow Paige ended up taking on a lot more responsibility—more than usual—and Ariel's latest idea was a big benefit concert. There was no way Paige was getting involved with that mess. Her temper was short, her nerves were frayed, and Dylan's sudden obsession with his image and getting the band back in the public eye was making her want to scream.

At every Literacy Now event or function they went to, he managed to turn it into a self-promotion event for himself and his band. At first, Paige had to focus to realize what he was doing—like he was so smooth about it most people might not notice the plugs he managed to slide into his talks.

But she noticed.

And she didn't particularly like it.

Not that she was against Dylan being excited about his work with Shaughnessy. She wasn't. What she was against was Dylan using their time with Literacy Now to promote his music, and not literacy and the importance of reading.

Like right now, she thought, they were at a regional library outside of LA, and Dylan was supposed to talk about the different library programs and get the kids excited about them. But was he? No. Right now he was answering questions about life in a rock band. She could reason that he was building a relationship with the kids in the crowd, so when he did mention the library programs, they'd be willing to listen to him and take his advice. Looking at the clock, however, she knew they were almost out of time, and if he didn't do an immediate change of subject, there was no way he'd get to the pertinent information.

It wasn't easy to get his attention, but she managed to snag it for a second and held up the library brochure and waved it at him in hopes of him getting the message and leaving his riveting band talk in favor of his love of reading.

"So what I'm saying, kids, is you need to have an interest in the arts. Whether it's playing an instrument or drawing or painting or writing, you need to find where your passion is and go for it," Dylan was saying, and Paige started to relax.

"Like I did when I figured out that I wanted to play the guitar," he went on, and she groaned, her head falling forward as she cursed him. Why now? Why, when they were so close to the entire campaign going national, did he have to go rogue? Seriously, why?

A loud round of applause burst out all around her, and she knew he'd missed giving out the real information. Jumping up, she ran to the front of the room before anyone could leave and immediately began talking as loud as she could.

"On your way out, please see Mrs. Duncan, the head librarian, at the front desk to get a schedule of the many programs they'll be offering here over the next three months. From story time to reading tutors, there will be something for everyone!"

By the time she spoke the last word, the room was almost empty. She turned to Dylan and glared.

"Good group today," he said with a grin as he grabbed his jacket and slipped it on.

"Are you for real?" she asked. "You do realize this was a promotional event for the library and not a press junket for Shaughnessy, don't you?"

He looked at her in confusion. "What are you talking about?"

"You!" she cried. "You spent the majority of the time talking about yourself—again—and about the band—again—and never mentioned any of the library programs! Dammit, Dylan, that's why we were here!"

"I *did* mention them," he argued, his grin fading.

"No, you didn't. Trust me. I was sitting here listening the entire time. You talked about world tours, Shaughnessy's catalog of songs, and who your favorite superhero is! And you know what you *didn't* talk about? Books! Any books!"

His expression hardened. "Okay, fine, so I went a little off script today. But don't you think building a relationship with the kids is important too? Now when they see me on TV talking about the importance of reading, they'll remember this day and how I was cool with them, and they'll listen."

"You're impossible," she murmured and gathered up her things. She was halfway to the door when Dylan caught up with her. She immediately spun out of his grasp. "What!"

Rather than say anything, he simply glared at her for a minute.

"We need to go. The library needs this room for another meeting," Paige said and walked out of the room. Dylan was right behind her; they had driven together and as much as she wanted a little space right now, she knew she was stuck in the close confines of the car with him for at least an hour.

They were in his car, and the first fifteen minutes of the drive were spent in total silence.

"Look," he began calmly, "I get that you're passionate about your job and I respect that. But everything can't go your way all the time, Paige. Sometimes you have to go with the flow. No one was harmed there because I didn't talk books."

"It's why you were there," she said wearily, her head turned away to look out the window.

He sighed, and she knew he was as frustrated as she was. "Even if I say I'm sorry, it's not going to change anything. I can't call all those people back and read from your script, so you need to move on."

The urge to haul off and punch him was almost too great to ignore. "Move on," she repeated. "Awesome. Thanks."

Dylan briefly looked at her. "You can keep harping on me and bitching at me, but like I said, it's not going to change anything. I'll read from your damn script next time—word for word. And I'll ignore any questions anyone has that doesn't pertain to books and reading, okay?"

It was his tone that was pissing her off. So cocky. So arrogant. "Do whatever you want, Dylan. I think from this point on, you can go to these things without me."

He gave a snort of disgust as he wove through the late afternoon traffic. "Wow, so I finally graduated to not needing a babysitter. Thanks."

It was right then and there that she knew any other exchange of words would be pointless. She was upset, he was defensive, and they were simply at an impasse. It was sweet relief when he seemed to come to the same conclusion and turned on the radio.

When they pulled into the PRW parking garage, Paige couldn't get out of the car fast enough. Dylan parked and she was surprised—she figured he'd pull up to the door and let her out. When she climbed from the car, he did the same. She certainly didn't want a confrontation here in the middle of the garage, but if that's what it was, she'd deal with it.

He came around the front of the car and stood in front of her. "I'm sorry," he said solemnly.

She let out a slow breath. In the moment, she knew she had been right to be upset, but Dylan had also been right—him going off script hadn't been the end of the world. "Me too."

He wrapped her in his arms and held her. Dropping her purse on the ground, she wound her arms around his waist and held him too.

And they stayed locked like that for a long time.

—⁓—

Music was flowing. The words, the melodies, every-thing. Dylan couldn't remember a time when he was this creative musically, and he was loving the hell out of it. It was giving him a sense of purpose again, and on top of it, he felt great.

Healthy—mentally and physically.

Everywhere he turned, people were praising him. Mick lined up several interviews for him with differ-ent media outlets—*Rolling Stone* magazine was one and Savannah Shaughnessy's former employer *Rock the World*. Then he had one television interview with a major network. They were all scheduled for after his completion with Literacy Now, so he could focus on finishing that up along with his community service hours. Mick thought it would be a good angle for the interviews because it would show that he took his com-mitments seriously.

And he did.

Like right now, he was committed to writing this song that he was anxious to share with the guys. The record label had given him access to one of the studios to record some demos for use once Shaughnessy was officially back from their hiatus, and it felt good to know he'd be making a major contribution to the band for the first time since their early days together.

Yeah, it was an amazing feeling.

Professionally, he felt like he was back on top.

Personally, he was floundering, and he knew it. This thing with Paige had been so good, so perfect for him… and now? Now he knew he had let her down. It had seriously been all downhill since that damn lunch day. It pissed him off because he felt, on some level, that she was still holding it against him, like no matter how hard he tried or apologized, she wasn't fully willing to let it go.

But he also had to accept the fact that he had screwed up, and since that point, he'd also been very distracted. They weren't spending the time together like they had in the beginning, and he missed that. Missed her. But this was how life was, right? They both had demanding jobs and they couldn't spend every day in each other's pockets. That wasn't good either, right?

Questions like this swirled in his brain a lot lately. Relationships were never his thing, and he had never given them much thought. But for some reason, Paige made him think—about her, about them, about…a future.

And it scared the heck out of him.

When this all started, he figured it would be casual and fun and then…over. He never saw them lasting beyond working together. But now, when things weren't going great, he wanted to try to make it better.

He just didn't know how.

Putting down his guitar, he got up and walked across the room to get something to drink. Bottle of water in hand, he walked onto his balcony and looked out at the city. Between rehab and now, this was the longest he'd stayed in one place. Granted, rehab was in Colorado and this was LA, but normally he didn't stay in any one place for very long. The road was always calling—in the past, a trip to get away and party had always been calling, but now it was just the music that was calling to him.

And Paige.

Sighing, he opened the bottle and took a long drink.

Her life was here in LA and he couldn't imagine her

being away from her family, no matter how much he thought that would be the best thing for her. And on top of that, could she handle dealing with him once the band did get back together and went into the studio to record and then on tour? Would she be willing to understand that he couldn't stick to her schedules and timetables?

And would he be able to stand having that argument over and over and over?

Probably not.

This was why he never did relationships—he was too wrapped up in himself and what he wanted to care about anybody else and their needs and wants. The last two months with Paige had opened his eyes to how good it could be to care about someone beyond the physical and be cared for in return in that same way. But was he feeling like that because he was feeling like that or because there was nothing else going on in his life?

He needed help. He needed direction. He needed a friend to talk to.

He could call Matt, but he wanted a face-to-face conversation with someone. Riley was a good option. Last Dylan heard, he and Savannah were in town but... their relationship was always solid. Even when they were broken up in the beginning of their relationship, everyone knew they'd work it out because Riley was a commitment kind of guy.

Walking into the suite, he picked up his phone and called Mick.

"Hey, Dylan," Mick said distractedly. "I'm getting ready to board a flight to New York. You okay?"

"Oh, um...yeah. Yeah, sure. Everything's good. I

just hadn't talked with you in a while and wanted to catch up."

Mick chuckled. "How about one night next week? I'll be back on Tuesday, so any night after that should work."

"Sounds great. I'll call you when you get back."

When they hung up, he decided to call Julian, not that he was holding out much hope there. Julian was reclusive on a good day and not one to talk about anything other than music. But…he decided to give it a try.

The main thing with Julian was… Well, Dylan loved him like a brother, but he was also in complete awe of him too. Julian was intense and brilliant and…always in control.

Bottom line, they were complete opposites.

Maybe this wasn't the best idea.

"Screw it," he murmured and hit Julian's number before he could second-guess himself any more than he already was.

An hour later, they were sitting opposite one another in Dylan's suite over a chessboard. For whatever reason, talking over a game of chess was easier than having a regular conversation.

"Can I ask you something?" Dylan began.

"Sure."

"What was it about Dena that made you want to… you know…make it a thing?"

Julian lifted his head and quirked a brow at him. And that was another thing about Julian—he was intimidating as hell, built like a linebacker, eyes so dark they were almost black, and hair so black it was almost blue. Dylan was always glad they never clashed over anything because there wasn't a doubt in his mind that Julian could crush him with minimal effort.

"A thing?"

Oh, and his voice was scary too—deep and gravelly and always so unbelievably serious.

"Yeah. You know, like that you wanted to marry her."

"But I haven't married her." He moved his rook, scratched his stubbled chin, and let out a sigh that was almost a growl. "Why?"

"You met Paige."

Nodding, Julian stared at the board. "She's nice."

"I know. Almost too nice for a guy like me and yet…"

This time Julian did look up. "Don't do that."

"Do what?"

"Don't pull that 'aw shucks, I don't deserve to be happy' crap. It makes you sound ridiculous. And annoying."

Dylan rolled his eyes. "Dude, how long have you known me?"

"Too long."

"And have you ever seen nice girls come around me? Ever see me date one?"

Julian chuckled. "All kinds of girls come around you. You've just never been interested in the good girls. You always needed someone who was willing to be wild with you. You scared the nice ones away."

"Okay, fine. Maybe. But…I didn't scare Paige away. If anything, she was the aggressor in the relationship."

Another quirked brow. "Nice."

And Dylan couldn't help but smile at the memory. "Yeah, it was. But two months ago, I had nothing. I was barely leaving the house, and now? Now I'm starting to engage in life. Our schedules are crazy, our personalities are opposites, and yet…"

"And yet you still want her," Julian finished for him. "So? What's the problem?"

"This is all foreign to me, man. Like seriously foreign. Am I latching on to her because it's convenient? Or because she's safe?"

"How is she safe?"

Dylan moved his pawn and sighed. "She didn't know me before," he said gruffly. "Don't get me wrong, she knows what I was like—she researched me when I tried to sign on for the campaign—but she didn't know me then. With her, I almost have a clean slate."

"D, if this thing the two of you have is solid, then your slate shouldn't matter. Clean, dirty, shattered, none of it. Is she harping on you about staying sober?"

Dylan shook his head.

"Does she throw your past back in your face?"

He shook his head again.

"Then what's the holdup? Is it her, or is it you?"

"That's just it… Right now, I feel like it's both of us. Like we're drifting and I don't know if I'm supposed to keep fighting for it."

Julian looked down at the board again and moved his knight. "Yeah. I get that."

"Which brings me back to my original question—you and Dena."

With a curse, Julian reached for the can of soda Dylan had given him earlier and took a drink. He put the can down, but Dylan could almost feel the rage vibrating off him. "In the beginning, it was all lust. I know that now. I was so hot for her, and the things she did with me? Man, it was like living in a fantasy."

Settling in his chair, Dylan waited to hear the rest.

"Then she started talking about music and how she was interested in it—all aspects of it. And I found we had a lot in common. So here was this beautiful woman who was my every fantasy in bed and who also held my attention with intelligent conversation out of it. It was a heady combination."

"I'm sure," Dylan said, doing his best not to sound too jaded. None of the guys in the band liked Dena. None of them. They all felt she was using Julian, and everyone saw it—except Julian.

"Then she tried making a go of a music career for herself as we were finishing the tour. I had been working with her on it, but as soon as she knew I was going to have time off, she decided to up her game and record an album, and she wanted me to give it to Mick and the label and…" He raked a hand through his hair. "I hated it. I hated being put in the middle, and the thing is, she wasn't very good. I did everything I could to polish that project—I wrote the music, the lyrics, I played on the demo, but she's not a strong performer, and I could tell no one was interested. That's when things got really bad."

It was on the tip of Dylan's tongue to remind Julian how bad it was long before then, but again, he kept it to himself.

"She started using sex as a bargaining chip. She began flaunting her relationships with other guys in the music industry, and I was blown away by who she was becoming. And not in a good way. But we'd been together for so long that I thought we could overcome all of it. So I proposed, thinking it was what she wanted. She liked the ring. She liked the attention and the thought of a million-dollar wedding. It was me she didn't like."

Okay, this time he couldn't stay quiet. "So if you know that, why do you keep trying?"

"Honestly? I hate admitting defeat." He let out a mirthless laugh. "I'm convinced she's going to come to her senses and realize she's been screwing with me for no reason and we can get back to where we used to be. That's the couple I want to be."

For a minute, Dylan could only stare. Had he really thought Julian was closed off and unwilling to talk about stuff? This was almost more than he even wanted to know. It was one thing to go along and think that his friend was clueless and being taken advantage of; it was another to know he was willingly torturing himself with a crappy relationship.

Damn.

"So...you're just going to wait her out and hope she comes to her senses?"

Julian shrugged. "I've got nothing else to do."

"Jules, come on!" Dylan cried. "That's ridiculous. Do you know how many women out there would kill to be in Dena's shoes? Do you have any idea how much time and energy you've put into this relationship and it all might be for nothing? You're wasting your life on something that maybe isn't even meant to be."

Another shrug. "I think it could be—that in the end, she'll see I'm what she wants. And I think it's some-thing worth fighting for."

Well, that was...insane. Dylan knew he had feelings

for Paige and he enjoyed standing up for her and working for what they had. But it hadn't been work, and he hadn't done all that much standing up for her.

Basically, he was a slacker.

Could he possibly do all the things Julian was doing? Was he willing to put in that kind of time and energy into a relationship?

He looked over at Julian, who was studying the board, and almost felt sorry for him. Dylan missed out on a lot of living because he was drunk to the point of oblivion most of the time. Maybe missing out wasn't the right term, but he hadn't appreciated his life. He was living, but he was living dangerously. But Julian? Julian was alive, but he wasn't living. He was in a constant state of limbo, and Dena was the one playing with the height of the bar.

He hated that bitch.

All that being said, it brought him back to the same question—was he willing to put the time and energy into a relationship, especially now that he was living his life cleanly and clearly for the first time since he was a teenager?

"Your move, man," Julian said.

Unfortunately, it was. He hadn't been paying close enough attention to Julian's moves, and there was no way for him to win now.

Julian laughed quietly. "Yeah, man. You're screwed."

Yeah, he was. And not only on the board.

The next night, Dylan showed up at Paige's with Chinese food. They'd talked earlier in the day and made the plans, and at the time, he'd been excited by the thought of seeing her. Now, as he stood at the door, he felt more than a little nervous.

Actually, he felt like nothing about this whole thing was natural anymore.

He had to think about what to do, what to say, how to act. Maybe it was just him putting pressure on himself and overthinking everything. Like now that the thought had been put in his head that you have to work toward making a relationship…work, he felt he couldn't relax and be himself.

"Totally overthinking this," he muttered and knocked on the door.

Paige opened it and he relaxed. She smiled at him as he walked in, and he stopped and kissed her—not their usual over-the-top, frantic kisses, but a soft one that lingered a little. She had amazing lips and that simple act put him back on even ground.

Stepping around him, Paige led the way to the kitchen, where she had the table set and ready for the food. She was dressed casually—barefoot and in cropped yoga pants with a plain white T-shirt—and though they clung to her and showed all of her amazing curves, he found he missed the sight of her in her skirt and boots. "How did the studio work go today? Did you work on anything good?"

As they worked together to serve up the takeout, Dylan talked about the different songs he'd played on and how he'd gotten a couple of hours to himself in a studio to lay down some tracks he was hoping to use with Shaughnessy.

"Do you guys have a timeline for when you're going to get back in the studio?"

"Not yet," he said with a sigh. "I don't want to nag everyone. I know it's going to be at least another couple of months until Matt's ready. He wants to be close to home and ready to travel with Vivienne to all her gallery shows."

"That's so sweet," Paige said with a wistfulness he'd never heard in her voice before. He was going to question it, but she spoke up first. "And all her shows are on the East Coast, right?"

He nodded. "So let's say, in my mind, it's going to be three months for him to be ready. Then we'll be dealing with Riley and Savannah and them expecting a baby. The studio is close to home for him, but he's not going to be as focused with that going on. So we'll add another couple of months to that."

"Realistically, it could be at least six months before you guys even start," she said, reading his thoughts. "Wow. That is a long time. Will studio work be enough for you in the meantime? I mean, creatively?"

He shrugged and realized he liked this—liked how she took an interest in his music and that they could talk about it.

Just like Julian and Dena…

Okay, that wasn't something he wanted to deal with or even think about. Paige was nothing like Dena. This relationship wasn't batshit crazy like Julian and Dena's.

Paige's hand touched his, and he looked up to see concern on her face. "Are you all right?"

"Um…yeah. Why?"

"You got this weird look on your face, like you were going to be sick."

Shaking his head to clear it, he replied, "No. No, I'm good. Sorry." He took a bite of one of the dumplings on his plate. "So, yeah. Waiting is going to suck, no doubt. But I'm hoping during that time we'll all manage to get together and talk and jam and plan, so that when we do get into the studio, we'll be so prepared that it will be a no-brainer."

"Is that even possible?" she asked, nibbling on her own dumpling.

"Yeah, definitely. Our third album was like that. We had been touring for so long and working things out on the road that when we finally got home and into the studio, we were able to lay everything down in ten days. We were pumped and knew exactly what everything was going to sound like, and we got it done."

"That sounds awesome."

"It was."

She studied him. "But…?"

He laughed softly—she knew him well. "But…I love the time in the studio. Sometimes working stuff through is amazing because you end up with so much more— more music, more ideas. I love when we have to talk it out and try new stuff. If we go in with everything done in our minds, it's just…"

"I get it. You like putting the puzzle together with them," she said simply.

Yeah, she got him.

And damn if that wasn't a turn-on in and of itself.

"Exactly."

They talked about music while they ate and how he'd like to see the next Shaughnessy album go, and she asked all the right questions and seemed so genuinely interested that he had to ask: "You're not looking into doing anything in the music business, are you?"

She looked at him quizzically. "Like what?"

"Like…making a record yourself or anything like that, right?"

She laughed out loud—actually snorted at one point—before she put down her fork and looked at him. "Are you out of your mind?" she asked around another round of laughter. "You've heard me sing, right?"

He had, and now he laughed with her. "You're right, you're right. Sorry."

Paige was still chuckling as she picked up her drink and asked him, "Why would you even ask such a thing?"

He shrugged. "I don't know. Tonight you had a lot of questions about the music and the process, and well…it seemed like you were a lot more interested than usual."

"Dylan, I'm interested because it's what you do for a living. I'm curious. I want to know what you do and understand it so we can talk about it and so I don't sound like an idiot when we do."

And that was so like Paige—considerate in everything she did. He didn't deserve her—he knew that.

"You do the same with me," she said, interrupting his thoughts.

"I do?"

She nodded. "Those first two weeks of us working together? You asked me, like, a million questions!" Smiling, she reached out and caressed his cheek before going on. "At first I thought you were being annoying, but then I realized that's how you are—you like to figure out how things work. It's probably why you're the way you are about time in the studio. You like the whole learning process and I think it's really cool."

All Dylan could do was blink at her because she put

it all in a way that completely made sense to him and managed to make him feel…worthy. He wasn't a selfish prick. He was someone who put in an effort, just not in the way most people did. And what was wrong with that? Nothing.

Suddenly he felt lighter, happier than he thought possible. This could all work! He and Paige? They could work because…they already were. That wasn't to say there weren't going to be times when they'd get pissy with each other or fight, but they'd done that already too and look at them—here they were, having dinner and talking and wanting to learn more about each other.

Pretty. Freaking. Cool.

"Are you okay?" she asked for the second time in a matter of minutes.

Reaching for her hand, Dylan took it in his and brought it to his lips and kissed it. "Yeah. I'm good."

And he really was.

For the life of her, Paige didn't know what had suddenly changed with Dylan, but things were definitely different.

Better.

At some point over dinner, it was as if a switch had been flipped. Things had been a little strained between them as of late, and she knew part of it was due to their different schedules and pressure from her job, but whatever it was that happened, she was enjoying the benefits of it.

They were cleaning up the dinner dishes and he was touching her and kissing her every time he got near her. It was sweet and playful and so much everything she loved about him.

A small gasp escaped and she froze in her tracks.

She loved him.

She absolutely loved him.

Swallowing hard, she looked over her shoulder to where he was standing and putting the leftover Chinese food away in the refrigerator, and her heart began to race.

This tattooed, dirty-talking bass player—the kind of man she never in a million years thought she'd find attractive—was the sexiest, most caring and considerate man she'd ever known. He understood her, he challenged her, and he made her want to go out and…and do things! Lately, she was so dissatisfied with her life—the life she'd chosen for so darn long. He'd taken her out to new restaurants and concerts and clubs, and it was obvious she had been living such a boring, sheltered, and structured life before he came along.

And while she knew they never talked about it, the original plan was for them to be a couple until the end of the campaign. But she knew this was never about appearances for the press for her. It was always about how she felt.

"Dylan?" she asked cautiously and waited for him to shut the refrigerator door and turn around. He smiled at her and everything in her melted like it always did. "Do you remember the day I came to your hotel room?"

His smile fell a little as he thought about her words. "Which one?"

"Not the night of the gala but the next time," she said slowly, cautiously.

And his smile was back. "Hell yeah. That particular visit is burned into my brain."

With a soft laugh, she took a step toward him. "You

know…" She paused and cleared her throat. "You know it had nothing to do with the press and the tabloids, right?"

Dylan's head tilted ever so slightly as he studied her. "Of course I know that. Why? What's this about?"

Taking another step toward him, Paige focused on looking at her feet rather than him because…well… she wasn't sure how he was going to react to her little epiphany.

"It occurred to me that we got thrown into a situation together under one set of rules, so to speak, and then things…changed."

Dylan stayed where he was and waited for her to look at him before he spoke. "Right…"

"And I was standing here thinking about all the things we've been doing together and how much I enjoy our time together, and now that the campaign is almost over…" She shrugged. "I don't know. I guess I was wondering if this was all going to stop."

Now his expression was like stone. She couldn't read him, and one of the things she had learned about him since they'd become involved was how she could always tell what he was thinking.

"Do you want it to stop?" he asked, and his voice was borderline fierce.

She took a steadying breath and let it out as she shook her head. "No. No, I don't want it to stop. But—"

He closed the distance between them. "Enough," he said, cupping her face in his hands. "Don't say another word. There is no *but*. I'm here with you, Paige, because I want to be. This was never about the press. I know it was the push that put us both…here," he added, pulling her in until her breasts were pressed firmly against his chest, "but I think we would have gotten here on our own eventually."

Tears stung in her eyes as she nodded. "I'd like to think that too."

"It's true." Caressing her cheek, his dark eyes scanned her face. "I'll admit that I didn't like you being assigned to babysit me in the beginning, but you never made it feel that way. You were the first person in a long time to treat me like me—Dylan—and not a celebrity. I enjoyed our talks and watching you work and…just being with you."

"I feel the same way. I hate how I was such a snob to you in the beginning."

"Well, to be fair, most people act that way when they first meet me. I'm the poster boy for bad behavior. You were seriously the first person in my career to see past the tattoos and the attitude and the reputation to see me."

It was impossible to hide how pleased she was; her smile couldn't be contained. "I like who you are, Dylan. I like how you make me stop taking myself so seriously and step away from my job and go out and experience new things."

"So it sounds to me that we like each other," he said softly.

"Yes, it does."

Paige was certain he was going to kiss her, that he was going to dip his head and give her the kind of kiss that made her knees weak and her heart race.

But he didn't.

Instead, he caressed her cheeks one more time before wrapping his arms around her and holding her close.

And that's when she knew it was more than just *like* for him too. As much as she wanted to scream out that she loved him, she didn't. This moment was so good, so perfect, she didn't want to change a thing.

When he stepped back a few minutes later, Paige looked around the kitchen and saw everything was clean and put away. Taking one of Dylan's hands in hers, she led him straight to her bedroom.

They walked slowly and silently. Next to her bed, she turned and slid her hands under Dylan's T-shirt and lifted it up. He took over and pulled it over his head. The sight of his tattoos did it for her every time—she loved to look at them, to touch them, to kiss them. And she knew he loved it when she did because every touch of her lips and hand had his breath going ragged.

One of his hands anchored in her hair and gripped it—not too hard, but with enough pressure that she knew he wanted her to keep doing what she was doing.

So many times they rushed this part—the exploring and the touching—but tonight, she wanted to take her time.

And hoped he'd want to do the same with her.

Her hands caressed his warm skin. Her lips kissed and explored all his ink. Her senses were on overload as she inhaled his clean scent. There wasn't an inch of him that wasn't perfect to her.

"Paige?"

"Hmm?"

"I want to touch you."

"I want that too." Their words were like breathless whispers. "But I'm enjoying touching you too much to move right now."

Dylan reached out and stilled her hands, and Paige looked up at him. "How about we crawl onto that bed two feet away and touch each other?"

Her lips curved up in a sexy grin. "I do like the sound of that."

Before she could move, he reached down, grasped the hem of her shirt, and pulled it up and over her head, exposing the white lace bra. She held her breath as she waited for him to touch her, to cup her breasts with those magnificent hands.

But he didn't.

Instead, he slid his hands into the waistband of her yoga pants and slid them down her legs. She stepped out of them and loved the look on his face when he saw the matching white thong she was wearing.

He muttered a curse before saying, "Get on the bed." She took one step back toward it when he stopped her. "Uh-uh. I want you to crawl on the bed. I need to watch that sexy ass as you do it."

Oh. My. Dirty talk was also something she didn't know she loved until Dylan.

Turning, she did as she was told. Her moves were slow and deliberate, and she was rewarded with a growl from Dylan.

"You are such a good girl, listening to me like that," he said gruffly.

She was on all fours in the middle of the bed when she turned and looked at him over her shoulder. "Should I lie down now?"

He was kicking off his shoes and unzipping his jeans as he said, "Fuck yeah."

Dylan's eyes never left hers as she stretched out on

her back and waited for him. "Promise me something," she whispered.

"Anything."

"Promise you're going to touch me now. That you'll do it with your hands and your mouth."

His boxer briefs hit the floor and he climbed on the bed, stretching out beside her. "Baby, I'm going to do all that and so much more."

And he was true to his word.

For the rest of the night.

～～～

The next morning, Paige was getting ready for work as Dylan lay in bed watching her.

Something had changed last night. He couldn't put his finger on it, but there had been a point when he simply knew he didn't want to leave and go back to his hotel alone. So here he was, in her bed, watching her scramble around the room. It was a favorite pastime of his—watching her. She was efficient in everything she did, but watching her get ready in the mornings was completely different.

For starters, it was a complete transformation—she went from soft and sleepy to composed businesswoman in thirty minutes.

It normally took him that long to get out of the bed.

He loved watching her come out of the shower wrapped up in nothing but a towel as she moved around grabbing articles of clothing, trying to figure out what to wear. He'd lost count of the amount of time he sat and silently prayed for the towel to fall.

It never did.

Once her outfit was picked, she'd slip on her underwear.

She could rival an entire Victoria's Secret store with the selection she had. They'd been sleeping together for almost two months and he couldn't remember seeing the same selection twice.

It was a complete turn-on.

Then, in nothing but a bra and panties and her hair wrapped up in a towel, she'd put on her makeup.

So. Damn. Sexy.

She'd be on her tiptoes to get closer to the vanity mirror as she put on mascara and then step back and study herself before going on to the next task. Hair. He remembered the exact day she stopped pulling it back in clips and combs and bands and let it hang loose and wavy. He loved her hair and watching her dry it was far more erotic than it should have been—mainly because she spent a lot of time bent over to dry the layers, so he was either getting a fantastic view of her ass or her cleavage.

Yeah, he made sure he was positioned perfectly on the bed to see it all.

And he had a feeling that Paige left the door open for his entertainment.

She was so perfect it was almost like it was too good to be true.

As if reading his mind, she turned and looked at him. Today's lingerie was a deep shade of purple. The bra was sheer and the panties were too. Sitting up, he gave her a sexy leer. "How about going in late today?"

With a smile, she walked across the room to her closet and then... Holy hell. She bent over and slipped on a pair of stilettos. Dylan almost swallowed his tongue.

"Where…? When…?" he stammered. "Baby, why are you torturing me so early in the morning?"

"It's almost nine and I didn't think this was torture," she replied, but he knew that tone. She was teasing him and loving it. Standing there in sheer lingerie and heels? Who was this vixen?

"Please, you're almost preening over there. So what gives? Why the shoes?"

She shrugged and then turned toward the closet and pulled down a skirt. "Ariel keeps harping on me about my wardrobe so…I don't know. I thought I'd try it her way."

That's it, he thought. Jumping up from the bed, he stormed across the room and spun her around to face him. "Take it off," he growled. Paige misunderstood him and gave him a playful shove. "I'm serious, Paige. You're not changing who you are because of anyone. There isn't a damn thing wrong with you and how you dress. You don't need to be your sister's freaking clone!"

"That's not what—"

"It's exactly what you're doing!" he yelled. "Take the shoes off, take the skirt off and…and…get rid of them. Burn them. Throw them out. I don't care. But don't you dare change who you are because of some nonsense Ariel's throwing at you."

Her eyes were wide and her expression was…well, more than a little shocked. "Dylan, I…I don't know what to say to that."

"Say you'll get rid of this stuff," he spat.

"Dylan, please. Not now," she said wearily. "I need to present a certain image if anyone's going to take me seriously. So if I have to dress in a power suit and heels, then I'm willing to try."

"Paige," he began as he pinched the bridge of his nose and willed himself to calm down, "that is ridiculous. There isn't anything wrong with your wardrobe that would make people not take you seriously."

"Then why aren't they?" she demanded. "I do everything right! I handle everything for everybody, and it's not enough. So maybe, just maybe, I can try this and see if it works because I'm out of ideas, Dylan."

He saw the tears in her eyes and cursed himself. Wrapping her in his arms, he held her tight and did his best to keep his opinion to himself. He hated this—hated what her family was doing to her. The way they made her doubt herself.

With a small shove, Paige stepped out of his embrace, and he saw the fire back in her expression. Fine. He'd take the heat. He'd be her sounding board or punching bag or whatever she wanted—after all, he'd opened Pandora's box.

"Do you think I want to do this?" she said hotly as she rummaged around for a blouse. "I had to go shopping and have people tell me what to get and what goes with what because this isn't my style!"

He was about to remind her—again—that she didn't have to do this.

"The quality of my work isn't getting me anywhere. My punctuality and never missing a day's work isn't getting me anywhere. I've yet to prove my leadership skills because no one will let me lead! So if a skirt and shoes makes people take me seriously, then it's what I have to do!"

"Paige, you have great leadership skills and people know it. Every event I've gone to with you, people say it. Every meeting I've sat in on, people listen to you," he said soothingly. "You are great at what you do."

"All those things—the events and meetings—have not been within PRW," she countered. "I've got an office because I'm Robert Walters's daughter. And on top of that, I have Ariel to compete with, who manages to outdo me in everything. She's never come up with a campaign idea on her own. Don't get me wrong. She comes up with stuff—like the way she changed the Literacy Now lineup—but she doesn't follow through on it. She tosses out ideas and sees if they stick. She doesn't work. She makes everyone else do the grunt work."

Okay, now he couldn't keep his mouth shut. "That's because she knows you're going to do it!" he yelled with frustration. "Ariel knows you're always going to be there to do the grunt work because you want the approval, the attention, the pat on the fucking head! Dammit, Paige, don't you get it? This is like a sick game now! She keeps holding up the hoop and you keep jumping through it. And no matter how many times you jump or how high you jump, no one's going to congratulate you. So if you're waiting for that, if you're waiting for your sister or your coworkers or your father to pat you on the head and say it, you're wasting your damn time!"

"You're one to talk," she spat.

"What does that mean?"

"It means you're no different than I am. You were desperate for your parents' approval too!"

"Not the same thing," he argued. "And we've been over this already. We both know our need for approval is destructive. I chose to numb myself to it and not give a damn anymore. But you just keep going back for more!"

"Oh, please," she said with annoyance. "Don't try and play armchair psychologist. I'm trying to do my job. That's all."

The entire time he spoke, she dressed. Navy-blue pencil skirt and nude-colored shoes and blouse. She stormed past him into the bathroom, and when she came out, her hair was pulled back in a sleek ponytail in a silver clip.

The sight pissed him off.

Without uttering a single word to him, Paige moved around the room and collected her things. If she was leaving, he knew he needed to go too.

As it was, he was beyond ticked off and was ready to storm out right now.

So he quickly got dressed and was pulling his shoes on when she left the room. Before he could go after her, he heard the front door slam closed.

With a muttered curse, he walked out to the living room and found his keys. He had his hand on the front door handle when it opened and nearly hit him in the face. Paige strode by, mumbling under her breath. "Forget something?" he asked snidely, figuring maybe she'd come in to tell him to leave.

"My tire's flat again," she said without looking at him. "I have the card with the dealership's number on it somewhere in here. I forgot to program it on my phone."

When he saw her with the business card in her hand, he let out a huff. "You can call them from the car. I'll drive you to work so you're not late." Because God forbid she be late on her first day of dressing like a freaking Ariel clone.

They walked out of the house together, Paige already

calling the car dealership about the tire. Apparently, it was the one they had replaced only a few months ago, and she was demanding someone come to the house to replace it. She was direct, and if he hadn't been so annoyed with her, he'd have been seriously impressed with how she was firm while still polite.

Clearly, it was only him she felt comfortable enough to get ugly with.

And yeah, her words damn near killed him.

Not only because they were mean, but also because they were right.

But what did he expect? He'd hit her below the belt and she was returning the favor.

He sped out of her driveway and neighborhood and onto the highway. She slipped her phone into her purse after confirming the tire would be replaced before lunch. Again, he had to give her props for getting them to come and make a house call like that.

Traffic was a bitch, but that wasn't anything new. He wove around where he could and was doing his best to get her to work because he wanted to be alone. His emotions were too raw, too close to the surface, and it was normally when he was angry about something that he drank. So yeah, right now he was dealing with *that* demon as well.

"You might want to slow down," she murmured. "There's no prize for getting me to the office in record time."

"Wanna bet?" he said under his own breath. The prize was he'd get to have time to calm down and not have to look at her after having lost some respect for her.

He pulled off the highway at the exit to PRW and

went through the light as it was turning red. Hitting the gas, he wove around the slow-driving Honda in front of them and got behind a Dodge pickup. They were at least doing the speed limit now, he thought to himself. Their turn was up ahead, and he moved to the left to the turn lane as the arrow turned green.

Almost there, he chanted in his head. He cut the wheel and could see the PRW building when his head hit the driver's side window and the sound of Paige's scream filled the air.

And then everything went deadly silent.

Chapter 9

"I WANT ANSWERS, DAMMIT!"

Dylan's head was pounding, and he tried to move but he couldn't. "Easy, Mr. Anders. Give us one more minute."

Who was that?

"Test him! I want him tested for alcohol! He's done this before!"

This time he tried harder to sit up. Who was yelling like that?

"Sir!" the nurse said firmly. "I'm not going to tell you again. You have to leave. You are not allowed in here!"

Whoever it was must have left because the yelling stopped, but Dylan could tell there were still a lot of people in the room. Opening his eyes hurt—the light was far too bright. Wait…where was he?

"What's…what's going on?"

An older man came up beside him and started shining a light in his eyes. "You were in an accident, Mr. Anders. You need some stitches in your head and we need to x-ray your arm."

An accident?

"Where's Paige?" he said frantically, trying to sit up and look around the room. "Where's Paige? Is she all right?"

"We're going to need you to calm down," the nurse said from the other side of him. "Is Paige the woman who was in the car with you?"

"Yeah," he said, feeling sick to his stomach. Oh God…what if something had happened to her? What if something bad had happened and the last things they'd said to each other were those snarky remarks? "You have to find her! You have to see if she's okay!"

Nodding, the nurse walked away and was instantly replaced by another one. All around him, people were taking blood and checking his vitals while the doctor examined the cut on his head. Dylan blocked it all out. The only thing he could think about was Paige.

No, that wasn't true, he was trying to remember what had happened. They were driving on the highway, and she'd snapped at him for going too fast. Was that what had happened? Had he been speeding and crashed? No, that wasn't it, because he remembered getting off the exit ramp and getting to the light to turn onto the street where PRW was located. He was turning and then…nothing.

"Is he awake? Is that son of a bitch awake now?"

Great. Yelling guy was back.

But why is he looking to yell at me? Dylan wondered. He hadn't done anything wrong. Someone must have hit them. That was the only explanation he could think of.

"Sir, we have asked you repeatedly. Please don't make us call security," one of the nurses said, and Dylan wished he could turn his head and see who she was talking to.

There was more yelling, and from where Dylan was, he figured security had indeed been called. Good. The last thing he needed was some crazy person yelling at him when his head already felt ready to explode.

"We've got someone coming to do your stitches, Mr. Anders," the doctor said. "Once that's done, someone will take you down to radiology so we can look at your arm. In the meantime, try to relax. Do you need anything for the pain?"

"No," he said emphatically. The last thing he needed right now was anything to dull his senses. He could deal with the headache, and the pain in his arm was tolerable. "Can someone please tell me where Paige is and if she's all right?"

The doctor looked across the bed to the nurse who, in turn, looked toward another.

Unease began to trickle down his spine. Why wouldn't anyone tell him anything?

"Mr. Anders, as soon as we know something, someone will come in and talk to you," the nurse beside him said. And there was something in her tone. Something... very sterile—almost void of emotion.

Oh God. Something was wrong. Something was really wrong!

"I'm going to be sick," he said as he turned and retched.

It was an hour before the doctor showed up to stitch up his head, and then he was immediately taken to radiology. His left wrist was fractured and he was going to need a cast. He nodded and let them do whatever they needed to do, but still no one came to talk to him about Paige.

He was in the triage room when two police officers came in.

It was like he was in that hospital in Vegas all over again. Panic threatened to overwhelm him as he had a flashback.

Were they here to arrest him?

Had he killed someone?

Even though there was no alcohol or any narcotics in his system, Dylan still had no recollection of what had happened that morning. With no other choice, he sat and waited, willing to accept his fate.

"Mr. Anders," the first officer said as he stepped forward, "the doctors said they're going to release you soon. Can we ask you some questions?"

Dylan nodded, too afraid to speak.

He sat back and listened as the officer described the accident to him—someone had run the light. They had been speeding and hit the passenger side of Dylan's car, which had caused it to spin and hit a light pole.

He hadn't been at fault.

He hadn't caused the accident.

Tears stung in his eyes. "Paige," he said, his voice gruff and cracking. He looked up at the officer pleadingly. "No one will tell me what happened to her. Is she all right? How badly was she hurt?"

The officers looked at one another before facing him. "Um…last we heard, she was in surgery."

For a minute, Dylan thought he was going to be sick again. "Does… Did anyone call her family?"

The second officer nodded. "They're here. We had to escort her father out a little while ago."

Ah. So it was Robert Walters who had been yelling earlier.

"Mr. Anders, I'm sorry but…we have to ask—were you under the influence of any drugs or alcohol at the time of the accident?"

"No," he said firmly as it all started to make sense— why Robert was yelling and what he was trying to prove.

"The doctors and nurses took my blood. I'm sure they can verify that. I've been clean and sober for six months."

And what killed him was how neither looked like they believed him. It didn't matter that the other guy had run the light—once an addict, always an addict.

"Will you need a ride home? Your car was towed," the first officer said.

"No, but thanks. I'll call a friend to come and get me."

Once they were gone, Dylan found his phone and immediately called Riley—the first person he thought of. It didn't take long for him to explain the situation before Riley said he was on his way.

That left Dylan with nothing to do but wait.

And wait.

And wait.

A nurse came in with his discharge papers and explained to him the importance of not being left alone tonight with his head injury and instructions to follow up with his doctor as soon as possible. When she turned to leave, he reached out and touched her arm and said the only thing he could. "Please."

"She was taken to surgery for internal bleeding," the nurse said. "Beyond that, I don't know. I don't have any updates."

Emotion clogged his throat as he nodded and fought back the tears. "Thank you," he whispered.

With his discharge papers in hand, he walked to the waiting area to wait for Riley. His head was pounding, his wrist was throbbing, but more than anything, his heart ached. Paige was somewhere in this hospital, and he had no idea where. And what was worse, knowing it had been her father carrying on and making a scene earlier, Dylan doubted that he'd be welcome even if he found out what floor she was on.

Carefully, he walked to the corner of the large sitting area and took a seat. His whole body hurt now that he thought about it, and he knew it would only get worse over the next few days. He'd survive, he knew he would, but the temptation to swallow something to take the edge off was strong. Closing his eyes, he tilted his head and prayed Riley would get there soon.

———

"Dylan?" Riley said as he touched Dylan's shoulder.

Slowly, Dylan opened his eyes and his friend came into focus. "Oh. Hey. I must have fallen asleep. Sorry."

Riley smiled sympathetically and sat beside him. "I would have gotten here sooner, but you know LA traffic."

"I do, I do. I'm just glad you're here."

"Any update on Paige?"

Dylan told him what the nurse had shared with him. "I have no idea how she is, Ry. They're not going to get updates down here and—I hate to admit it—but I'm afraid to go upstairs."

"Why?"

"Her father was down here making a scene earlier, demanding I be tested for alcohol since I've done this before."

"Holy crap."

"Yeah, I know. So I think the last thing anyone wants is for me to go up to wherever she is and create a scene."

"Dylan, you have every right to see her. You weren't drinking. Someone ran a red light. I'm sure by now he knows that. He's upset. Any parent would be in that type of situation."

"I guess, but…" He looked at Riley helplessly. "I hate this. I hate that even when something's not my fault, I'm the first one everyone looks to blame."

"It's not like that, Dylan. This was a bad situation. Come on. Let's go find Paige and see what's going on."

"I don't know if I can."

Riley stood. "Then stay here and feel sorry for yourself. I'm going to find out what's going on. If her old man wants to start a fight, I'll gladly fight with him. You were hurt too, Dylan. You're a freaking mess, and there's nothing Robert Walters can do or say to keep you away from Paige. She's a grown woman and you're involved with her."

Gingerly, Dylan rose to his feet. The room began to spin, and he immediately reached out for Riley.

"Whoa. You okay?"

"I need a minute," Dylan admitted.

"They must have given you some strong stuff."

He shook his head. "I wouldn't let them give me anything."

"Are you crazy? You've got about fifteen stitches in your head and a broken wrist!"

He shook his head again. "I can't do it, Ry. I can't take the chance of letting myself get addicted to something again. Right now, I'm weak, man. It wouldn't take much to push me over the edge. I'll deal."

They walked slowly together through the emergency area and around to the main entrance of the hospital. At the front desk, they inquired about Paige and were directed to the sixth floor. Wordlessly, they walked to the elevators and rode up.

"I'll handle Paige's dad," Riley said firmly. "You're in no condition to go toe-to-toe with him, so promise me you'll let me do the talking if it's needed."

"Sure."

On the sixth floor, they followed the signs to the nurse's station, and once there, they spotted Paige's parents, Ariel, and Daisy in the waiting area. Robert immediately jumped to his feet, but his wife reached out and grabbed his hand before he could take a step.

Daisy got up and walked over to them. Dylan could tell that part of her was excited to meet Riley, but she kept her focus on him.

"How is she?" Dylan asked.

"She's getting moved to recovery," she replied. "A nurse came out a few minutes ago to update us."

"Do you know the extent of her injuries?"

Daisy shook her head. "Not really. All we know is Paige suffered blunt trauma from the force of the crash—the airbag deployed so that saved her from it being worse, I think." Then she registered how he looked. "And what about you? You're a mess!"

"Stitches, broken wrist, and all around banged up," he said quietly. "But I'm still able to leave and Paige isn't." He muttered a curse. "I hate this. She's going to hate me."

Reaching out, Daisy touched his good arm. "Dylan, it wasn't your fault at all. How could she hate you? We all know the other guy was speeding and ran the light."

Unable to help himself, he glanced in Robert's direction. "Really? Does he know that?"

Daisy looked over her shoulder briefly. "Dylan, it's his daughter who was hurt. Of course he was going to be upset. I was sitting downstairs with them when the police officers arrived and talked to him. Everyone knows the accident wasn't your fault."

It should have made him feel better, but it didn't.

He was about to comment on it when another couple around the age of Paige's parents walked over.

"Daisy," the woman asked frantically, "how is she? Is she out of surgery yet?"

"Hi, Mrs. Brown. Mr. Brown," she said softly. "They're moving her to recovery. The doctor will be out shortly to talk to us."

Mrs. Brown's hand rested over her heart. "That poor girl."

Mr. Brown nodded solemnly.

"Mr. and Mrs. Brown, this is Dylan Anders. He's Paige's boyfriend," Daisy introduced.

Dylan shook both of their hands. "Nice to meet you."

"Oh, you were in the car too?" Mrs. Brown asked, and Dylan nodded. She took in his appearance and her expression turned sympathetic. "How are you feeling? Do you need to sit down?"

"He probably should," Riley added, and motioned for all of them to sit down.

A minute later, they were all seated on the opposite side of the waiting room from Paige's parents. The Browns asked about the accident, and Dylan told them what he remembered. Unfortunately, Daisy decided to relate Robert's outburst but not why he specifically attacked Dylan.

"As a parent who's been through a situation like this,"

Mr. Brown said, "I can understand that. You need to find the person who hurt your child. I would imagine that, until he knew all the details, you were an easy target."

All Dylan could do was nod.

Mrs. Brown put a hand on Dylan's knee. "People say things in the heat of the moment they don't mean. I'm sure once emotions aren't running so high, it will be better. The important thing right now is Paige and her recovery."

He nodded again, unable to speak because the thought of her lying unconscious and injured was too much.

"We're going to go over and see how they're doing," Mrs. Brown said as she and her husband rose. "We hope you feel better, Dylan."

"Thank you."

Once they were out of earshot, Daisy leaned in so only he and Riley could hear her. "The Browns' daughter, Marni, was killed in a car accident several years ago. She and Paige were best friends. So really, they completely understand this situation. I'm sure they'll talk to the Walterses and calm them down. But they were right—we need to focus on Paige right now."

Dylan knew that, but all he wanted was to get an update on Paige and see her.

It took another fifteen minutes before the surgeon came out to talk to them. Everyone rose and walked over to hear the news. He looked at the group as a whole before focusing his attention on Paige's parents.

"She did great," he said. "She suffered blunt trauma, which caused the internal bleeding, and once we were able to go in and assess the extent of it, we did a partial splenectomy."

"What does that mean?" Robert asked.

"It's a partial removal of the spleen," the surgeon said before he explained the whole procedure to them.

"Is she awake yet?" Ariel asked.

"No, not yet. I expect it could be a couple of hours before she's awake, and then we'll move her to a room." He looked at the group again. "The procedure was done laparoscopically, so she has several small incisions she'll need to take care of while they heal, but this is less invasive than traditional surgery, and her healing time will be a little shorter."

"How soon until she can go home?" Robert asked.

"We're going to keep her here and monitor her for about three days. The recovery time from the procedure is generally four to six weeks. However, the internal bleeding wasn't her only injury from the accident, so I'd say Paige is looking at a six- to eight-week recovery."

"What other injuries?" Daisy asked, and Robert glared at her.

The surgeon smiled at her before mainly addressing the Walters. "She has a concussion, and her right ankle is broken. Considering the circumstances, it could have been a lot worse. She's going to be sore and bruised for a while, but because of the surgery, she'll be forced to take it easy and rest." He paused. "Any other questions?"

"When can we see her?" Robert asked.

"A nurse will come out when Paige is awake. Until then, why don't you grab something to eat? I'd say it will be at least an hour before she starts to wake up, and at that point, we'll need to check on her and talk with her before we let any family members visit." He gave them all a reassuring smile. "Paige is young and in good health, and we're confident she'll be on her feet in no time." Then he waved and walked away.

Now what? Dylan wondered.

Ariel was the first to step away from the group, announcing she was going to make some calls before getting something to eat. The two sets of parents stood off to the side talking while Dylan, Riley, and Daisy stood together.

"I think I'm going to head to the office," Daisy said quietly. Then she looked at Dylan. "Will you call me when she wakes up and let me know how she is?"

He nodded and noticed she was still cautiously keeping her gaze averted from Riley, so he took pity on her. "Riley, I don't think you've ever met Daisy before. She's Paige's assistant."

Riley gave her his famous grin as he took one of her hands in his and shook it. "It's a pleasure to meet you, Daisy. I'm sure Paige appreciates you taking the time to be here."

She blushed to the roots of her hair and let out a small giggle. "Thank you. It's so nice to meet you. I just wish it weren't…you know…like this."

Riley nodded. "I agree."

With one last giddy look at Riley, Daisy looked at Dylan again. "Are you going to be okay? You look like you should have been admitted."

"I'm more banged up than anything. Nothing life threatening. And as soon as I know Paige is awake and all right, I'll feel much better."

"Still," she replied. "You need to rest. Do you need anything? Can I do anything for you before I go?"

He smiled at her. She was a sweet woman. "I appreciate

the offer, but I'm good. I'm sure if I need anything, there are plenty of doctors and nurses around to help, and when I leave, the hotel should be able to get me what I need."

"Dude," Riley said, "you can't stay by yourself tonight. You'll come home with me and stay for a couple of days."

Normally, Dylan would have appreciated the offer, but right now, he wanted to be alone. No. He wanted to be with Paige. He wanted to turn back the clock and go back to this morning, before their argument.

Right now, he'd settle for sitting next to her bed and holding her hand until she woke up.

Robert Walters walked over and looked at Daisy. "Will you talk to the staff and let them know what's going on when you get back to the office?"

"Of course, sir," she replied. "No problem."

"Thank you."

Squeezing Dylan's good hand, she said goodbye. When she was out of sight, Robert turned to Dylan.

"May I speak to you for a moment?" Then he looked at Riley. "In private."

"You can talk to me in front of Riley," he said with as much bravado as he could muster at the moment.

Robert sighed and gave Riley a look of annoyance before focusing on Dylan again. "The police officers explained to me the cause of the accident."

Dylan nodded and waited for the apology.

"However, after some careful consideration, I think it would be best for Paige if this…affair the two of you are having came to an end."

Dylan's heart simply stopped for a moment.

"Um…excuse me?"

"Paige has a long recovery ahead of her," Robert explained. "And to be honest, she needs someone who is stable and reliable and able to be there for her."

"And you don't think I'm capable of that?" Dylan asked incredulously.

"No, I do not. I think you are someone who requires help and assistance. I think Paige has spent a lot of time taking care of you, and I haven't seen that reciprocated."

Riley went to speak, but Dylan cut him off.

"If you'll remember correctly, you assigned her to take care of me and babysit me even though no one asked you to," Dylan countered.

"The Literacy Now people asked," Robert said smugly. "You have a reputation, Dylan, and we needed to make sure you didn't embarrass anyone."

"And have I?"

"No, but that was Paige's doing. We're at a point in the campaign where your commitment will be done, and then how you behave will no longer be a concern," he went on. "So there's no reason for you and Paige to keep seeing each other."

"I hate to be the one to break this to you, but Paige and I weren't seeing each other only because of the campaign. I'm spending time with your daughter because she's an amazing woman. I like her, I respect her—I love her!"

Robert gave a snort of disgust and looked around to make sure no one was paying attention to them. "I'm sure you think you're in love with Paige, but in time, you'll realize it would be a mistake."

"And why is that?" Dylan sneered.

"Because you could never fit in with her life. Paige is a girl who works a nine-to-five job. She goes to a book club and has a small circle of friends, and she's happy that way. You, on the other hand, are a recovering addict who plays in a rock-and-roll band and travels the world and is promiscuous," he added with disgust. "I'm sure my daughter was infatuated with you, but it will pass."

"Now wait a minute," Riley interrupted. "Who are you to pass judgment on us?"

"I didn't say—"

"Yeah, you did," Riley snapped. "What you just said went beyond insulting. Do you think we're sitting here looking at you and assuming you're a closed-minded tight ass because you wear a suit and tie and work in an office?"

Robert sighed. "Mr. Shaughnessy, I don't know any such thing about you. Nothing in all my recollections tells me that's the type of person you are. In Dylan's case, however, it's all public knowledge. Any Google search of his name will bring up his every indiscretion for all the world to see." He paused. "That's not the kind of man I want for my daughter. She deserves someone better."

"That's Paige's decision to make," Dylan said, anger and adrenaline coursing through him.

For a moment, Robert studied him. "How is it going to look when your name is dragged through the headlines for causing yet another accident? What if your sobriety is brought back into question? The public is only willing to be forgiving so many times."

"Everyone knows I didn't cause that accident," Dylan argued. "The cops, the doctors, everyone!"

"The press hasn't caught wind of it yet. But one phone call could start the speculation," Robert said with deadly calm. "Tell me, Dylan, are you willing to deal with all of that again? Are you willing to put your band back in the spotlight for your bad behavior? Will your record label be willing to have you associated with them? Or your insurance companies? Tell me."

Dylan had never known rage like this before. His hand was clenched at his side, and it took every ounce of strength not to lash out, but that would add fuel to an already out-of-control inferno. Robert Walters was good at what he did—he had proven that to Dylan already. And there wasn't a doubt in his mind that he would do his best to destroy Dylan in the public eye and succeed.

"Leave, Dylan," Robert said. "Finish your commitment to Literacy Now as you're contracted to do, so we don't have to go after you legally for that. I'd hate for your hours of community service to come into question too. That could lead to jail time, right?"

Son of a bitch.

"I'll talk to Paige," her father went on. "I'll tell her this all became too much. That you're injured and need to go heal someplace and can't come and see her. She'll understand. She doesn't argue with me."

"Dylan, don't go along with this," Riley said urgently. "We can fight this! He's threatening you with slander!"

"Mr. Shaughnessy, I have a great many connections, and I'd hate to have to drag you into this too. I think we both know that with Dylan's past, it wouldn't take much for people to believe he'd fallen into his old ways." Then his eyes narrowed as he continued to look at Riley. "You have a daughter, don't you?"

Riley went stock-still.

"Wouldn't you do everything in your power to protect her? To make sure no one hurts her?" When Riley didn't respond, a smug smile crossed Robert's face. "You know you would. Don't fault me for doing the same."

For several minutes, they all stood in silence and Dylan was at war with himself. He didn't want to leave Paige—not like this. Not ever. Unfortunately, he knew Robert would make good on his threats.

"If I leave," he began gruffly, "if I stay away from Paige…"

"The topic of you being at fault will never come up from me. And I'll handle the press to make sure it doesn't go any further. Are we clear?"

Even though it killed him, Dylan nodded.

"Good," Robert said. "Good day to you both."

Without a word, Dylan turned and made his way to the elevators. Riley was at his side. As they rode down to the main floor, neither spoke.

Walking out to Riley's car, the only conversation was about getting some of Dylan's things from the hotel and then Riley taking him to stay with him and Savannah.

At this point, it didn't matter to Dylan where he stayed or what happened to him.

Nothing mattered.

Because he'd just lost everything.

———~~~———

For four days, she waited.

Every time someone walked into her hospital room, she hoped it would be Dylan. Every time the phone rang, she thought it would be him.

But it wasn't.

Now, as a nurse was wheeling her down to her mother's car, she felt nothing but an overwhelming sense of sadness. Everyone had told her about Dylan's injuries, and she ached for him. She knew that right before the accident, she'd been mad at him, but she also knew she would have gotten over it.

Now? Not so much.

On top of all her other injuries, her heart was broken too.

The entire way down to the car, the nurse chatted with her about the weather and current events. Paige knew she answered when she needed to, but she just wanted to get out of the hospital and go home. After many conversations on the subject over the last several days, she had finally convinced her family that she wanted to spend her recovery in her own home. They had argued how it would be better for everyone—meaning them—for her to stay with them, but Paige had held firm. So her father hired a home health aide to stay with her for the next week.

Between the cast on her foot and the discomfort from the incisions, she knew she was going to need the help. But the doctors had confirmed that as long as she took it easy, there was no reason she couldn't be on her own after that.

The weather was a cool sixty degrees and the slight breeze felt glorious after being in the hospital for four days. Paige breathed in deeply, and even though LA didn't have the freshest air, it still felt wonderful.

Getting into her mother's Mercedes wasn't easy or graceful, but with a little help, she finally managed to sit in the passenger seat. Letting out a breath, she closed her eyes and waited for her mother to join her.

"Are you sure you don't want to come and stay with us for a couple of days?" her mother asked as soon as she sat behind the wheel.

"Mom, we've been over this. I want to be in my own home and sleep in my own bed. I know you're worried, but with the aide Dad hired coming to stay with me, it's going to be fine. I'm sore more than anything, so I think it's going to be better for me to be someplace where I'm comfortable."

"I know, I know. I worry. It's a mother's natural instinct and right to want to take care of her children."

That made Paige smile. If only her father were this compassionate, they'd be the perfect parents. "Honestly, Mom, I am so tired from not sleeping well in the hospital, I'm probably going to sleep for days."

"That's not the worst idea, Paige. Your body needs rest. I know you normally get antsy and want to get up and run around and work, but you have to force yourself to stay put and let your body heal."

"Trust me, no forcing will be necessary. I'm so sore that I plan to move as little as possible."

Her mother reached over and patted Paige's knee. "My poor baby. I hate this for you. Do you have your prescriptions?"

"They're all called in to the pharmacy and being delivered later this afternoon. I told them not to come until after three."

"It's only noon now, so you'll be home and settled in by then. Your father said the aide should be arriving by four. I'll stay with you until then."

"Thanks, Mom."

They drove the rest of the way in silence, and Paige couldn't wait to be alone in her own home. Even though there was going to be an aide there, Paige didn't think that would be an issue. More than anything, she wanted time alone to call Daisy. The few times they had spoken, her mother or her sister or her father always showed up, so Paige didn't feel free to talk. They would yell at her for trying to work from her hospital bed.

What they didn't realize was she wasn't trying to work.

She was trying to find out information about Dylan: Where was he? Was he okay? And why hadn't he contacted her?

The day after the accident, her father had come to see her and tell her Dylan wouldn't be coming back. He'd been so apologetic and sympathetic, but...Paige knew her father and something didn't sit right with her about the whole thing. For starters, there was no way Dylan would break up with her through her father. Never. They had talked about her family issues enough times that she was confident in that fact. Then there was the way her father told her. He was never sympathetic about anything. He was kind, sure, but he was never particularly compassionate about things like this.

The whole situation stank, and she wanted to find out what was going on.

It was possible her fight with Dylan had been a breaking point for him. She also knew that even if it were, he'd still tell her to her face that it was over. Dylan didn't shy away from anything. Over the last several months, she'd noticed that about him—it didn't matter if a situation made him uncomfortable or if people made him feel like an outcast; he stood his ground and took whatever they had to throw at him.

So either he was injured more than anyone was telling her, or something else was going on. And if anyone could find out for her, it was Daisy.

Soon they pulled up to her town house, and Paige almost wept at the sight of it. Getting out of the car was a little easier than getting in was, but it also put a lot of strain on her abdominal muscles. Together, they got into the house and Paige immediately went to her bedroom door and froze.

Her bed was still unmade.

Dylan's things were still scattered around the room.

Not that there was a lot of them—he didn't believe in keeping too much there—but there was enough that it made her heart still for a moment.

A brush, a shirt, a jacket…

"Oh dear," her mother said as she came up behind her. "I guess we should have sent somebody over to clean up and put fresh sheets on your bed."

Probably, Paige thought to herself. But…the thought of sliding between the sheets they had last shared together gave her a little peace too.

"What can I do for you, Paige? Do you need help getting changed? Or are you going to take a nap right now? Tell me and I'll help you."

"I…I think I'm going to change into some pajamas and sleep for a little while if that's okay."

What she wanted to sleep in was Dylan's shirt. What she ended up sleeping in was one of her own. Her mother had pulled a nightshirt out of her drawer and helped her change.

"You know, when you're feeling better, we can take you to a plastic surgeon and I'm sure he can do something about those incisions," her mother said very matter-of-factly.

Paige didn't respond. She carefully slid under her blankets—no easy feat with her casted foot. Her mother fussed around and stuffed a pillow under the blankets to keep her foot elevated, but she knew in a matter of minutes, she'd end up moving it away.

"Thanks, Mom," she said instead, and within minutes, she was sound asleep.

She slept much longer than she thought she would.

When Paige woke up, it was dark out. Turning on her bedside light, she saw it was after eight. She called out and smiled when a middle-aged woman in scrubs poked her head into the room. "Ms. Walters?"

Paige carefully sat up and said, "Hi. You can call me Paige."

The woman stepped into the room and smiled back at her. "I'm Kathy, and I'm going to be your roommate for the next five days."

"I'm sorry I wasn't awake when you arrived. I didn't get much sleep in the hospital and it felt good to be in my own bed."

"I'm sure. Why don't I help you up, and you can use the bathroom? Your mother mentioned you needed fresh sheets on the bed, so if it's all right with you, I'll change them now."

It was on the tip of her tongue to say no, that the faint smell of Dylan's cologne helped her sleep, but she didn't want to seem pathetic. "Sure," she said instead. "That would be great."

The next few minutes were spent navigating around her bedroom and bathroom on crutches and making an attempt to freshen up by brushing her teeth and washing her face. Her reflection was enough to make her shudder, but really, who did she need to impress?

Out in the living room, she met up with Kathy.

"Are you hungry?" Kathy asked. "Your mother went shopping and stocked your refrigerator with some of your favorites." She walked over to the refrigerator and opened it so she could tell Paige what was there. "I'm sure you'll have a hard time choosing from all these wonderful dishes."

Somehow Paige doubted that. Her mother was a health-food fanatic and thought everyone was. "Did she get any cake?"

"Um…no."

"Any ice cream?"

Kathy opened the freezer. "No."

"Anything to make a sandwich? Cold cuts? Cheese?"

"Um…I don't see any."

"Frozen pizza?"

With a chuckle, Kathy closed the refrigerator and turned toward her. "So this was a case of your mom buying her favorites."

That made Paige laugh too. "Bingo!"

"Okay, I can go to the store for you, or I can call in an order for some takeout. Which would you prefer?"

Paige hobbled along on her crutches into the kitchen and over to her pantry. She pulled out a bag of tortilla chips and handed them to Kathy. Then a jar of salsa and another of queso dip. Next, she went over to the refrigerator and pulled out a can of soda and turned and smiled. "Chips and salsa—not exactly the loaded nachos I prefer, but in a pinch, it will do."

"A girl after my own heart," Kathy said with a grin. "Why don't you sit down on the sofa, and I'll make you a tray and bring this out?"

"Thanks. I appreciate it."

Once on the sofa, she reached for the remote and turned on the TV. Flipping through the channels, she ended up on HGTV and settled in to hunt for houses with tonight's couple.

"I love these shows," Kathy said as she came in and put the tray down beside Paige. "Some of the houses these people look at are amazing."

"Oh, I know. I love my home, but I wouldn't mind some of those million-dollar houses," Paige said as she reached for a chip.

"If I had that big of a budget, I would want a swimming pool, a gourmet kitchen, and a guesthouse for relatives. What about you?"

"Definitely with you on the pool and kitchen, but I would need a spa-like master bathroom. Something with a huge soaking tub and a shower that had a dozen jet sprays."

"Now that does sound nice. Very decadent."

They watched the show and commented on the couple's choices, and when it was over, Kathy changed over the laundry. Paige asked for her cell phone, and while Kathy was doing her thing, she took advantage of the time alone to call Daisy.

"Oh my God! Are you home? Are you okay? Do you

need anything? I could totally go on a bakery run for you! Do you want me to? It's not too late, I can—"

"Daisy," Paige interrupted.

"Oh, right. Sorry. How are you?"

"Sore but so happy to be home."

"I'm sure. Your mom picked you up from the hospital, right?"

"She did. And now I have a very nice home health aide staying with me. I fell asleep as soon as I got home, and my mom left as soon as the aide got here I guess. Not that I mind, but I feel bad that I slept for so long."

"Don't feel bad. It's good for you."

Paige asked about work and the campaign and general business stuff before she asked what she really wanted to know. "Have you heard from Dylan?"

On the other end of the phone, Daisy sighed. "Only when I called to give him next week's change of schedule."

"What change of schedule?"

"Ariel figured with his injuries, he wouldn't be up to doing the appearance at the Fishing for Books event at the pier. So she asked me to call and let him know he didn't have to do it."

"Oh."

"You haven't heard from him?" Daisy asked, concern lacing her voice.

"No."

"What did he say to you when you saw him at the hospital? Did he act funny?"

Paige paused. "I…I didn't see him at the hospital. He never came to see me."

Daisy was quiet for a moment. Normally that was a good thing, but right now Paige had to wonder why.

"Okay, I'm going to apologize if I'm out of line…"

"But…?"

"Your dad made a huge scene at the hospital. Seriously huge. He was yelling at the doctors to test Dylan for alcohol, and then he was yelling at the cops to arrest him for drunk driving, telling everyone how Dylan had done this sort of thing before."

Paige gasped in horror. "No!"

"Unfortunately, he did," Daisy said. "It took a while to calm him down and the nurses threw him out at one point. The police officers came and explained what had happened, and I thought he seemed okay with it…"

Paige sighed. "But…?"

"But when Dylan and Riley came up when you were having surgery, your dad was just…glaring at him. After the surgeon came out to give us an update, I was standing with them when your dad came over and sort of… you know…prompted me to leave. Last I saw, the three of them were standing together and Dylan promised to call me with any updates. When he didn't, I thought it was because he was recovering too."

"Do you… I mean… Do you think my father is the reason I haven't heard from Dylan?" Paige asked weakly.

"Honestly, Paige, it wouldn't surprise me at all. Things were tense, and while I don't blame your dad for being upset, he was sort of rough on Dylan." She paused. "Have you tried calling him?"

"No. I was so upset that he didn't come to see me, even though I know he's hurt too. I thought he would have at least called or…something."

"I'm so sorry," Daisy said quietly. "I really am."

"Yeah. Me too."

"So what are you going to do? Are you going to call him or…?"

"I don't know. Part of me wants to, but now that I know what happened, I'm even more confused about it."

"Why?"

"He should have called me and talked to me about this—about my dad. We've talked about how…complicated my relationship with him is, and I thought he would understand that by now. We…we fought about it that morning. If he's still mad about our fight, that's fine. But he should respect me enough to at least call and see how I am."

"I agree," Daisy said. "But…in his defense, he's hurt too, Paige. And not just physically. That had to be hard on him—another accident and then having your dad throwing accusations at him like that."

While Paige knew Daisy was right, she was still torn. And as much as she wanted to go to him and comfort him, as well as confront him, she couldn't. She was a mess in her own way right now and needed to think about all this and figure out what she was going to do.

"I can't believe I'm going to miss the big launch," she finally said, deciding to change the subject.

"There's no way you can do it," Daisy agreed. "I think if it were only your ankle, it would be one thing, but you need to take it easy for a while."

"What's going on with the campaign? Is everything set for the launch?"

Daisy sighed. "I don't know. Ariel took it over and I'm out of the loop. But I can find out for you tomorrow if you'd like."

Did she even want to know, or was it better to put this whole thing behind her? By the time she was able to go back to work, the Literacy Now campaign would be a done deal and PRW would be onto something else, another cause, another campaign.

"You know what? It doesn't matter. It's probably best if I take myself out of work mode and focus on getting better."

"I think that's a great idea. Hey, how about I pick up lunch from your favorite deli tomorrow and bring it to you and we can eat together? It's been a while since we've done that."

Paige couldn't help but smile. "I would love that. Thank you. But are you sure? It would mean taking an extended lunch break."

Daisy laughed. "Are you kidding? I'm not even clocking out! I'm going to tell everyone I'm coming to see you to do work stuff." Then she paused and cleared her throat. "I mean...if that's okay with you."

"Tell you what, you bring me some cake pops and a Frappuccino and I'll tell payroll you need to take a four-hour lunch at least once a week while I'm recovering!"

"Yeah!" Daisy said excitedly. "It's a deal!"

When they hung up, Paige reached over and munched on her chips and salsa and thought about what her assistant had shared with her.

If her father had done what Daisy had said—caused a scene and accused Dylan of causing the accident—then she could understand Dylan being distant.

If Dylan was still upset over their argument from that morning, her father's accusations certainly hadn't helped matters.

But if she meant something to him—anything at all like he meant to her—shouldn't he have called by now?

"That's the million-dollar question," she said with a sigh.

Kathy came into the room with a smile. "I still think you need something a little more nutritious than nachos," she said and winked. "But we'll start to worry about that tomorrow."

That made Paige grin. "My assistant will be bringing me lunch tomorrow, and it's somewhat on the healthy side—turkey and avocado on whole wheat."

"And…?"

"And what?" Paige asked innocently.

Studying her for a minute, Kathy gave her a look that said she didn't think that was all.

"Okay, fine. It also has bacon."

"And…?"

Paige told her about the cake pops and Frappuccino. "They're my weakness."

Kathy's smile grew. "Mine too. Ask her to bring extra for me and I'll pay her when she gets here."

"Not a problem," Paige replied. "Did my mom show you to the guest room?"

"She did, and it's a beautiful room. I almost feel a little guilty sleeping in there."

"I wish I could go up and show you where everything is," Paige said. Her home was two stories, with the guest rooms upstairs. She loved the floor plan because it managed to give everyone privacy. "I know the bathroom is totally stocked, but if there's anything you need and can't find, let me know."

"It's all good, Paige. I brought everything I needed

with me and you keep your guest rooms stocked like a five-star hotel. This is almost like a vacation for me."

Somehow she doubted that, but she appreciated the sentiment. And as Kathy went about doing her thing, Paige sat and only half listened to the television, her mind immediately going back to Dylan. Should she call? Text? Wait him out?

"No," she finally said. From the beginning—or close to it—she had vowed to go after what she wanted where he was concerned, and she wasn't going to shy away now. Grabbing her phone, she pulled up his number and dialed. Her heart was racing madly in her chest as she silently prayed he'd answer and tell her this was all a mistake—his staying away.

But he didn't answer.

It went directly to voicemail.

"Hey, this is Dylan. You know what to do."

Even with the mental pep talk, Paige couldn't seem to make herself speak, and reverting to her old ways, she simply hung up and prayed that he'd at least see the missed call and know she was thinking of him.

Chapter 10

"HOW LONG HAS IT BEEN LIKE THIS?"

"A week."

"Doesn't anyone think it's…odd? That maybe something else needs to be done?"

"I think right now they're grasping at straws and doing what they can."

They paused.

"This can't keep going. Someone needs to be the voice of reason."

Savannah reached out to stop Vivienne from going down to Riley's man cave. "I'm one step ahead of you."

For a week, Dylan had been staying with the Shaughnessys, and he'd been under twenty-four-hour watch. Riley, Matt, Julian, and Mick had been taking turns being with him because he was so depressed and somehow had managed to find an unopened magnum of Grey Goose that he kept close to his body with his casted arm. No one was willing to argue with him about it, thinking he'd eventually snap out of the funk he was in, but he'd gotten more despondent.

"He's not sleeping," Savannah explained. "That's what triggered the 'round-the-clock schedule. He's so fragile, and all he does is stay down there in the recliner playing chess."

"Has he eaten?"

"Barely. I bring food, and he eats a little. I bring him

bottles of water, and he's drinking those. I keep waiting for him to let go of that bottle of vodka."

"How'd he get it?"

"It's not ours, so he had to have gotten it from the hotel when he and Riley stopped there on their way home from the hospital."

"Has he had any?" Vivienne asked.

"No, but it's the fact that he has it and is holding on to it that's worrying everyone."

"What's the plan, then? You said you were one step ahead of me."

"I'm going to interview him," Savannah said sweetly as she picked up her coffee mug and took a sip.

"Um…what?" Vivienne asked in confusion.

"The only way to fight against a bully is to take away the power. For the last couple of days, I've been strategizing with the guys and my old boss, Tommy, over at *Rock the World* and managed to get some press time to present Dylan's story. He hasn't given any interviews about his past addiction, rehab, or either accident, and we're going to give him the outlet to do it."

"Wow, but…what if he doesn't agree?"

Savannah grinned. "I can be very persuasive. Trust me. And I'm not afraid to fight dirty either."

"Savannah, no offense, but the last thing Dylan needs right now is one more person manipulating him."

"I'm not going to manipulate him. I know how to do my homework."

The look on Vivienne's face showed she wasn't convinced. "What are you going to do?"

The doorbell rang and Savannah gracefully got up from her seat. "You're about to find out."

—⁓—

"Checkmate."

"Unreal," Riley said as he collapsed in his seat. "Beat me again."

Dylan glared at him. "You weren't trying."

"Dude, I've been playing chess for six days and I don't even know how!" Riley said with a laugh. "You should be impressed the game lasted longer than twenty minutes this time." He looked at his watch. "I'm ordering pizza tonight. Why don't you go grab a shower before Matt gets here?"

With a shrug, Dylan stood and stretched, the magnum of vodka still in his hand. He knew it was pissing everyone off that he had it, but he didn't care. He wasn't going to drink it. That wasn't why he had it. He had it to prove he was strong—stronger than he'd ever been—and it didn't matter what temptation was right there in his lap, he could beat it.

On the surface, he was fine. He was healing. His bruises from the accident were fading, and his wrist wasn't throbbing quite so much. It was his heart that wasn't healing.

Why. Why had he let Robert Walters put him in this situation? Why had he caved?

Because you already knew Paige was too good for you and didn't deserve a lifetime of dealing with your past and reputation.

Oh, yeah. That's why.

There wasn't a minute that had gone by when he hadn't thought about her. Worried about her. Longed for her. Unfortunately, there wasn't a doubt in his mind that if he tried to reach out to her, Robert would hold true to his threat and annihilate him in the press. How could he, with a clear conscience, let that happen? After all, it wouldn't only affect him. It would also affect the band. His friends. His family.

And Paige.

He'd seen the missed calls, and each and every time he had to fight with himself to keep from calling her.

Maybe there'd come a day when he'd be able to think about her without his heart squeezing painfully in his chest, or maybe, just maybe he'd get to see her, even from a distance, so he could know she was okay.

But that day wasn't today.

So he went into the bathroom and showered. He brushed his teeth. He changed his clothes. It was about all he could handle. God, his friends were probably so tired of this. Of him. It was probably time for him to leave Riley's and move back into his suite at the Beverly. Dylan knew he was strong enough. If he could sit here with a bottle of vodka in his hands all day, every day for a week without the slightest urge to drink it, he knew he could handle it alone.

He looked at his reflection in the mirror and grimaced. Yeah, the bruises were fading, but he hadn't shaved, and he looked worse than he ever had after a bender.

Something had to give.

Just not today.

He opened the guest bathroom door and stepped into Riley's basement living area and froze. "What the hell?"

In front of him stood…everyone—Riley, Savannah, Matt, Vivienne, Julian, Mick, and a couple of people he didn't know. He was tempted to step back into the bathroom and slam the door, but Savannah's words stopped him.

"We are not going to let you destroy yourself, Dylan."
Wait…what?

She looked at the people around her and then took a step forward. "What Robert did and threatened to do wasn't right. It wasn't fair, and it certainly wasn't ethical. And what's worse is it left him in total control—he'll be able to dangle that threat over your head forever." She paused. "Unless you beat him at his own game."

Panic threatened to overwhelm him as he looked from one person to the other. No, he couldn't do this—couldn't do anything! The thought of fighting Robert and losing and hurting Paige even more was too much.

"I can't beat him," Dylan said gruffly. "My past speaks for itself."

"Dylan," Mick said as he came to stand next to Savannah, "our PR people already took care of the accident story. No one thinks you caused it. There were so many witnesses, and it's public record the other guy was at fault."

"Mick, I saw the news."

"Yeah, yeah, yeah…you got one or two of the sleazier tabloids who wanted to try to get some attention by bringing up the Vegas incident, but no one took the bait and the story died." He smiled and took another step forward. "Allow me to introduce you to some people," he began, and motioned toward the group of people behind him.

"There on the end in the black jacket? That's Erik Anderson. He's the head of the legal team at the label. Next to him? That's Michelle Jacobs, head of PR. Beside her is Richard Patrick, our insurance broker. Over there next to Julian? You know that's Tommy from *Rock the World*. And sitting on the arm of the sofa is Anthony Litchford, the best damn photographer in the entertainment industry."

Dylan was confused. He looked warily at Mick. "And? I don't understand what this all means."

"It means," Riley said as he took his turn stepping forward, "we all have your back. For every threat that Robert made, we have someone here to counter it."

But Dylan shook his head. "I don't want to fight him. I don't. I…I can't."

"Yes, you can," Savannah said firmly. "You're going to sit down with me, and we're going to talk, and then your story is going to be told. Why? Because the longer you stay silent, the more power he has."

"We can sue him for slander," Mick said. "Actually, we can do more than that—we can make sure PRW is done in the PR industry."

"No," Dylan insisted. "Don't."

"Why not?" Mick asked with annoyance. "That prick threatened you and pretty much everyone in this room. Give me one good reason why we can't crush him."

His shoulders dropped as his entire body went lax with defeat. "Because he's Paige's father. If you destroy PRW, you're destroying her, and she doesn't deserve that."

Everyone grew quiet.

"I appreciate how you're all here and that you want to do this for me, I really do, but…I don't want to stoop to that level."

"Will you do the interview?" Savannah asked softly.

He nodded. "That I'll do. But I don't want this to be an attack piece on Robert. Promise me that."

She frowned. "Okay, fine. But…"

"Am I late? Oh my God, am I late? I got lost and…"

Dylan looked up as Daisy raced down the stairs. Everyone turned and looked at her, and Dylan had to wonder what she was doing there.

"Sorry, sorry, sorry," she said breathlessly. "I got a little lost."

Savannah walked over and hugged her and took a folder from the young woman's hands. Then she turned and faced Dylan with a grin. "We're not going to need to do an attack piece on Robert," she said as she waved the folder. "Not anymore, anyway."

There was a time when Dylan remembered Riley talking about how brilliant his wife was, and it looked like he was about to have a front row seat to finding that out for himself.

"I have to admit, I never quite got the appeal of this."

"I think it's something you either enjoy or you don't," Paige said as she studied the chessboard. She'd loved playing the game with her grandfather, and she loved playing it with Dylan. With Kathy? Not so much. "Sorry. We can do something else."

Kathy sat back and smiled. "Can I ask you something?"

"Sure."

"I've been here with you now for the better part of two weeks," she began, "and physically, you are doing great. Your incisions are healing well, you've said you're not uncomfortable, and you are maneuvering around on your crutches like a pro."

"O-kay…"

"You've been taking it easy and getting plenty of rest, and I was wondering why you're not more interested in getting back to work."

Paige looked at her in confusion. "What do you mean?"

Shifting in her seat, Kathy was quiet for a moment. "Okay, most of the younger patients I work with are champing at the bit to go back to work. I know your assistant has come here several times and—excuse me if I'm being too bold but—you never let her talk to you about work. I guess I'm curious. Don't you like your job?"

"Not really," she said and then gasped. It was the first time she had ever admitted it out loud. "I mean… I…um…"

Reaching toward her, Kathy tried to put her at ease. "Paige, it's all right. Really. I know it's none of my business, but if you want to talk about it…"

And then it was like opening the floodgates. For the next thirty minutes, she told Kathy about her positions in the company and her hopes and frustrations and how she felt like no one took her seriously and how it was like being undermined at every turn. "I know that must sound awful because I'm talking about my own family."

"Sometimes family can be the worst offenders," Kathy countered. "Paige, if you're miserable, you should do something about it. You've got at least another month at home—use that time to do a little soul-searching and a little job hunting. You can spend your days thinking about what it is that would make you happy."

"I wish it were that simple. My father—"

"Isn't going to be happy," Kathy interrupted. "There's no doubt about that, but he'll get over it. If he hasn't appreciated your hard work by now, then it really shouldn't be an issue." She paused and then a big smile crossed her face. "Okay, let me ask you something—and you have to say the first thing that comes to your mind. No thinking about it, okay?"

Paige nodded.

"If you could have any job you wanted, what would it be?"

"I'd have my own small PR firm where I could work directly with clients."

Then Kathy spread her arms in front of her as if to say, *There you go! What's stopping you?*

"I don't want to be in direct competition with my family. How would that look?"

"I would imagine you wouldn't be taking on the same kind of clients. Where your father's company takes on big corporate accounts, you'd get to work with the small business owner or the new business owners and help them create their image. I think it could be very exciting!"

And it could. Paige knew that. She'd dreamed of it, but…could she do it? "I don't know… I'm not good at that sort of thing."

"What do you mean?"

"You know, standing up for myself and making waves. I tend to just…" She shrugged. "I'm the push-over of the family, and I tend to do what I'm told and not argue about it."

"Hmm…maybe it's time to change that up a bit,"

Kathy said. Then she rose and went toward the kitchen. "What are you thinking of for dinner tonight? Want me to whip something up, or did you have something specific in mind?"

Paige heard the question, but her mind was on their conversation. "You decide," she answered distractedly. Relaxing against the sofa cushions, she let the idea take root. Change things up. Could she do that? It was the perfect time for it. Forced to stay home and recuperate, she wasn't in the office to take care of everyone and make sure work was being done. And though she refused to let Daisy come over and talk about work, Ariel had called enough to complain and ask questions that Paige knew they were foundering a bit without her.

And boy did it feel good.

It was petty but…there it was.

Her iPad was on the coffee table, and she reached for it and began doing a little research on what she would need to get started. Office space would be nice, but if she had to, she could work from home to start out and convert her second guest room into an office. That would save her some money. And she was involved with a lot of different groups, so she could start looking for clients, and it wouldn't mean taking anyone away from PRW.

She had no idea how long she had been searching and scrolling when Kathy came into the room with a tray of food.

"I decided to go with the enchiladas I picked up from Whole Foods yesterday. I hope that's all right."

Paige blinked at her a few times as she tried to remember why Kathy was bringing in food. *Oh, right.*

It was dinnertime. As if on cue, her stomach growled. "That sounds great and smells even better. Thank you."

"You seemed pretty engrossed in what you were doing, so I thought you'd want to eat out here. Or we can eat at the dining room table if you'd like?"

"No, no, this is fine. Thanks!" It was beginning to make her feel a little lazy to keep enjoying her meals while sitting on the sofa, but it was the easiest way to keep her ankle elevated while still being comfortable. Positioning the tray over her lap, Paige inhaled the wonderful aroma of the meal. "I think I'm going to get spoiled."

"Why?"

"Between you cooking for me and all the takeout, by the time this cast comes off, I'm going to forget what it's like to cook!"

That had Kathy laughing. "I'm sure it will come back to you soon enough, like riding a bike." She looked around at their dinner trays. "I'm going to grab some drinks, so don't wait on me. I'll be back in a minute."

Manners that had been instilled in her since childhood prevented Paige from picking up her fork. The tray had just about everything she could need on it—napkins, silverware, a small cup of sour cream—and as soon as she had a drink, she'd be all set.

Kathy came into the room and placed their beverages down before picking up the TV remote. "How about a little TV while we eat?"

"Sounds good to me. And if we can find something that is not house-hunting related, all the better." They had watched a marathon of the show the day before, and Paige was completely burned out on the whole concept.

"I'm with you on that one," Kathy commented as she began scanning the channels. She stopped at one as she situated her own dinner tray. "I hope you don't mind, but...I'm addicted to these entertainment news shows."

Paige waved her off. "That's fine. I could go for a little mindless TV right now. My brain is too full of ideas about office rental space and..."

Dylan's face was up on the television screen and Paige simply froze.

Shaughnessy bassist, Dylan Anders, addresses rumors that he's heading back to rehab...

"Isn't that a shame?" Kathy said as she looked up at the television. "From what I've read in the papers, there was no proof he's gone back to drinking. Why can't people accept that and leave the poor guy alone? Sheesh."

Indeed, Paige thought.

Her appetite was gone as she listened to entertainment reporter Julie Mize question Dylan.

"Three weeks ago, you were involved in another car accident. What happened?" she asked.

Paige could tell he had makeup on his face to cover the bruises—she knew his face so well—and her fingers twitched with the need to touch him. Her heart raced as she listened to him recount the events of that horrible morning—not that he mentioned their argument...

"I was driving my girlfriend to work. We were a block away from her office, waiting to make a left turn," he said calmly. "We had the right-of-way, the arrow turned green, and I pulled out into the intersection and..." He paused. "I remember the sounds. I remember hearing the metal crunching, the glass breaking, and Paige screaming."

"And then?" Julie prompted.

"Then...nothing," he replied. "The next thing I knew I was in the hospital with a team of doctors and nurses around me. I was confused and terrified, and I had no idea how I had gotten there."

"Dylan...were you drinking? Were you under the influence of any alcohol that morning?"

"I haven't been under the influence of alcohol in almost a year," he said firmly. "I successfully completed my time in a rehabilitation center, I go to weekly AA meetings. I've met every term of my community service, and I find it painful that people refuse to see who I am now because they want to keep looking at my past."

"It's a very colorful past," Julie said. "You have to admit, it's hard to believe that in a year's time, you've become a pillar of the community."

Dylan chuckled. "I'd hardly call myself that. I know what I am and I know what I've done. But the accident was the fault of the driver who was speeding and ran a red light. He managed to walk away with very few injuries. Paige and I were less fortunate."

Hearing him say her name had her tearing up.

"Tell us about your injuries," Julie said sympathetically, and Paige wanted to punch her. Her words were sympathetic, but the way she was openly admiring Dylan was pissing Paige off.

"I had a concussion and cut my head open," he said and pushed his hair back to show the scar. "I broke my wrist, so I haven't been able to play any music and won't be able to for another month or so. I've got bruised ribs and the impact really banged me up from head to toe."

"And your girlfriend? Is she all right?"

He shook his head. He was visibly shaken up and took a moment to compose himself. "When I woke up, no one would tell me where she was or what had happened to her. I had to wait for hours before someone would tell me. She ended up needing surgery for internal injuries, and she broke her ankle and was bruised and banged up pretty bad. The passenger side took the hit so..." He stopped and shook his head. "It was awful."

"Did she blame you?" Julie asked, and Paige wanted to jump up and scream at the TV. Why would she ask something like that? She wanted to cry out for Dylan not to answer, but she knew this wasn't live TV.

"I don't know," he said honestly. "Her family did. I know I blamed myself for it, even though I know it was someone else's bad decision that caused the accident, I blame myself because I couldn't keep her safe."

"What's next for you, Dylan?"

Paige found herself leaning forward a little in anticipation. What was next for him?

"I need to finish healing," he said. "I'm taking life one day at a time. And I plan on proving a lot of people wrong—I'm not the same man I was a year ago. I'm not even the same man I was three months ago."

"What happened three months ago?"

He gave a small smile—it was the kind he used to give to her when they were in a meeting or in a crowd, and she knew it was private and meant for her.

"That was when I first met Paige," he replied. "She was the first person to believe in me." He stopped and laughed softly. "Although, at first she didn't like me. Like so many other people, she took one look at me and thought she had me all figured out."

"And she didn't?" Julie asked with amusement.

Dylan shook his head. "No. She didn't. And I was okay with it because I did the same thing to her. Then we started spending time together, and…well…she makes me want to be a better man. She's shown me how good my life can be, and I can't imagine what I did to be lucky enough to have her in my life."

"But you don't," Paige whispered. Her hand instantly flew to her mouth to cover it, but not before Kathy turned to her.

"So…wait…you're the Paige he's talking about? You were in the accident with Dylan Anders?"

Paige never looked away from the television screen as she nodded. "I was."

"But…he's talking as if you're still together."

Tears welled up in her eyes. "I know."

Both women sat in silence as Julie Mize thanked Dylan for his time and the show went to a commercial break. Paige hated how she couldn't see his face or hear his voice. She began to look frantically around for her phone because she knew she had to call him, had to find out what he meant by what he'd said. If he still felt that way about her, why was he staying away?

Kathy jumped up and grabbed Paige's phone from the coffee table and handed it to her. "Oh, this is so exciting! You're calling him, right? You're going to call him!"

With trembling hands, she pulled up his number and called.

It went directly to voicemail. Again.

"Hey, this is Dylan. You know what to do."

"Son of a bitch!" she hissed.

This time, however, she left a message.

"Dylan, it's Paige. I want to talk to you. I saw your interview on TV and…well…I think we… I mean… We should … Dammit." She paused. "I miss you. Call me. Please."

And then she hung up and placed the phone on the sofa beside her.

Kathy sat and sighed. "I'm sorry, Paige."

"Yeah, me too. It didn't even ring. It went directly to voicemail again."

"How many times have you tried to call him since the accident?"

"A couple of times." She shook her head. "I know I should have tried harder but…I was hurt and I thought he'd come to me. I don't understand—how can he say all that on national TV and not call me?" she asked with dismay. "How could he sound so believable when it's all a lie?"

"Oh, sweetie, I don't think it's all a lie. Maybe he thinks you're mad at him because of the accident."

"If he answered his phone, he'd know that I wasn't!"

Rather than say anything, Kathy changed the channel, and they ended up on HGTV. Tonight's marathon was on tiny houses.

And suddenly, they didn't seem like a bad idea. If she could hitch her house to a pickup and drive away right now, Paige knew she'd do it in a heartbeat.

"Keep the faith."

That was the text she had received from Dylan, and for the life of her, she had no idea what it meant. She wanted to take it as a good sign, but when he didn't respond to her texts or her repeated voicemails, it was hard to.

On Monday, Paige asked Kathy to drive her to the PRW offices. She wanted to get out of the house a bit and had finally come to some hard decisions. For starters, she didn't want to go back to work for her father. She had always loved doing PR work, but if she stayed with PRW, she knew she'd end up hating it. Right now, she almost did. Her creativity was being stifled, and even more than that, she was being stifled. Paige knew she deserved more—had more in her to give—and this wasn't the right fit for her any longer.

Kathy had not been one hundred percent on board— she thought the stress of a confrontation would be too taxing on Paige—but she'd eventually caved and agreed to take her. As they rode up to the sixth floor in the elevator, she seemed ill at ease.

"If you want, there's a coffee shop on the corner. You could go and wait there," Paige suggested. "I don't know how long I'll be, but I promise not to make this an all-day event."

"No, no, no...I want to be supportive. I egged you on about this and I'm excited to see how it all plays out. Plus, I need to know you're okay. I know I'm a temporary part of your life, just an aide helping you during your recovery, but I've come to think of you as a friend too."

"Thanks, Kathy," Paige said as she balanced on her crutches and reached over to squeeze one of Kathy's hands.

"I picture you going all badass on your dad and making him grovel a little," Kathy said with a hint of amusement.

"I think you're going to be disappointed," she replied

with a small laugh. "We don't make scenes in the Walters family. My father will give me a disapproving look and try to intimidate me by saying we'll talk about this when I'm better, but Daisy's already packing up my office for me."

"Maybe I'll help her with that, so I'm not in the way."

"I'm sure she'd appreciate it. She's supposed to get someone to assist us. We'll probably need a hand truck or something to get everything to the car."

Kathy nodded. "I'll be sure to help her with that too."

When they arrived on their floor, Paige made her way out into the hallway and took a steadying breath.

"Do you want me to walk with you to your dad's office?"

Paige shook her head. "No. I'll be okay." Then she gave Kathy directions to her office, where she'd find Daisy. "I'll text you when I'm done."

"Okay. Good luck!"

It took Paige a little longer to finally get to her father's office because so many people stopped to talk to her. It was so good to see everyone and she appreciated all their well-wishes, but for every minute she was delayed, the more she began to second-guess herself. When she finally had a clear path, she made it all of ten feet before Ariel spotted her.

"Paige! What are you doing here? Are you ready to come back to work, because there are some things you need to look at—"

"I'm not here to work, Ariel," she said with a sweet smile and kept on hobbling. "I'm here to see Dad."

"So…that's kind of like work. I know he's going to want you to look at this stuff and—"

Paige stopped in her tracks and looked at her sister. "I'm not here to work," she said slowly, carefully enunciating each word. "There is nothing I have to look at. Now I really need to go."

"Oh," Ariel said as she took a step back—almost contritely. "Okay."

And as Paige started moving away, she couldn't help but marvel at how quickly her sister backed down. "Must be pregnancy hormones," she murmured.

She was immediately ushered into her father's office, and he stood and smiled at her as she made her way in.

"There's my baby girl," he said as he came around the desk to kiss her on the cheek.

"Hi, Dad." She smiled and was relieved to ease into a chair.

Robert walked around the desk and sat. "You sounded pretty serious on the phone, Paige. Is everything all right? Are you feeling better? Will you need Kathy to stay with you another week?"

"Kathy has been wonderful but I think I'm going to be okay from here on out. I'm feeling so much better and stronger, and I'm able to get around fine. I still can't drive, but I don't think I'm going to have a problem finding a ride if I need one."

"Well…if you're sure. I don't mind paying for her to stay for another week."

"It's fine, Dad. Really."

"Then what's on your mind? Are you anxious to get back to work?" he asked with a small, and somewhat awkward, laugh.

"Work is on my mind, but not in the way you think," she began slowly.

Robert looked at her and some of his jovial and relaxed manner slipped. "Meaning?"

Taking a steadying breath, she let it out and looked him square in the eye. "Dad…I'm leaving PRW. I won't be coming back after I get clearance from my doctor."

"I see." He paused. "Is this because of Dylan Anders?"

"What?" she asked incredulously. "No! No, Dylan has nothing to do with my decision. Why would you ask that? I haven't talked to him since the accident." It did seem like an odd comment for him to make. Since the crash, Dylan's name had never come up in any conversation with her family, so it was weird that her father would choose now to mention him.

"You've never been defiant before, Paige. Suddenly you get involved with this musician and you're taking time off and refusing to work and—"

"I was in a car accident, for crying out loud! It's not like I took off to go backpacking through Europe or something! God, do you even hear yourself?"

Robert held up a hand to stop her. "You're right. You're right. I'm sorry. That was a complete misrepresentation of the situation."

She rolled her eyes. "Dad, can you please talk to me like a normal person? I'm leaving because I'm not happy here. It's obvious I don't fit in with what you're looking for at PRW, and honestly, I'm tired of trying to prove myself."

"What on earth are you talking about?"

"Let's start with my appearance. I'm never going to dress like Ariel," she said, her heart beating like mad in her chest. "This is the person I am. I don't think being someone else's clone makes me a better employee."

"Paige, honey, I honestly don't know what you're talking about. I don't have an issue with how you dress." He shrugged. "And no one's ever said that they did."

Figures, she thought. Yet another way her sister was trying to undermine her.

"Okay, never mind. I know where that one came from. But I'm also talking about how you never let me lead a campaign, how you think it's okay to pass me over time and time again, how you put Ariel in charge of everything and then she dumps all the work on me and she still manages to get the credit!"

He sighed. "Are we back to this again? Sweetheart, this jealousy thing you have with your sister is getting old."

If she didn't have a cast on her foot, she would have stormed out. Now she had no choice but to stay put and see this thing through to the end. "This isn't about jealousy, Dad. This is about what is fair. I work very hard for you, and you have yet to acknowledge that. I have so much to offer, and I need to work someplace where that is appreciated. I am more than someone's assistant and gofer." She paused. "And I think it's time—"

Ariel came bustling through the door. "We have a problem," she said nervously.

"What's going on?" Robert asked.

Frustration boiled up in Paige. Awkwardly, she got to her feet and reached for her crutches. "Is it really too much to ask to have five freaking minutes with Dad without you having to come in and demand the attention?"

"Paige!" Robert admonished. "Is that kind of language necessary?"

"As a matter of fact, it is," she snapped. "This is *exactly* the kind of thing I was talking about. *This* kind of behavior! Why can't I have a private conversation with you without Ariel being here?"

"It's not like she knew—"

"Yes, she did!" Paige cried. "I ran into her out in the hall and she was trying to get me to work and I told her no! And now here she is having—surprise, surprise— some crisis! Why can't she manage to handle anything for herself? I always have to!"

Her father and sister were both silent for a moment, looking at her as if she'd grown a second head.

She looked directly at her sister and figured she's already opened Pandora's box, so she might as well go all the way with it. "And you," she snapped, "go ahead and tell me again how Dad asked you to talk to me about my wardrobe because I'm not management material. Please."

Ariel's eyes went wide and she stared at Paige and then their father.

"Ariel?" Robert asked. "Why would you tell your sister something like that? I never asked you to—"

"Dad, we have a problem," Ariel quickly interrupted. "I got a call from legal about the Literacy Now concert and—"

"Wasn't that supposed to take place a week ago?" Paige asked, but neither of them were listening to her.

"There was a problem with the contracts, and everything else is ready to go for Friday night."

"So what's the problem, Ariel? Whatever it is, tell Darren and the team down in legal to handle it!" Robert said with frustration.

"That's just it," Ariel said with a sob. "They can't handle it!"

"Why not?"

"Because we don't have any bands to perform at the concert!" she cried. "The contracts were never signed and—"

"What?!" he roared.

"I…I thought someone else was handling getting the revised signatures from the bands, and now they've all backed out, and we don't have any way of making them—"

"How is that possible?" Robert yelled. "How could you have forgotten to get the contracts signed? That was the first thing you had to do! What on earth were you thinking, Ariel?"

"Paige was supposed to—"

"Oh, no!" Paige quickly interrupted. "Don't you *dare* put this on me! I was completely out of the concert talks and I've been away from the office for almost a month. This is *your* fault, Ariel. For once in your life, take responsibility for your own screwups."

Ariel looked at her and then their father and began to cry. "I'm sorry, Daddy! This pregnancy has been so hard on me. And…and…I don't know how to fix this."

"We'll see about this," Robert growled as he walked around his desk to pick up the phone. "We had a verbal agreement, dammit, and that bastard will honor it or else."

"Or else what?"

Paige turned at the sound of Dylan's voice. He was standing in the doorway and looking sexier than anything she'd ever seen in her life. His eyes met hers, and she saw all the emotion she was feeling too. He walked over to her and gently caressed her face.

"Hey, beautiful," he said softly.

"Hey, you," she said, sighing at how good it felt to be near him again.

"Give me five minutes," he said, "and then I want to talk to you. Okay?"

Nodding, she took a careful step back and watched in fascination as Dylan walked up to her father's desk. A sound from the doorway drew her attention away, and she spotted Riley and Mick and about a half-dozen other people standing there. What in the world?

"Or else what?" Dylan repeated, looking at her father sternly.

"You were to finish the terms of your community service," Robert said snidely. "And that includes the benefit concert."

Dylan shook his head. "That's where you're wrong. You see, the contract for my community service did not include the benefit concert. I think Ariel was supposed to draw that one up too and dropped the ball on it. Again. Now if Paige had been in charge, I'm sure this would be an entirely different scenario."

Paige watched as her father sneered. "You think you're so smart, don't you? A verbal agreement will hold up in court. And all the things I told you I'd do to you that day in the hospital? I promise you I'll do all that and more."

"Dad!" Paige cried. "What is wrong with you?"

"This…this *punk* thinks he's going to come in here and get the better of me? I don't think so!"

Paige moved toward the desk. "I don't think he's getting the better of you. You simply screwed up."

"Paige!" her father snapped. "That is enough! As my daughter and an employee of PRW—"

"But I'm not an employee of PRW," she reminded him. "Remember? I quit ten minutes ago."

"You did?" Dylan asked, turning to look at her.

She nodded. "I did. But we'll talk about that later." Then she nodded toward her father. "Finish what you were going to say."

Leaning in, Dylan gave her a quick kiss on the lips before returning his attention to Robert. "You can try to do the things you threatened me with, but you'll only make yourself look like a fool. You probably haven't noticed because you thought you were done with me, but I've been in the news. Actually, I've been in the news a lot. I had a feature story in *Rock the World* magazine, and I did a television interview with *Entertainment Extra*—you know, the top-rated entertainment show with Julie Mize? Well, that interview was their highest-rated episode last week. Needless to say, a lot of people saw it."

"I saw it," Paige said softly and blushed when Dylan smiled at her.

"You see, the public wasn't looking at me like I'd relapsed. No one thought I was to blame for the accident. And all those people standing behind me? That's my legal team and my label's legal team and our insurance broker and the president of PR for the label. None of them see me as a risk."

Robert's jaw ticked, but he said nothing.

"Now, considering my arm is still in a cast, I knew I wasn't going to be playing at any concert, and there was no way you could hold me liable for that. But considering *your* firm dropped the ball and *you're* the ones who are going to end up looking foolish…well…I would think you'd be a little careful with what you say and do next."

Turning, Dylan motioned for someone to come forward. Paige noticed the man in the Armani suit make his way over to the desk.

"Mr. Walters, I'm Erik Anderson of the law firm Anderson and Carter. From what I've learned from Mr. Anders and Mr. Shaughnessy, we have grounds for a case of slander against you. Normally that sort of thing can be handled without a whole lot of fuss, but in your case, I'd be willing to make an exception and make the biggest deal over it and drag your name through the press like you threatened to do to my client."

"You can't do that!" Robert cried.

"And when I'm done," Erik went on as if her father hadn't said a word, "do you think you'll be getting many clients here at PRW? Do you think anyone will want to be associated with a firm that was going to lie and destroy a man's reputation? And for what?"

Paige watched as her father slowly sank to his seat. "I was trying to protect my daughter," he said quietly.

"No," Paige said before anyone else could speak. "You were trying to control me. And I'm done with that. You don't know me, and you certainly don't respect me. And that adds to the list of reasons why I can't work with you anymore."

"But what about the concert?" Ariel cried.

Both Dylan and Paige rolled their eyes.

"Shaughnessy's not performing," Dylan said adamantly. "And not only because we don't have a contract, but because we don't want to do business with you. As for the other bands who were going to perform, they won't be available either. Once we told them why we were pulling out, they said they would support us. And considering they didn't sign anything, they're in the clear as well."

You could have heard a pin drop.

"But…but the concert was to benefit Literacy Now," Ariel said weakly. "It wasn't about PRW."

And in that moment, Paige thought it was the most logical thing her sister had ever said.

"Dylan," Paige began softly, "she has a point."

But he shook his head. "I'll talk to the people over at the Literacy Now office and explain to them that if they'd like to hold an event in the future, we'd be a part of it. But between this whole mess and my arm, it's not possible right now."

"And what about the other bands?" she asked.

Dylan studied her for a long moment. "If you—and only you—were working on it, I think we could make something happen. But I can't make any promises."

She nodded. As conflicted as she was about the entire situation—especially because this campaign had started out as something near and dear to her heart—Paige knew it was time to stop cleaning up everyone else's mess.

"Considering I'm no longer an employee of PRW, it would not be for me to take over and organize another concert," she said carefully. Then she turned to her father and sister. "I'm sure you'll find a way to make something work. After all, you seem to think Ariel has all the answers and connections."

Taking a step back, she looked at Dylan expectantly. "I need to head to my office to get my things. Daisy's packing it all up."

His smile was slow and sweet and sexy. "I'll give you a hand."

Riley stepped forward and kissed Paige on the cheek. "Why don't you two go on ahead? I'll help Daisy and get the things to your house, Paige. I think you guys need some time alone."

They both nodded and said their goodbyes to Dylan's support group. When Robert called out her name, Paige stopped and turned.

"Paige! You can't simply leave like this!" he said heatedly. "Don't you have anything to say for yourself?"

She thought about it for a minute and then smiled. "Tell Mom I'll call her in a day or two." Then she waved and left.

Silently, she and Dylan made their way to the elevators. When the door opened, she preceded him in and did a little happy dance inside when he stepped in close beside her and hit the button for the lobby.

Dylan pulled up his phone and smiled but said nothing. The doors opened on the main floor, and she stepped out ahead of him and then out the front doors. She had no idea where they were going, but when he walked straight ahead to a waiting limo, she stopped.

"What are you doing?"

"This is one of the cars we all took over here. Mick texted that we can take it and everyone else will fit in the other cars. So…"

A giggle escaped before she could stop it. "The last time I rode in a limo was for my senior prom," she said as she carefully climbed in. Dylan held her crutches and then handed them to the driver as he slid in beside her.

"The Beverly Hills Hotel," he said to the driver before closing the door.

The Beverly. They were going to his suite. The grin that crossed her face was too powerful to hide. A million thoughts raced through her mind—along with as many questions for him. But for now, she was content to be beside him. She wanted to hold his hand, but the casted one was the closest.

"Are you hungry?" he asked softly. "I can call the hotel and have food sent up."

Before she could say no because she wanted to focus on talking to him, her stomach growled loudly.

Beside her, he chuckled. "I guess I have my answer."

"In my defense, I didn't eat this morning. I was too nervous about going to talk to my father."

He nodded, pulled his phone out, and called the hotel. Paige listened and let her head relax against the seat cushion as he ordered for them—nachos, cake pops, and cookies. With a happy sigh, she turned to him, "You remembered."

Dylan turned fully to face her so his right hand could caress her face. "I remember everything, Paige," he said softly.

With that one statement, she knew they were going to be all right. It didn't matter what had happened over the past month—the time they were apart. After hearing what she did at her father's office and the things Daisy had told her, she could pretty much figure out what had happened and why he had stayed away. And all that mattered now was that they were here together.

At the hotel, he helped her from the car, and together they made their way up to his suite. She hated the fact that they were both so banged up and in casts because she envisioned their reconciliation going much differently.

She sat on the sofa and Dylan put pillows under her foot and then got her something to drink. And when he sat beside her, she knew she couldn't wait any longer. She reached for him and cupped his face in her hands and kissed him.

Casts or no casts, it was the exact kind of kiss she needed—hot and wet and needy.

On both their parts.

"Food…is…going…to…be…here…soon," he said between kissing the line of her jaw.

The last thing she cared about now that they were touching and kissing was food, but as she was about to say so, there was a knock at the door. Dylan jumped up and she wanted to be offended, but he grinned at her.

"The sooner I answer it, the sooner they'll leave."

It was a good plan.

Dylan let the waiter put the tray on the coffee table for him and then tipped him and showed him out. When he returned, as much as Paige tried to ignore the food, she simply needed to eat something.

"Don't hate me for opting for food at the moment," she said and helped herself to a tortilla chip.

He chuckled beside her. "Never. Besides, I didn't eat earlier either." Together, they ate for several minutes in silence and Dylan was the first to speak again. "I never should have let anything keep me from you."

She loved that he didn't out-and-out blame her father—though they both knew he was at fault. "Dylan…"

He shook his head. "That day was hell, Paige. And so was every day after it until today." He paused. "I wanted to come to you, to call you and talk to you, but I needed this whole threat to be out of the picture. I didn't want that hanging over our heads."

"I wish I had known sooner," she admitted. "Daisy told me the things my dad accused you of the day of the accident, but I never thought it went beyond that. I thought you were mad at me because of our argument and...and..." Emotion clogged her throat, and she couldn't speak.

"Hey," he said, cupping her chin. "Never. I could never stay mad at you, Paige. I'm so sorry I put you in a position where I made you choose. And who am I to say what's a healthy family relationship? It took me spending three months in rehab to finally tell my parents that they need to talk to me and how it's okay to tell me when I screw up and disappoint them." He released her chin and raked a hand through his hair.

"And have they?"

He nodded. "Granted, I've practically been a choir boy since rehab, so there hasn't been too much for them to be disappointed about." He chuckled. "Although they did tell me they were disappointed I was taking so long to go to you and beg for forgiveness."

"You don't have to beg, Dylan," Paige said shyly. "You had good reason to stay away. I'm so sorry my father put you in that position. I'm so embarrassed."

"Don't be. That's all on him and he's going to have to deal with the consequences."

She stiffened slightly. "Are you really going to sue for slander?"

Shaking his head, Dylan reached for his drink and took a sip. "No. That was never the plan. We needed to make him see he wasn't holding all the cards. I don't want to make things worse for you and your family. And if I destroyed PRW, that was going to hurt you."

She shrugged. "I know it sounds cold but...not really. It felt so good to walk—well, hobble—in there and quit today!"

He smiled broadly at her. "I bet it did. I'm proud of you, Paige."

No words had ever sounded sweeter. She leaned in and kissed him gently. "Thank you. I think this is going to be good for all of us."

"What are your plans? Do you have another job lined up?"

"Not yet. I was thinking about starting up my own, much smaller, firm. But my focus right now is on recovering."

"How are you feeling?" he asked, his tone laced with concern. Then he muttered a curse. "You had surgery, and you were so hurt and—"

She placed a finger over his lips. "My recovery has been great. I stayed an extra day in the hospital and I've had a home health aide staying with me ever since. Her name's Kathy and..." She gasped.

"What's the matter?"

"She went to help Daisy and I never texted her to let her know where I was!"

"I'm sure Riley took care of it, and Daisy knew what was going on."

"Wait...what? How did Daisy know?"

"If you were still working for PRW, I'd say you need to give that girl a raise," Dylan said before popping a cookie in his mouth. "She was the one who brought to our attention that Ariel had never sent over the contracts for the concert. It gave us the leverage we needed with your father."

"Wow, I...I can't believe. It's so crazy to me."

"Savannah planned a mini-intervention. I was staying with her and Riley and barely living, and she gave me the wake-up call I needed. She was the one who arranged the interviews and had the idea of reaching out to Daisy to try to get you to come. What the two of them ended up talking about—because you know how easily your assistant gets distracted—was how PRW was falling apart without you."

"I don't know if I'm upset or seriously impressed," Paige commented.

"Go for seriously impressed because without her, I don't know if we could have pulled off what happened today as magnificently as we did."

Resting her head on his shoulder, she sighed. "I wish it didn't have to come to that—for either of us."

"I know, baby. And I'm sorry."

"So what happens now?" she asked carefully. In her mind and her heart, she thought she knew where they were going—back together. Back to where they were before the accident. But she needed to hear it from him.

He was quiet.

And he kept being quiet.

Her heart started to race. Maybe she had gotten it wrong. Maybe she had misread the signs. Their kiss had been as hot as it always was, but maybe that was all this was going to be. Sex. Lust. Fooling around. They'd never exchanged house keys with each other or talked about a future so...

"Excuse me for a minute," he said as he stood up.

Paige watched in confusion as he walked out of the room and into the bedroom, and she let out a weary breath. Would she be able to handle going back to the way things had been and knowing they weren't ever going to progress? Could she realistically handle living in the moment and not having a plan? She looked toward the bedroom and saw him walking around, looking for something, and knew her answer.

Yes.

For Dylan, she could.

When he turned and walked toward her, she braced herself for what he had to say—the talk of how he needed them to go back to the way they were and how he'd be busy with the band and wouldn't have a lot of time for her.

She took a deep breath and released it slowly.

You can do this, she told herself.

The last thing she expected was Dylan to scoop her up into his arms.

"Dylan!" she cried. "Your arm! What are you doing?"

"You asked what happens now and I figured you knew—I was taking you to bed and not letting you leave for a long time."

His words were both thrilling and depressing.

He laid her on the bed and stood and looked at her—at her cast—and then to his own. "You know we're going to have to get a little creative here, right?"

She couldn't speak, so she smiled at him and nodded. Wanting Dylan was never in question, but her heart hurt right now as all her fears were proven to be true.

This was sex.

This was lust.

This was…Dylan down on one knee.

What?

"What are you doing?" she whispered, afraid she was seeing things.

"The area by the couch was too confined for what I knew I was going to do immediately after." He gave her a sexy wink. "Paige Walters, you gave me hope when I thought I had nothing to live for. You made me smile when my world was gray. You showed me how this man that I am is all that I need to be. I don't need the fake public persona—I don't need to pretend to be anything else. Who I am is good enough. You challenge me, you push me, you sometimes aggravate me, but more than anything, you complete me."

"Oh," she said breathlessly.

"I love that you're this prim and proper business-woman during the day and behind closed doors you turn into this sexy, dirty girl just for me. I love how I'm the only one who gets to see that side of you. And I want to see that side and every side of you every day for the rest of my life." He paused. "Paige Walters, will you let me love you, through good times and bad, through happiness and tears, and through every day and every challenge life throws at us?"

She nodded anxiously, her hand pressing over her fluttering heart. "I will, Dylan. I will!"

He stood and leaned over her and kissed her. It wasn't the dirty, erotic kisses she craved.

It was better.

It was slow and tender and…everything. She pulled him down on top of her and reveled at the weight of him there. So long. It had been so long since she'd felt him there and it was everything she wanted.

When Dylan lifted his head, he studied her face. "I'm afraid we can't go any further."

She looked at him with confusion. "Because of the casts? I think we can make it work."

Chuckling, he rested his forehead against hers. "No. Although that's still going to be an issue, I'm sure."

"Then…why?"

"Do you love me, Paige?" he asked, and she could hear the vulnerability in his voice, and she realized she had never said those words to him. Ever.

"Dylan Anders," she said solemnly, "I love you. I look at you and I still can't believe you're mine. In a million years, I never would have thought a man like you, so strong and sexy and confident, would want someone like me. You scared the heck out of me when we met, and you helped me see that I was only living half a life. I can't wait to see what life has in store for us. It's exciting and scary and all that, but because you're going to be by my side, I know I can do it." She paused and caressed his stubbled jaw. "I love you."

He grinned. "That's my girl."

Then it was a flurry of clothes flying and pillow placement and lots of sighs and cries of pleasure.

And yeah. Everything was going to be okay.

Epilogue

IT WAS THE MOST BIZARRE FORM OF FOREPLAY, BUT neither seemed to care.

"Oh God," Paige moaned. "More. Harder."

Dylan chuckled. "Baby, if I go any harder you won't have any skin left on your ankle." She had gotten her cast off and was enjoying being able to scratch her foot after six weeks. "And I really enjoy you having skin on your ankle so…" He went from scratching to caressing and then held his hand out to her. "Your turn."

Coincidentally, he was able to get his cast off at the same time and was enjoying the freedom of scratching at his own wrist. And right now, Paige's nails felt fan-freaking-tastic. They were in the back of a town car he had hired to take them to their appointments because neither could drive—at least not to the appointment. Now he was thankful because they could relax and indulge in this…whatever this was.

A few minutes later, Paige looked out the window and frowned. "I thought we were going to my place."

"We will."

"But…we're going in the opposite direction," she said.

"We're taking a slight detour. I wanted you to see something first, and then we'll go to your place."

"Oh. Okay." Then she paused. "What are we going to see?"

He laughed. He loved how impatient she could be

and this was one time he wasn't going to give in. "You'll have to wait and find out."

With a slight pout, she pulled her hand from his so she could cross her arms. He mimicked her pose and she shot him a look. "No fair."

"Extremely fair," he countered. "You know the old saying: 'You scratch my back, and I'll scratch yours'? Well, that applies here. But…you know…with ankles and wrists."

"Dylan," she whined, but he wouldn't be swayed. He did go back to gently scratching and caressing her ankle—it was almost as much for his enjoyment as hers—and he fought the urge to grin when she reached for his hand and gently resumed her scratching.

They made quite a pair.

The past two weeks had been a bit on the wild side. There had, of course, been a little fallout from their interactions with her father. Robert had temporarily disowned Paige. She hadn't seemed too bothered by the whole thing, but Dylan had been ready to strangle the man. Her reasonable nature won out, and it had been less than twenty-four hours before Robert had called her, begging for forgiveness and for help. And Paige being Paige, she had agreed to help.

As a consultant.

The little minx had managed not only to stand up for herself, but had also found a way to stay in control of the situation.

Dylan was beyond proud of her, and when she had gotten back from their meeting, the sex had been off the charts. His girl liked being in control, and he had been more than willing to let her have it to her heart's content.

There were so many things he loved about Paige, but it was her ability to transform that turned him on the most. In the three months he'd known her, he'd watched her go from a quiet and meek woman, who totally had a badass side she didn't let people see, to this sexy and confident woman who refused to take any prisoners.

He was a lucky man.

The car turned and drove through a pair of gates, and Paige stopped what she was doing and stared out the window. "Whose house is this? Is this Mick's new place?"

His manager had bought a new place in the city—he already owned one at the beach but wanted a smaller place closer to the office. "Nope. Mick's got a condo downtown."

She turned to him with those perfectly arched brows furrowed. "Then whose is it?"

The car came to a stop, and Dylan climbed out and helped Paige to come and stand beside him. "Right now, it's no one's home. It's new construction, so I guess it belongs to the builder."

It took her a minute to catch on to what he was saying. Then her eyes went wide and those luscious lips formed a perfect little *O*.

He took her hands in his. "I know we haven't talked about it, but I'm tired of living in a hotel and you living in your town house. I'd like us to find a place that's ours. If I'm jumping the gun here and moving too fast, tell me and we'll leave. We'll put this on the back burner until—"

"Oh, no," she cut him off. "I want to go inside and check this place out. It looks amazing from out here."

It really does, Dylan thought.

The exterior had a bit of a Mediterranean look and the inside had five bedrooms, six bathrooms, and forty-eight hundred square feet. Honestly, it was much bigger than what they would need, but…he was hopeful about filling that space up.

Soon.

They walked through the front door, and Paige looked at him quizzically. "Is the agent here?"

"He unlocked the place for us and he'll meet us here in thirty minutes. I asked if we could have a chance to walk around alone."

"That was generous of him."

"He's a friend," he replied as they both stopped to admire the hardwood floors and the high ceiling in the entryway. "Wow. This is way more impressive in person than it was in the pictures."

"I love this space," she said wistfully. "I always wanted a grand entrance, a transitional space that doesn't immediately take you to the living area. It's beautiful."

They marveled at the first of three living rooms and then the gourmet kitchen. The master bedroom was on the main floor, and this was the space Dylan couldn't wait to show her. Taking her by the hand, he led her into the massive bedroom, which could easily fit a king-sized bed and had two walk-in closets, a sitting area, and a fireplace. One wall was comprised of glass doors that slid open to take you out to the pool.

Paige slid open the doors and gasped. "Oh my God, Dylan. This is amazing! And look! There's a hot tub right here!"

It was a private hot tub for the master suite and was well hidden from the pool area—something Dylan knew he'd love to take advantage of with Paige if they bought this place. They walked around the yard and commented on the seating area and where they could grill and entertain, and he had to admit, her excitement level about the whole thing was making him feel better.

He led her back into the bedroom and toward the master bath.

This was the make-or-break room and he knew it.

Paige took one step in and looked to her right, where there was a glass shower that had two showerheads and about ten different jets. In the middle of the room was a massive soaking tub he knew they'd both fit in. To the left were dual vanities, so they'd each have their own space.

She crossed her arms and frowned, and he was confused. How could she not love this? It was perfect. It was everything she had said she wanted!

"Well, this sucks," she said.

He almost choked at her words. "Excuse me?"

She nodded and looked at him, her expression bored. "You heard me. This. Sucks."

"I… Paige, come on. This space is incredible! It's even better than the one at the hotel!" His voice echoed as he stepped into the room. "The floors are heated and so are the towel bars. You see the blinds on the window there? They're remote-controlled. And did you see the shower? It's got more bells and whistles and jets than the one at the Beverly!"

"I know," she said simply.

"Um…what?"

She smiled slowly, sweetly. "I said, I know."

"Then…what sucks? I don't get it."

Then she sighed dramatically. "It sucks because now I don't want to leave here. I want to move in right now!" she said excitedly. "How am I supposed to go back to my tiny, little town house after seeing this place?"

"So you like it?" he asked, still unsure of her reaction.

"Yes!" she cried. "Dylan, I love it!"

"We can look at other houses," he explained. "I just thought this was a great way to get us motivated to start. I wasn't expecting you to fall in love this quick."

Then she stepped in close to him and wrapped her arms around him. "Something about you makes that happen for me," she said.

Now that's more like it, he thought. "Good," he murmured and kissed her.

"Don't get me started," she said when she broke the kiss a minute later. "I'm already tempted to strip down and test out the hot tub. If you start kissing me, we'll be testing out a lot more than that."

"You know it's going to be like a sexual circus when we get home later, now that we're cast free," he said with a lecherous grin.

Swatting him away playfully, she laughed. "I know. And I can't wait!"

They toured the rest of the house, and with each room they walked through, they talked about what they would do with it. There were enough bedrooms and bathrooms that having guests wouldn't be an issue.

"I don't think any of them will work for a studio space," Paige commented as they made their way down the stairs. "I really liked the setup Matt and Vivienne had in North Carolina."

Dylan smiled serenely and led her outside again,

to the backyard. In the far corner of the property sat a guest cottage. "I know it's supposed to be for guests, but...I have some plans for this place," he said when they walked inside. There was one room that was a combination living area/dining area/kitchen on the main floor and one bedroom upstairs. "Technically, we can still keep the upstairs as a guest room, but I'm picturing redoing the downstairs to soundproof it and set up equipment and doing a smaller kitchen."

"I think that sounds perfect," she said beside him, her hand still in his. "But it also sounds like a lot of work. It would take some time before you could realistically move your guitars in here."

He shrugged. "Most are in storage, so I can wait."

Paige let out a small laugh, and when she went to move away from him to explore, he held her back.

"What was that laugh about?"

"I was thinking about how you apparently excel at waiting."

He looked at her quizzically.

She laughed again. "You took your time and made me wait before kissing me for the first time, you were fine with waiting it out before sleeping with me, and need I remind you about how long you waited before coming to see me after the accident!"

She was still laughing as she roamed the room, and Dylan stood and watched her. She had a point; he did take his time a lot more now than he ever had before. But he was finding that it made everything that much sweeter when it happened. There wasn't one thing he would change about the pace he and Paige had with one another.

Walking over to her, he gently spun her around and kissed her until she was boneless in his arms. And when he lifted his head, he smiled down at her. "C'mon. Let's go."

"But…what about the agent?" she asked breathlessly.

With her hand in his, he led her out of the guesthouse. They were halfway across the yard when the agent in question came out to greet them.

He could wait…

Or he could be a man of action.

"Hey, Brian," Dylan said, shaking his hand. "Draw up the papers and make a full-price offer."

"Oh…um…I didn't think—"

"I'm going to want to do some extensive renovations on the guesthouse and a few things inside, but I'll send that all over to you tomorrow," Dylan said as he led Paige back to the house. Looking over his shoulder one last time, he said, "And thanks for letting us look around. We love it."

"Uh…great!" Brian stammered, clearly flustered at the quick decision.

And once Dylan had Paige in the car, he pulled her into his lap and kissed her again. His hands began to roam, and she playfully swatted them away.

"Dylan!" she whispered with a giggle. "Stop! We're not alone."

It was tempting to keep kissing her and touching her, but he knew she was right. And besides, they'd be back to her place soon enough.

And he knew once they were alone, it would definitely be worth the wait.

*Keep reading for a sneak peek of
Samantha Chase's next book!*

Until There
Was Us

"Dammit," Megan Montgomery cursed as she tried to pull her phone from her bag and ended up nearly tripping over her own two feet. She might be in a new city, but she was the same old klutz she'd always been. The airport was crowded, and she wasn't paying attention to where she was going, and all in all, she felt like a disaster. She murmured an apology to the people around her before stepping aside to read her texts.

Her cousin Summer Reed was meeting her outside baggage claim, and according to the text, she was circling the airport, trying to put her baby daughter to sleep.

Great.

The flight to Portland had been crowded, there had been a crying baby behind Megan, and the last thing she wanted was to be sitting near another crying baby — even if she was incredibly adorable and related to her. *Ugh*...her nerves were frayed. As if moving across the country wasn't stressful enough, it had to get off to a rocky start? She let out a breath and joined the throngs of people again—careful to pay attention this time—and joined the stream heading to the exit.

Fifteen minutes later she had her bags and was searching for Summer's red SUV. Spring in Portland was nicer than in Albany, Megan thought as she waited. She was practically bouncing on her toes as she watched the flow of cars. Her emotions were doing their own version of a tennis match, flowing between being nervous and excited about this new adventure.

Leaving the job she'd had for the past three years hadn't been hard—especially since she knew from the beginning it had an end date—but opting to work for her cousin Zach on the other side of the country was definitely out of her comfort zone. Megan liked to keep things simple. Orderly. She had been settled in Albany and figured that even when her job ended, she'd find another in the same city.

That hadn't happened.

Instead, she had been handed an opportunity she'd always wanted but never thought she'd get—working within the family business.

It was crazy. After all, she *was* a Montgomery, and it shouldn't have been a big deal. The only problem was… she didn't understand finance, she wasn't particularly suave, and she didn't have the business savvy of the rest of her family. She was a computer girl—a techie—but she was really good at what she did!

Still, the planets seemed to have aligned perfectly for this job with Zach to open up just as she was in need of one. Who was she to question it? It was the perfect solution to her employment dilemma, and it was going to be a good thing for her to do something new.

No matter how terrifying it currently felt.

The sound of a horn broke Megan from her reverie, and she saw her cousin pulling up in front of her. With a big smile on her face, Megan waved to Summer and immediately loaded her bags into the hatch. With a shriek of excitement, Summer gave her a fierce hug.

"I am so glad you're here!" she cried. "I have been counting the days until I could see you and squeeze you and look at your face!"

Summer had always been the excitable one in the family. She had a heart of gold and a zest for life that Megan never quite understood, but she was hoping to have some of her excitement rub off on her.

"Come on, come on, let's get you in the car! I want to hear all about your flight and how you're doing and if you're excited about starting work on Monday and—"

"Summer?"

"Hmm?"

"Breathe," Megan said with a smile.

With a nod, Summer walked around to the driver's side and climbed into the car. Megan did the same on the passenger side, but not before peeking into the rear seat at her niece—that sounded much better than "first cousin once removed."

"I have some super-cute stuff for Amber in my suitcase," Megan said as she climbed in.

"You didn't have to do that. You already sent that precious crocheted baby blanket when she was born."

"So...how far are we from your house?"

"It's about an hour's drive," Summer said as they pulled away from the curb. "Amber's a good sleeper, so we can talk all we want without worrying about waking her up."

Was it wrong that Megan wanted to let out a sigh of relief and a hearty "hallelujah"?

With a sigh because all she wanted was to close her eyes for a few minutes and unwind, she turned toward Summer. "Would you mind if I give my mom a quick call? I should have done it while I was waiting for my luggage, but…"

Summer laughed. "Go for it. I know my mother went a little crazy when I moved here and was on the phone with me constantly at first. So I understand."

With a quick nod, Megan hit Send on her mother's number and waited for her to answer.

"Are you there? Was your flight okay? Are you with Summer?" her mother said as a greeting.

Her anxious tone had Megan laughing softly. "Hi, Mom. Yes, I'm here, my flight was a little less than ideal, and I'm in the car with Summer and Amber right now."

"Oh, she brought Amber with her? How sweet! You'll have to send me some pictures!"

"We're in the car, Mom."

"I didn't mean right now," her mother said with a bit of a huff. "So you're there and you're on your way to Summer's, and…when are you going to start looking for an apartment?"

"Mom, we've talked about this. I'm only going to stay with them for a couple weeks, and I thought it was okay for me to get here and relax for a few days before I had to spring into action."

"I'm just saying…you shouldn't rely on them for everything because they're already so busy with Amber and Summer going back to work, and…maybe you should ask them if they know of any vacant apartments near people they know. Plus, you'll need to make some friends of your own and maybe start socializing so—"

"You know what…our connection…bad…call you… weekend…"

It was childish, and she wasn't proud of it, but now was so not the time to deal with a lecture on her social life.

Beside her, Summer started to laugh, and Megan smacked her playfully on the arm.

"Megan? Megan, are you there?"

"Can't hear…go…soon!" And then she hung up and immediately turned her phone off.

About the Author

Samantha Chase is a *New York Times* and *USA Today* bestseller of contemporary romance. She released her debut novel in 2011 and currently has more than forty titles under her belt. When she's not working on a new story, she spends her time reading romances, playing way too many games of Scrabble or Solitaire on Facebook, wearing a tiara while playing with her sassy pug, Maylene...oh, and spending time with her husband of twenty-five years and their two sons in North Carolina.

Also by Samantha Chase

The Montgomery Brothers
Wait for Me
Trust in Me
Stay with Me
More of Me
Return to You
Meant for You
I'll Be There
Until There Was Us

The Shaughnessy Brothers
Made for Us
Love Walks In
Always My Girl
This Is Our Song
A Sky Full of Stars
Holiday Spice

Shaughnessy Brothers: Band on the Run
One More Kiss
One More Promise

Holiday Romance
The Christmas Cottage / Ever After
Mistletoe Between Friends / The Snowflake Inn

Life, Love and Babies
The Baby Arrangement
Baby, I'm Yours
Baby, Be Mine